DEAD IN WINTER

An Addy van den Bos Mystery

J. NOL

iUniverse, Inc.
New York   Bloomington

iUniverse books may be ordered through booksellers or by contacting:

iUniverse
1663 Liberty Drive
Bloomington, IN 47403
www.iuniverse.com
1-800-Authors (1-800-288-4677)

ISBN: 978-1-4401-6996-0 (sc)
ISBN: 978-1-4401-6995-3 (ebook)
ISBN: 978-1-4401-6994-6 (hc)

Printed in the United States of America

iUniverse rev. date: 01/27/2010

CHAPTER 1

In order to make Professor Natalie Cruz's going-away party, I had to race across town during a full day of psychotherapy sessions at Bertha Reynolds Mental Health Center. Usually I try to avoid those kinds of affairs. The atmosphere among my colleagues at the Janette Rankin School for Social Work was less than collegial. And as much as any good social worker should understand the reasons for such gatherings, I hate good-byes. Besides, something about the party had been nagging at me all morning and I had almost convinced myself that it was best to avoid it. But, despite my misgivings, Natalie was worth it, and she would see my absence as a snub. So I put off making notes on the most recent session, threw on my coat, shook off the uneasy feeling and sped across town to Rankin. What had begun as a cool gray morning in December had transformed by midday into what felt like a predictable northern mid-February. Only a few somber naked trees dotted the flat grounds of the school, offering little break from the biting wind. Those of us who made our way from the parking lot to the building had to scurry over what felt like an expanse of Yukon tundra. The ground was in the process of freezing and it crunched spongily underfoot.

I arrived at the faculty lounge just in time to see Professor Ralph Brewer leaning over the food table. His tie followed the contour of his protruding belly, the tip of it hanging perilously close to the bowl of salsa, as he scraped at the steaming enchilada tray. I was surprised to see him. Natalie had often told me she and Brewer were on opposite sides of almost everything. Brewer, the head of the Field Office, believed the tried-and-true methods of the last twenty-five years were more than sufficient. Natalie, who knew that fieldwork was crucial to the education of social work students, reasonably felt the whole system should be tweaked regularly. It didn't make for friendship between them. Oh well, maybe Brewer was celebrating Natalie's departure. Or maybe he was here for the free food.

Nearby, Professors Francine Anderson and Martin Enriquez stood in whispered conversation. Anderson towered over him like an old weathered telephone pole and had to bend herself almost double. One would have thought that Natalie and Martin, both being from Mexico, would be compadres. However, Enriquez taught macro-practice classes, and Natalie's area was individual psychology, what we in the profession called micro-practice. There had always been a tendency by people in big systems to look down their noses at those of us who specialized in working with individuals. Yeah, this was going to be a fun party.

I spotted Natalie Cruz surrounded by a cluster of students. Normally a robust caramel color, her face was latte pale and drawn, thanks to a long bout of cardiac trouble, but she was still smiling. Natalie had been a force in my life, the chair of my dissertation committee and an essential support for me at Rankin. I suspected I might have relied on her too much at times. Or perhaps not enough. She'd never been able to help me move from my position as an adjunct professor to a faculty line. I thought I was slowly making peace with it. But that day was Natalie's and I had vowed to put my own troubles on hold. Still, a reminder of her retirement was a reminder of the loss of my strongest ally. I headed in her direction, weaving through knots of students and faculty balancing paper plates of Mexican food. Some also juggled plastic flutes of champagne. I recognized many of the students from the classes I had taught over the years at Rankin, and several faculty members gave me friendly nods.

Natalie loved to hold court, which, even in her poor health, and sitting down, she still managed to carry off. The little group broke into guffaws at something Natalie said. As I approached, I barely looked at the others, but instead caught Natalie's eye and she paused with her fork hanging in mid-air between her lap and her mouth.

"Addy. It's about time." The same old affection was still in her voice. But I noted she remained seated, a cane leaning against her chair. I grabbed her outstretched hand and held it, aware that it felt weaker than I'd known it to be. I was suddenly afraid of hurting her, but that was too painful to consider.

"Dr. Cruz, I wouldn't miss it," I said. "I can only stay a while, but I wanted to make sure to see you before you left."

She laughed and pulled me into her arms. "Adrienne van den Bos, what is this Dr. crap? There's no one to impress here. Go get yourself something to eat. And, Addy, come and see me at the house, sometime. Soon."

"I will, Natalie. Promise." I unfolded from her hug and turned toward the food table.

Anderson and Enriquez were still talking with hunched shoulders as if to protect their plates and conversation from being snatched away. On the other side, Ralph Brewer had joined a group of three junior faculty members who were glaring at Martin Enriquez. I couldn't help but glance back over at Anderson and Enriquez to see that they were staring daggers back. I wondered what recent skirmish had occurred to lead to the jockeying for position.

Dean Patrice Forsythe and I smiled at each other as I walked by her. She had always supported Natalie and, by extension, me. She was talking with Professor David Kayson and a couple of staff from the field office. It looked to me like Kayson wasn't attending so much to what a young office assistant was saying as to what she was wearing. Or not wearing. I made a bet with myself as to how long it would take him to bed her. I gave it a few hours. Despite my wish to be PC about Kayson's rumored dabbling with the student set, I couldn't help but notice how his downright pretty face was aging into a mature, dark male beauty. At least it seemed so to me. I quickly checked around to make sure nobody had caught me eying him, and then I made my way to the food.

"Too bad the plates are so small," I grumbled, to no one in particular as I ladled. Somebody next to me laughed and I turned to see my colleague, Georgia Enfield, a fellow adjunct, at the trough as well. I shrugged and smiled but kept loading. We exchanged some small talk about it being the end of the term, and how much work we had yet, and that we were both looking forward to collapsing.

As we moved along the table, Georgia asked, "Do you believe that Kayson?"

For a moment, I wasn't sure what she meant, but then I remembered that Georgia had been one of Kayson's dalliances, although I wasn't sure how it had gone. "Oh, you mean his appreciation of the defining mammalian characteristic?"

"Yeah."

"He's such a …"

"Pig?"

"Oh come on, Georgia. They're not all bad."

"Well when you find a good one, let me know."

"Point."

A huge chocolate sheet cake with blue and yellow icing sat at the end of the food table. The message was piped in tiny letters of yellow icing:

Fare Thee Well Natalie Cruz—
With Love, the Rankin School of Social Work

Just as I was in the middle of hacking off a piece, someone called out my name. Cutlery in hand, I swiveled around, and the knife swept right into the mass of Ralph Brewer, drawing a wide swath of cake and icing across his white shirt. The idea of signing my name flitted through my mind, before the enormity of what I'd done dissolved that thought away. Somebody handed me a clump of paper towels and I tried to undo my piece of modern art. I thought I heard a few snickers.

Brewer stood gaping down at his front and wrenched the wad of towels from me. "I'll take care of it. You've done enough."

I left him mopping up and went to find something to clean myself up. I felt a hand on my shoulder as I stood over the sink, wiping the cake crumbs from my sleeve. It was Natalie, leaning heavily on me and struggling to stifle her laughter.

"A fitting upholstery for such a fine figure of a man," she said quietly.

I dried my hands. "Well I'm off. My work here is done."

"And so well too." She smiled. "I'll be here for the rest of the week, but then I'm gone. Come and see me at the house."

I told her I would and made a retreat, pondering a silent question about my recent blunder. Would there be some fall out? Some people's memories were long.

The next morning I arrived at the school, breathing heavily, for my first class, to find a cluster of students huddled around the door like piglets fighting for the sow's teats. I was panting because once again, the ancient elevator was on the fritz, and I had just hauled an overflowing briefcase and a sack of goodies up three flights of stairs. It was a reminder of my broken promise to myself to get into better shape.

"What's … up?" I asked.

Marissa, one of the faculty secretaries, turned to me. "Addy, this doesn't look good. I was walking by and they called me over, but I don't know what to do. I'm afraid to go in."

"What is it, Marissa?" I pushed my way through the group into the nearly empty classroom and plunked down my cargo on the closest table. I could feel my arms aching with fatigue.

Marissa followed me in. I turned to look at her as I massaged my arm. She stopped just inside the door and pointed to the front of the classroom while cringing from what she saw.

One lone occupant was slumped over the instructor's desk. Empty rows of long dark Formica topped tables, looking like cheap narrow coffins, laddered the space between the still figure and the two of us.

I walked slowly along the side of the room, toward the motionless form, tapping once on the tables as I passed them. Stabs of reflected light from a table blinded me intermittently during what felt like an agonizingly long walk. My heart began to thud as I drew closer. I was vaguely aware that the clump of students had come in but stood in a knot close to the doorway, as if to guarantee a quick getaway.

Drawing up to the person, I saw the close-cropped graying hair, with a thinning circle. I noted the powerful hands and wrists on which the man's head gently rested. A heavy gold necklace glimmered from around the back of his neck. When I walked around to stand behind him, I knew for sure that he wasn't sleeping. For some reason, I noticed the fine black hair parted by a jagged line of a faded scar on the back of his right hand.

The brown plastic handle of a knife protruded from his back at a right angle with the blade submerged to the hilt. A dark rusty stain radiated out from the wound across the pastel blue of the man's shirt. His face was buried in the crook of his arms, which were folded around his head. However, I recognized the well-sculpted, muscular body of David Kayson, senior professor on the faculty here at Rankin School of Social Work.

CHAPTER 2

"**S**o then what happened?"

Even over the phone, Kris's intensity came through. Since we had met in undergraduate school, fifteen years ago, Kris Conner had jumped into everything vigorously, often leaving me behind. And that was on days when I wasn't exhausted.

What had started out as a regular teaching day had quickly deteriorated into a blur of police interviews and shocked responses by one person after another. Several of the school support staff had dissolved into tears upon hearing about Kayson's death. The student body had been shaken as the news rippled through it. My first class had obviously been canceled and I had only gone through the motions of the second one that naturally met in another classroom. The site where David Kayson had taken his last breath boasted yellow police tape draped across it.

Murder is not an event that one expects in an academic setting, especially in a school of social work. The Rankin School was small, with about a hundred and fifty students, ten full-time faculty—eight now without Natalie and Kayson—and around six adjunct faculty members. Through the shared experience of academic life and a commitment to the profession of social work, a sense of camaraderie tended to develop among the students, if not the faculty. As an adjunct professor, I wasn't as deeply involved in the life of the school as the full-timers were, but still, I did have a few nice ties with some faculty and students. I sensed the whole system go through a slow shudder at this ghastly event.

And now I had to go over the whole thing again with Kris.

"So, Addy," she said, "what's the scoop with this guy? What is he known for among the students?"

"I don't know him very well, so what I say about him has to be taken with a big grain, you know."

"Yeah, yeah, just tell me. You've got to know something. I mean you've been over there for, what? Eight years?"

I nodded, and then realized she couldn't see me. "Yeah, I've heard stuff. But who's to know if it's true. Anyway, okay, let's see, he had a reputation for having favorite students and breaking the rules as it suited him. He's known to be smart. He's a big name in the field because he's published a lot. In fact, one of his areas is ethics and another is families, I think. I've heard that he didn't tolerate other points of view very well."

"That's no motive for killing him, is it?" Kris asked.

"I wouldn't think so or we'd go through faculty members like tissues. I was surprised that there were so many people who are genuinely sad about his death. Anyway, I don't really know that much about him."

She didn't take my hint. "So, Addy, do you think it was a student who did it?"

"I can't begin to ... No, Kris. No no no. We're not going to get mixed up with this. The police will take care of it." I tried to sound firm. The memories of the other crime in which we'd gotten entangled, a couple of years ago, were never far away. And I knew Kris, as well as my tendency to allow her to talk me into doing things I live to regret.

"It's okay, Addy. Don't get your underwear in a bunch. I'm just playing with it." I heard her laugh. "It's a good mystery, isn't it?"

"Yeah, Kris. So you write it. I'm going to bed."

Before we hung up, we made plans for dinner later in the week. A few minutes later, with toothpaste foaming around the corners of my mouth, I stared at my image in the mirror. A winter pasty face, a legacy of my Dutch genetic line, along with the sandy-blond hair and blue eyes. A real contrast to the sultry darkness of, say, Marissa or

Natalie. Georgia, on the other hand was an Irish redhead. I wondered if that was why Kayson was drawn to Georgia. I hoped that I'd been right about the police and that they would solve his murder quickly. I couldn't imagine the uproar stretching into the next term.

Unbelievably, somebody called me at five minutes after eleven. I'd been sitting up in bed, enjoying a favorite end of the day activity—surfing the cable channels and awaiting sleep. The female voice on the other end was high pitched and agitated. It took me a minute to recognize Amy Arnold, a student from the term just ending.

"Professor van den Bos. I'm so sorry to call you so late, but I'm very worried about my grade in your class. I'm sorry that I wasn't in class today or last week."

"Yes, I had wondered about that." Two sorries in a row, neither of which, I suspected, were actually heartfelt.

"I couldn't make it because I had to work."

"I see." I remembered that Amy was the kind of student who was stretched so thin that she couldn't attend to anything adequately.

I also wondered how she'd gotten my home number. "Listen, Amy. This isn't really a good time to talk. Could we set up a time to get together? It's really too late now."

"No. I mean, I can't wait. I mean, I'm hoping that you could just tell me what grade I got and if I give you my address, you could send me my paper. I mean, I wasn't there today to get my assignment back and you could just check and see what I got. I got a C on the first paper and a B on the second and I really need an A for the term. I actually think I deserved a better grade for that first assignment, like I told you before."

I remembered our previous conversation, also by phone, with her pleading with me to add points to her score. I had reread her paper and indeed decided I could eke out another couple of points. However, since she'd already been at the low end of the C-range, I couldn't really justify changing her grade. I had toyed with offering her a chance to do some extra credit work—okay, so I'm a softy—but she flew into a rage before I could make the offer and it had felt futile to let the conversation continue.

I took a deep breath and, as calmly as I could, said, "Amy, I really can't do anything about it now. If you want to call me at the school

9

or my office and leave your number, I'll be in touch with you to set a time to talk."

"I really need to know now. Why can't you just check it now? And how come you can't go out of your way for me a little more? I mean I told you that I had a full-time job, and I have to take care of my mother who lives with me. She's sick, you know. So I thought you would be more understanding. You call yourself a social worker."

She was beginning to rev up for a full-blown tearful tirade, not what I wanted before bedtime. It came to me suddenly that Amy was often absent or slinking into class twenty minutes late. Her work was substandard and she deserved the grade I'd given her for the term.

"Amy," I tried to remain firm and not slide into punitive mode, "this is not the time to have this conversation and now that you've gotten yourself so upset, it is even less appropriate. As I said if you want to set up a ..."

"Shit. What kind of social worker are you?" The phone was slammed into silence.

Damn. Social workers are assumed to be more compassionate and empathic than other people and we try to be. But a sniveling, angry student at bedtime would challenge Gandhi's patience. And it wasn't just Amy. I'd been having variations of this conversation with students more and more frequently. The sense of entitlement got to me, sometimes. Perhaps it was good Amy had ended the conversation when she did.

This certainly didn't help with my campaign to get to sleep. It took two chapters of *Smilla's Sense of Snow* to do that.

CHAPTER 3

I awoke with a jolt and searched the dark for what had yanked me from my sleep. A siren clamored faintly in the distance, but not loudly enough to have dragged me into wakefulness. Remnants of a disturbing dream hung raggedly in my subconscious, but much as I focused on trying to retrieve it, all I could recall was an image of a man hanging prone in the air. He was face down and a dark fluid dripped from his back to the ground below. I couldn't make out the features but I knew that I knew him. Curiously, I was certain it wasn't Kayson.

Glancing to my left, I saw that it was 4:32 AM. My alarm was set for 7:00, so I turned on my side and waited for sleep to reclaim me. However, after about an hour of tossing, I decided it wasn't going to happen and reluctantly got up. I grabbed my scruffy yet still serviceable blue flannel robe, pulled on some heavy socks, and padded through my apartment to the kitchen. Might as well get the coffee going. I wondered if the paper had been delivered yet so I crept down the stairs, past the door of my landlady, Mrs. Kaldione.

I was in luck. I picked up my copy of the *Whitefield Chronicle* and placed Mrs. Kaldione's paper outside her door. As I turned to climb the stairs again, her door opened and she stepped into the hall. Her gray hair, which was usually neatly combed and cemented in place with pins and hair spray, now stood out at odd angles. There were pillow wrinkles on her face. She pulled her pink flowered robe around her as if to ward off a Canadian gale and bleared at me.

"Addy, you're up?" she said. "I thought I was the only early bird around here."

"Well, it's unusual for me; you know that." Since I'd lived in this house for eight years—had it really been that long?—Mrs. Kaldione knew much about my rhythms and rituals. And she was well aware that if I could, I would sleep late.

"What's wrong, Addy? I know there's something," she clucked at me. "You want to come in, Addy, and keep me company while I finish making this casserole?" She had such a nurturing nature, I often felt the need to keep her at arm's length. However, this morning I decided that I could do with just a bit of her offering. As a social worker, I spend my days concentrating on the intimate details of other people's lives and I often relish the quiet of my empty apartment.

Mrs. Kaldione waved me into her place as if I was royalty, and I half expected her to bow as I passed her in the narrow hallway that led to her living room. She liked to do things with a flourish.

Since the Italianate building was actually a refurbished single family home, each apartment had a unique floor plan. What had originally been the first floor, living room, dining room, kitchen, parlor and pantry areas had become Mrs. Kaldione's apartment. She'd had the renovation done after her husband, Aldo senior, had died and her brother, Marco, who had been living with them, ran away with one of the counter girls at the family bakery.

Mrs. Kaldione's decorating scheme consisted of fragile-looking tchotchkes and family pictures covering every vertical and horizontal surface. One had to be aware at all times of the placement of every appendage in three-dimensional space so as to avoid one unintentionally flailing out and smashing some delicate little piece of kitsch. I always took a little breath and held it whenever I entered her apartment.

The smells of earthy oregano and the acidic bite of tomato sauce permeated the apartment. I could let myself enjoy these smells alone, since I knew that the food itself would not quite satisfy. How she did it I didn't know, but whatever she cooked had promising aromas but ended up tasting as if she'd left out something important.

But blending with this false promise was the distinctive smell of good strong coffee like only Europeans know how to make it. I settled down at her kitchen table and she poured me a cup of the brew. I held the fragile flowered china cup in both hands for warmth as much as out of concern over crushing the delicate object.

After taking a few comforting sips and exchanging some pleasantries I reached for one of the rolled papers, which I'd dropped on the table. Spreading the first section I was hit with the headline "Social Work Professor Stabbed." The story that followed outlined the basics and I cringed when I read my name in the second sentence as the discoverer of the body. Further down, the spokesperson for the homicide unit of the police, Captain Arnold Redstone, was quoted as saying that they had several leads already and an arrest was imminent. It seemed a bold statement to make so soon but I assumed Arnie knew what he was doing.

Arnie and I had dated for a while just after we'd met. After several evenings together, we'd drifted apart for no reason in particular, except maybe because there had been no spark between us. He was a nice man, good at his work, and a little too low key for me. I never told him, but he might have picked up on that fact on our last date. It had been the first time that I'd been in his apartment. We both knew what was about to happen, but I had fallen asleep on his couch while he had gotten up to answer the phone. Ah well.

"So you knew this guy who was murdered?" Mrs. Kaldione asked as she poured me another cup. I watched the brown liquid flow out of the spout of the dainty white-flowered china pot. Only Mrs. Kaldione would use a teapot for her coffee.

I frowned. "Well, I wouldn't say I knew him. We'd had a couple of run-ins and I've heard stuff about him, but we never spent any time together if that's what you mean. The adjuncts are never involved in faculty meetings or anything much to do with the school other than just teaching our classes, so we were just two people who happened to work at the same place. But he's a big fish there. Everybody knows of him if they don't know him personally. He's always getting this or that academic award. I think he's written a couple of books as well."

"That was awful, what happened." She leaned over the table to look at the paper. Even after a night's sleep, her eau de toilet, scent of gardenia, was present enough to mingle with the smells of the coffee. "So you knew him? Eh?"

"No, I did not." I said to her profile.

"But you knew him to see him and maybe even say a few things. I've never known anyone who was killed." She shuddered and moved to the sink to finish deboning a chicken. This from a woman who had a large extended family back in Sicily. "What kind of life is this when a professor gets killed?" She posed the question to the beheaded, pink-skinned poultry, holding her momentarily idled knife over it. Drops of diluted chicken blood fell from it into the sink, making a tinny tapping sound. "You have to be careful, Addy. There's some crazy person out there."

"I will, but I'm sure that this was a one-time thing. Nobody goes around killing university professors."

"You had that Unabomber guy."

"I can't see social work professors being singled out."

I thought about what could have driven someone to kill Kayson. School politics? I was ABD—all but dissertation—from another school of social work. I had been teaching one or two courses a term at Rankin for years. But Kayson had successfully blocked my attempts to get on to the faculty. He was of the old school and one of the more powerful members of the faculty with a coterie of supporters who backed him up no matter what. And they had drawn the battle lines against, among others, Natalie and by extension, me. Either he would be on the search committee or other faculty members from his camp would represent his position. It may just have been that he wanted to hire new faculty who could be recruited to his political point of view. No one would ever acknowledge such a thing, of course, instead speaking of how important it was to have a diversity of perspectives on the faculty for breadth as well as depth. But no one murdered over school politics.

Unhappy love affair? According to rumor, he'd had enough of them. Even Georgia had been involved with him some time back. Because we weren't that close we had never talked about it. I just remember that I had heard through some now forgotten source that they were an item and then later I became aware that it had ended.

But if unhappy affairs were enough, I'd have left a trail of bodies behind me.

As if on cue Mrs. Kaldione asked, "So, do you ever hear from Brody?"

I shook my head. Living downstairs, she'd had a front row seat as our relationship unfolded and then crashed and burned. I grew to love him but I didn't trust him. It had gotten pretty tawdry by the end. He would smell of another women but say that he'd been to see his sister. When I challenged him about a credit card purchase of a necklace, he told me it was a gift for his mother. I had actually searched his stuff to come up with the receipt, which made me blush every time I thought about it. Then the phone call had come from the mysterious female. "You're never going to keep him. He's too much for you. So you might as well give up."

So I complied. I packed up all his things and set them on the front porch. Four years down the drain.

Ah, but he was gorgeous. His olive skin, smooth and unmarred, his dark wavy hair, and that five o'clock shadow that never stopped.

"No, I think the gentleman has moved on."

I sat back after finishing my second cup of coffee. Mrs. Kaldione switched to the latest news from her family in the old country. Drama, sexual peccadilloes, and secrets accidentally unearthed were so frequent that I found it hard to keep up with them. This morning it was her niece's latest affair, discovered by her father, with the mayor of the town. The scandal was that he was married and old enough to be her father. As scandals go, it seemed tame. I half listened for a while and scanned the rest of the paper. Under the fold there was another story about a six-year-old girl being beaten to death by her state-approved foster mother. I stopped reading at the point where the commissioner of social services was quoted as saying, "We have suspended the social worker who was responsible for overseeing this case."

Having lost interest in the paper and sitting with a now-empty coffee cup, I sensed that Mrs. Kaldione was about to begin another chapter. I knew it was time to go upstairs to prepare for the rest of the day.

CHAPTER 4

I showered, dressed, ate a piece of toast with a chunk of Gouda, one of my indulgences, and took the twenty-minute drive to Bertha's. Bertha Capen Reynolds, a hero in the profession of social work, had lent her famous name to our agency. We shortened it to make conversation easier, and because we sometimes felt the agency was more than just a place to work. Thoughts of Kayson faded with the drive, as I made the mental transition to begin my workday.

I arrived to find yet another memo in my box about a new cost-cutting strategy the board had designed. I smiled ruefully as I read it. It was hard to believe anyone would try to turn a profit on good mental health service to low-income people. But, apparently, there were those who were forever hopeful.

Between my back-to-back morning appointments, I made a few notes and checked my voice mail for messages. Most of the time I hope there aren't any, because they usually mean more work for me. Either some kind of crisis or the beginning of a series of phone calls back and forth, often bleeding into the following weeks. There was one message from someone named Virginia Early. She said that somebody at the School of Social Work had suggested that she call me. After my next appointment left, I returned her call.

"Good morning, Virginia," I said. "This is Addy van den Bos, from The Bertha Reynolds agency. I understand you wanted to talk with me?"

"I guess. I mean, I think I want to talk to you."

"You're interested in setting up an appointment for therapy?"

There was a pause, and just before I was about to say, "Are you still there?" she spoke again. "Well, I've been told that it might be a good idea."

This didn't sound too promising. Clients who want you to talk them into therapy always make the job more complicated.

"I'd be happy to talk about that with you if you want. Perhaps you have some questions now?"

"Yes. I mean no. No, I don't have any questions, and yes I do want to talk about it."

"Would you like to set up an appointment?"

There was a pause, and then in a barely audible voice, "I guess so."

We agreed on a day and time. I didn't hold out much hope that Virginia would actually appear. But people can still surprise me.

The day felt longer than nine hours, and by the time my last client left, I was wrung out. However, I knew that if I was ever going to finish up my dissertation I had to put in at least a couple of hours at the computer when I got home. I didn't look forward to it at all. Before I went back to school, most evenings found me eager to put my work aside and hang out with friends or maybe even go on one of those occasional dates. Usually, during the academic term, I also had to devote some time over the weekend to grading papers or pulling together some material for my next class. This late in the term, though, I didn't have much teaching-related work beckoning me.

But my pesky dissertation hung over my head like a nagging spouse. My never-ending burden, Burdy for short. Every time I snuck a few minutes or an evening of plain old fun time, it tweaked me, sitting on my shoulder, poking me, reminding me that it was unfinished. I worked in bursts of concentrated focus and then set it aside until the guilt accrued again. I was now coming to the end of one of those breaks.

So I was thinking about my need to return to Burdy when somebody walked up to me and said, "Adrienne van den Bos?"

It threw me off that the person accosting me was wearing a uniform. And that Edith Camden, the director of the center, was standing a little to the side and behind him with a frown on her mahogany-colored face.

"What's going on?" I said more cheerfully than I actually felt.

"Adrienne van den Bos," the officer said somberly. "I've been instructed to ask you to come to the police station with me."

"Why? For what? I don't understand. What's this about?" I looked at Edith and then back at the officer's implacable face. How had someone so young been able to perfect this unflappable visage?

"Ma'am, I'm Officer Perkins, and Captain Redstone instructed me to bring you back to the station for some questioning."

"Questioning? About what?"

"That's not up to me to discuss with you, Ms. van den Bos. Could you please come with me?"

He spoke firmly and it seemed clear that he didn't expect any answer but "yes." Edith shrugged behind him and seemed to be saying that my best bet was to go along quietly.

And so I did.

Arnie and I sat in his office facing each other over the desk. He wore his usual casually tailored look—dark slacks, olive green shirt, and matching tie with contrasting jacket. I wondered if I should be worried or reassured by his familiar, dark, handsome, mustached face. I noticed that his razor-cut short hair had developed tinges of gray at the temples. I searched myself for any hint of romantic feelings for him, but there were none that I could sense. He had greeted me with some reserve and told me that we had to wait for another detective to arrive so we sat for several minutes, without a word being spoken, in his cramped office. As the time passed, I wondered if this was deliberate on his part to wear me down. But about what? I'd already answered all their questions about Kayson, and I didn't really know very much about it.

"Arnie, what's going on here?" I said, at last.

He shook his head. "Addie, it's a bit awkward, I know, but this is official business. I would prefer not to begin until Detective Kelly arrives. I'm sorry."

He did seem genuinely concerned about the weirdness of this situation. I sat looking around his office, wondering what could make this normally affable man retreat into official noncommunicative silence. Perhaps he was thinking about appearances, which another person could mitigate against. I began to closely examine some of Arnie's plaques and commendations hanging on the wall nearest me, as if my deliverance hung among the words there.

But deliverance from what?

Finally, just before I worked myself into a full-blown state of anxiety, the door opened and a woman entered wearing black slacks, blue turtleneck, gray blazer, and a bulge suggesting a full shoulder holster. She nodded at Arnie and sat down. Did she hold the glance at him a little longer than was called for? I quickly dismissed the thought. I found myself admiring her short wavy blond hair, carefully swept back for the casual look. It's odd what you can find to focus on when you're sitting in a police station awaiting an interrogation. She was completely expressionless as she said, "I'm Detective Fran Kelly. I assume that Captain Redstone has already told you that we needed to ask you a few more questions about Professor Kayson?"

I looked at Arnie as I spoke, "Actually he hasn't told me anything, although I understood that this had to do with Professor Kayson. But frankly, I don't know any more about it than I told the officer who interviewed me at the scene."

Detective Kelly leaned toward me, "So, how long had you known Professor Kayson, Addy? It's okay to call you Addy?"

"Sure, that's fine, Fran."

I thought I detected a flicker of a reaction and it probably wasn't too smart to piss them off, but manner of address is one of those little things that have always been used to maintain a hierarchy and I wanted to minimize the power difference between us. In therapy, a power play can be a symptom and a message, but I suspected the police used them as weapons.

"And as I told the other officer, I didn't really know Professor Kayson. I knew him by sight and to say hi in the hallway. But that's it."

"We are under the impression that the professor made life difficult for you," Kelly said. Her tone was tepid, even if the statement wasn't. The nervousness that had receded somewhat was coming back in the form of a fluttering in my stomach.

So I cheated, resorting to the therapist's strategy. "What do you mean by that?"

"You know what I'm talking about and we'll be asking the questions."

It was her first outward sign of irritation. I made a mental note of her short fuse. She turned briefly to look at Arnie, who had been quiet during this interchange.

"Look, Fran," I said with deliberate calm, "You've just made a statement that you seem to believe is fact, and I don't recall saying anything of the kind. So I was asking you to clarify this. It is your line of thinking, not mine."

At that, Arnie said, "Addy, we've been doing interviews and several people have suggested that Kayson had made some enemies. Your name came up, among others, as having been burned by him. So that's what we want to clear up."

He glanced momentarily at Detective Kelly and then looked straight at me. Kelly seemed to acknowledge his look but remained silent.

I felt sullen and inclined to be uncooperative, but I knew that wasn't the best tack at this point. Perhaps I had more feelings about the way Kayson treated me than I was willing to acknowledge. "So, Kayson wasn't supportive of my joining the faculty. That's no reason for me to kill him."

"You have to admit," Kelly said, "now he's gone, he's one less obstacle. It's clear, you really wanted that position. How many times did you apply? Let me see …" She pulled out a notebook and flipped through the pages. "I understand that you applied twice and both times he put the kibosh on it." She looked up expectantly.

"I wouldn't say it was all due to him. There are other factors that enter into such a decision, you know. Actually, you probably give him more credit than he deserves, um, deserved. But even if he was … uh, had some influence, in my not getting it, as I said, that's no motive for murdering somebody."

I looked at her, silently wondering who had been so helpful to the cops. She was too close to the truth for comfort. Murderously angry was part of the range of feelings I'd briefly indulged in after the second rejection from the school. Perhaps someone had remembered this.

"Well, Addy," Arnie said, "the problem is that, although it's not a strong motive, along with the other evidence that we have it doesn't look so good."

Before this, I never knew the hair on the back of your head could actually stand up. "What other evidence?"

"For starters," Kelly said, "how did your fingerprints get on the murder weapon?"

Her words stung like a slap. Would I have touched the knife on that day? For what felt like several minutes, I worked to find words to ward off what she'd said, to deny their very existence or to go back to the moment before they'd spilled out.

Before I could speak, Kelly did. "Nothing to say now? Just tell us how it happened? Did you the two of you happen to be in that classroom and did he rub it in that you would never get on the faculty? Did it sting you? Maybe he was drunk from the party, and he did something to threaten you. Or maybe you'd had enough, and you followed him in there to threaten him and you were both drunk. Either way it ended up in a murder."

"I'm impressed with your imagination, Fran, but I didn't kill Kayson."

Suddenly it dawned on me that this might be a good time to stop talking without representation. I turned to Arnie, "Captain Redstone, am I under arrest?" The formality felt clunky on my tongue.

"Not at this time, Addy, but that could change."

I rose, my heart racing. "Well, in that case I assume that I am free to leave, and if you have any further questions please address them to my lawyer."

"Are you sure you don't want to come clean, now?" Kelly asked. "I'm sure that, if you are innocent, you would want to be more forthcoming. Once you get the lawyers involved, it can get messy. Besides, it doesn't look good for you, you know? I mean, you begin to look guilty when you hide behind some slick-talking attorney."

She wasn't bad at baiting me, but I had clients who were much better. "Much as you might enjoy the idea of my guilt," I said, "I have no intention of being sucked into this debate with you. I am leaving now. Kindly let me pass."

Kelly slowly scraped her chair out of the way.

I headed out as quickly as I could, feeling the need to get as much distance as I could between the police station and myself. It was clear that Kayson's murder was going to have a bigger impact on me than I had ever thought.

CHAPTER 5

I had been pacing my apartment for what felt like hours—realistically it was probably more like twenty minutes—while I waited for Kris to call me back. She had been on the line with somebody else and told me that she would get back to me as soon as she finished.

When the phone finally rang, you could say I leaped on it. I certainly yelled her name into the receiver.

"Jesus, Addy. Can it be that bad?"

"Kris, I think I'm a suspect. And what the hell am I supposed to do now?" I could hear my volume rise and it almost felt out of my control, like it had become detached from the rational part of me.

"Hey, Addy, is your ass on fire?"

"Kris, dammit, this is real. My whole life is practically flashing before my eyes."

"That must be quite a show. But tell me what's going on."

I recounted my grilling as best I could, ending with my suggestion to them to be in touch with my attorney. The problem, of course, was that I didn't have one, which was why I was calling Kris.

"Okay, okay," she said when I was done, "you're right. It sounds like they're serious."

"They thought I might have a motive to kill him because he blocked me from getting on to the faculty. That doesn't seem like enough, does it?"

"Yeah, it's kinda thin. But how the hell did your fingerprints get on the murder weapon?"

"I did not kill that man."

"I was kind of assuming that, Addy. But, even so, this is out of my league. I'm civil, not criminal. So, we've got to call on Toni Devonport. You know her. You met her at one of my parties. She's the best criminal attorney I know, and even better, she's in my firm. I'll give her a call, arrange a meet and in the meantime, don't say anything to anyone. And try to remember everything that happened on that Monday and Tuesday. It could be any little thing."

"What could be …?"

"Don't worry, Addy. That's what the lawyers are supposed to do. You just go on with your life and I'll be in touch."

We talked a few more minutes, although I'm not sure I could tell you what about. My anxiety was through the roof. And suddenly the weekend loomed vacantly in front of me. I anticipated spending it worrying.

Damn, I was a suspect in a murder investigation. How the hell had that happened?

Saturday morning, I awoke early and cursed the day. The evening before, I'd broken out a bottle of wine and had a couple of glasses to put myself to sleep. It wasn't much of a wine and I had to force it down but it had felt like an emergency. I hoped that the alcohol would work as a tranquilizer, and it hadn't let me down. But I'd fallen asleep at around nine o'clock so my eyes popped open at 6:30 AM, leaving a long day stretched out ahead of me.

To clear out my head, I did something I almost never do. I pulled on a T-shirt, a hooded sweatshirt, and a pair of sweat pants, and rooted around in the closet for a pair of track shoes. I had to blow the dust off them and they felt stiff on my feet from lack of use. After doing some stretching, which I'd heard somewhere was necessary before exercise, I set out on a slow jog. The air was cool and moist. My breath came out in steamy plumes. At first, my body protested against the unfamiliar activity and the cold, but as I warmed, my joints loosened and my muscles started to flex more easily. Although I felt as though I could pick up speed, I resisted, since I didn't want to tear anything that had gone so long unused. The running felt invigorating and at the end, surprisingly satisfying.

I chose a short route winding around my Eastside neighborhood and made it back to the apartment with a good sweat going. As I picked up my newspaper, I remembered yesterday's story and felt a shock. Suppose it had been me who was going to be imminently arrested? A chill started along my back and I wasn't sure if it was because I was wet or scared.

The phone was clamoring for my attention as I unlocked my apartment door. I debated about letting the machine pick it up, but my curiosity didn't let me. It was Kris. She'd been in touch with Toni and had set up a meeting for Monday afternoon.

I called Edith at home to tell her about the meeting and that I was going to have to cancel some clients to make it. Edith was more than a boss. We both worked with people whom society often rejects, and we tended to have similar reactions to them. You can't do this work without having a good support system because it can drain you. Edith was a large part of my support. We didn't always agree, but I could rely on her solid presence when I needed it.

I caught her in the middle of preparing breakfast for her two sons. I could hear her juggling the phone and the kitchen utensils while occasionally speaking to a child. Our conversation was disjointed and she didn't want to linger with me. When I told her about the meeting, she said it would be fine, and I told her I would call my clients over the weekend to give them enough notice. Any that I couldn't reach or leave a message, I'd call the receptionist on Monday morning and tell her to try calling them as well.

Monday afternoon I usually ran a group and saw four individual clients for therapy, so I had to call eleven people. After a couple cups of coffee and two pieces of whole grain toast with cheese, I started the phone work. It was actually very helpful, since it gave me something to focus on. I reached eight people and left messages for two. That left one more who didn't seem to have an answering machine, and I decided to try her again later.

It was a Saturday afternoon during winter break, and I had become a suspect in a murder. I knew that I couldn't just wait until

Monday and I was in no mood to work on Burdy. I had to find something to do that would at least give me the illusion that I could make a difference in my own situation. So Jerry came to mind.

Social workers tend to hang out with social workers, even off duty. We may be a little like firemen or cops in that way. Jerry Lake and I went way back. We had been colleagues in a substance-abuse agency once upon a time. I had moved to the outpatient mental health unit at Bertha's about five years ago. When there was an opening in a new substance-abuse unit I gave him a call, he applied, and shortly thereafter came aboard as well. Jerry was more than a support. I could count on him for clever conversation and reminiscing about those days when we worked together with addicts. Jerry taught me how to spot the con when working with alcoholics and drug users. Jerry was a master at it. After all, as a recovering alcoholic, he'd paid his dues.

We'd made a good team. One of our projects had been to go into the local jail and hold groups for the guys who had been picked up for drug- and alcohol-related offenses, mostly drinking and driving. So there we would be, once a week, sitting with a group of men in baggy orange coveralls in a grubby, locked, nondescript room. Even then, it was a tough road, since most of them had complicated, if not completely believable, stories about how they had been wronged. Denial, an alcoholic's intimate enemy. I thought about how I would look in orange overalls and I winced.

I had to talk to Jerry, so I decided to entice him with a free pizza and coke. We agreed to meet at Isadora's Pizza, a small hole-in-the-wall place up on Michigan Avenue.

CHAPTER 6

I sadora's wasn't far so I decided to hike it. Perhaps I was also seeking the comfort of familiar, even ordinary surroundings. The street was canopied by half-century-old trees and lined by brick and frame single-family homes that had aged with the trees. I could picture, in my mind, each house along my route, and with each one I passed, I waited for the reassurance that I sought. It didn't come, and so I set my sights on my meeting with Jerry. And a couple of drinks. He would have his usual soft drink and fortunately, he was no proselytizer.

The place was jammed with people since it was Saturday night, date night. Although the customers at Isadora's were usually students and locals, that night there were also small groups of people in business suits and a few couples looking like they'd gotten all dressed up for their own private special occasions. I scanned the room and moved through the crowd until I spotted Jerry already at a booth in the back. Isadora was leaning over the table, wiping it down and swinging her ample breasts in his face while laughing at something he'd just said. I could see that Jerry was enjoying the show.

Somebody had pumped the jukebox and Frank Sinatra warbled at me as I entered. Isadora kept the music box loaded with Italian songsters, without regard to style or talent—Pavarotti and Caruso to Frankie Valle and Mario Lanza. Heavy on the Sinatra though. I threaded my way through the crowd around the bar, which had swelled to cover most of the available floor space. The smells of oregano and tomato sauce wafted throughout, mixing with the sour odor of alcohol, a hint of perspiration and a strong dash of the many scents people wore to enhance their appeal.

Jerry spotted me and waved me over. Isadora greeted me with a hug. She pressed her bosom against me and I got a whiff of Chanel, sweat, and grease, a not-unpleasant combination. I slid into the booth and Jerry smiled at me with his teeth.

"Heh, how ya doin?" he said, and half stood so that we could awkwardly peck each other's cheeks. After we settled down and caught up a bit, we perused the menu, which I actually knew by heart. We settled on two salads and a large pizza with spinach, mushrooms, and artichoke hearts. And of course extra cheese. I also asked for a glass of Gianfranco Alessandria. After Isadora had taken our order, laughed some more with Jerry, and gone off to pass it to Juan, the Mexican pizza maker, I turned to look at my friend. Jerry was a man of slight build, with dark, chiseled good looks and a perpetual five o'clock shadow no matter how often he shaved. When I'd first met him, terrible, stumpy, brown, teeth had marred his handsome face, and when I'd gotten comfortable around him, I'd urged him to think about getting them fixed. He had struggled with the vanity of it, but once he'd had the work done, he'd been surprised by how much better he'd felt about himself. And the agency dental plan had helped take the financial sting out of it. Always a favorite with women, he now drew them in hoards. I had to admit that I'd had moments of wondering about the possibilities between us. But fishing off the company pier was a dangerous pastime.

He asked me about my work on Burdy and I answered distractedly.

"So what's up?" he said.

"What makes you think there's anything up?"

He just smiled.

I wasn't sure why all of a sudden I'd gotten shy. People often came to Jerry for help. He was a member of the sprawling network of AA and was seen as one of the elders. But I had never come to him for advice and it was an unfamiliar ground for us.

"I heard that there was a murder over at your place," he said. "Is it connected to that?"

"Who hasn't heard about it?" I said as I battled a cheese string. "And, oh by the way … I'm their prime suspect."

He smiled his lovely pearly white smile, "What? So they finally caught up with the infamous Addy van den Bos?"

I sighed, "That's what I said. I've never thought of myself as particularly violent, and now somebody out there thinks that I could actually kill a person."

"You're not serious, are you?" he asked, slice hovering in front of his mouth.

I nodded.

He shook his head. "This was no accident that you called me tonight."

"You caught me. I was feeling desperate to do something, to know something more. And you have access to people I don't. You haven't heard anything, have you?"

"Nothing but rumors."

"See, I was right to call you." I leaned forward. "You already have heard something."

"I hear lots of things, Addy, but I don't know how much of it I can trust. I had that guy, when I was in school, for classes, two or three, I think. I can think of at least a few people who would want to see Kayson dead. Why would they think it was you?"

"They found my fingerprints on the murder weapon."

His eyebrows rose. "That explains it."

"It's a bitch isn't it?"

"That doesn't make sense, unless you're a very stupid criminal or somebody is setting you up."

His suggestion hit like a bombshell. "Who the hell would I have pissed off that much?"

"You got a lawyer?"

His question felt odd, sounding more like a line from a B movie rather than a part of my modest little life. Still, I nodded, "I'm meeting with her on Monday. But I would feel better if I knew that you would give it a try."

"I'll see what I can do." He reached out and touched the back of

29

my hand. I felt the relief of his support, briefly, and then awkwardness swept over me and I withdrew my hand. "Thanks, Jerry. You're a good friend." Louis Primo finished up "Just a Gigolo" and Frankie Valle launched into "Volaré."

"Look, Addy. You've got everything you need to track this stuff down yourself."

I looked at him closely. "What do you mean?"

"All I'm saying is, why don't you try to figure out who killed him? You have an in at the school with the people most likely to know something. If the police are on the wrong track ..."

"What do you mean 'if'?"

"Hey, you know what I mean. You don't have the guts to kill somebody."

"So you think that's something that takes guts? I would think it's more like cowardice or panic or sociopathy."

He snorted, "Whatever it takes, you don't got it."

"Thanks."

We sat and ate for a time without speaking. I looked around the crowded restaurant and the smells and sounds that accompany such distractions swept over me. Chatter, glasses clinking, the scent of tomato and baking cheese and crust, and Connie Francis singing "Mama" blended together to form a thick layer of sensation. Normally I would have been able to let myself float on this blanket, but Kayson had intruded and I had to attend to him.

I turned back to Jerry, who was waiting patiently.

"I'm not a detective," I said.

"So what do you do when you're talking to a client? Aren't you trying to understand what's behind what's being said? This wouldn't be all that different."

"Except that few dead bodies show up in my sessions."

"Well, I've got this chronic depressive ... but seriously, you know people over at the school. Start asking around. Find out what people know. You know how to do that without triggering defenses."

I played with my glass. "Let me think about it. But keep your ears open, okay?"

He nodded. After that, we turned to other subjects, but I couldn't quite stop the noise in my head.

CHAPTER 7

Although I was somewhat relieved that I had a lawyer and support from a friend, the worry was still lodged in the bedrock. I felt unsettled by Jerry's suggestion, but I also knew he'd made some sense. And asking around on my own would give me something to hold onto. I wouldn't just be going along in passive silence.

I fought with myself until I felt mostly convinced that it was okay to cancel a few more clients. It would take time to ask around. I felt a twinge of guilt about this, both because I wasn't sure how well Edith would take it, and because it meant putting so many people out. Every time I didn't see a client, not only did my numbers go down, but also the agency didn't get the income. Not to mention how it affected the therapist-client relationship.

Still, I was accused of murder. I made phone calls to some of my morning clients and spent some time thinking about whom I should seek out in my quest for information.

I spent the rest of the day trying to concentrate on domestic tasks because it wouldn't have done any good to try to call people for a casual clandestine interrogation on a Sunday. Despite this decision to wait, I kept wandering by the phone, and late in the day, I succumbed.

I wouldn't be able to talk to people central to my search until Monday, but there were some more peripheral possibilities with whom I could touch base. Such as Rosalind Leblanc. She was another adjunct with whom I had once co-taught a course. I dialed and found she was home.

"Hey, Addy. What's up?"

I felt sheepish, because I had never really made an effort to keep in touch with Roz after the class had ended. Roz probably picked up on this, since my attempts at small talk left her wary and uninterested. I decided to forge ahead.

"I know this comes from out of the blue, but anything you can tell me might help."

"About?"

"David Kayson."

There was a pause. Then, "Why do you want to know about him?"

"Well, I assume you heard about what happened to him. Maybe you were there."

"When he was murdered?" If her voice had a temperature, the receiver would have frozen my ear. I was blowing this.

"No, no, of course not. But maybe you were at the school on Monday when he … his body was discovered."

"No, I wasn't there. But of course I heard. Actually I didn't hear until one of the other adjuncts called and told me."

Was this a zap? Did Roz harbor some leftover bitterness, or was I imagining this? How did we leave it when our course ended? Had I promised to get together? Who can remember these things?

It was my turn to pause. Now was the time to directly address how our relationship winds were blowing, but frankly, I didn't want to spend the time. I wanted to get to it—it being whatever she might be able to tell me. I had selected her because I knew that Kayson had recommended Roz for her first adjunct teaching assignment. He must have at least known her work.

Well, if I didn't have time to nurture the relationship, there was always shock and sympathy. "You may not have heard that I've been selected as a suspect in Kayson's murder."

"That's … unreal," Roz said. Shock was working. "I'm not sure how I could help you."

"Would you be willing to just give me some thoughts about him?

I mean, you knew him better than I ever did. I need some insight into who he was behind his public persona."

Another longer pause. "Addy, there's not much to tell." I felt disappointment begin to creep in. "I only knew him because I took a few classes from him. I don't think I know anything that isn't public knowledge."

"I thought he had something to do with you getting the teaching gig."

"Yeah, well, for some reason he took an interest in me. I wrote a paper for his class that he really liked and he told me so. And the next thing you know, I was getting a call asking me to teach this course."

Roz taught a Family Theory course, which was one of Kayson's areas of focus. I recalled that one of his books was on this topic. "So why do you think he did this? Do you think it was just because he was taken with your writing ability?"

I could imagine her shrugging. "Why not? He didn't really say much and I didn't ask." This made sense. It can feel flattering for your professor to ask you to teach, and who would ask why? Still, I thought there was a flatness to her that suggested there was more to this than she was letting on. I felt that I had pressed her as much as I could, so I decided to retreat and perhaps regroup for another try later.

"Okay. Well, maybe you can tell me what kind of teacher he was?"

"Well, it was more than four years ago, so I don't remember much. I think it went okay, I guess."

"Do you remember anything other students might have said about him?"

Was the pause unusually long? "Well, I did get the sense that some of them didn't like him so much. But you know how students talk."

"Any reason why they wouldn't like him?" Sometimes people will feel more able to talk about their own feelings through third parties.

"I guess they didn't like that he played favorites."

"How would he do that?" No sense reminding her that he had played her for a favorite by offering her the class she was teaching.

"I didn't know personally, but some people said that he would go easy on certain students. But I don't know anything about that."

So what was new about this? Professors are human and may without realizing it give more attention or leeway to students they liked. I've probably done it myself, much as I struggle not to.

"So you didn't actually see him do this?"

Was there another pause? "I really can't remember much. Look, I need to go. Sorry about your situation. I hope it works out." We said our good-byes.

She hoped it worked out. So did I. Did I learn anything from our conversation? It did seem that she was hiding something.

The rest of the evening passed uneventfully. I finished up my grade sheets for the term, which I would hand in during the week. I noticed that the grade I gave Amy, my night caller, would probably send her into another fit of entitled rage. No matter how I looked at it, she was getting a B-.

Then I read for a while. Kathy Reich writes a mean mystery and I could lose myself in the details of her forensic autopsies. I chose one of her books instead of some of the professional articles I should have read. No sense in torturing myself. Tomorrow would come soon enough.

CHAPTER 8

C heryl Taylor was the first of two clients I had not canceled for Monday morning. When she was one of my students at the school, she'd approached me for therapy. I told her we would have to wait either until she graduated or until she was no longer in any of my classes. She reluctantly agreed. We also had to work around the fact that several of her fellow students were placed as interns at Bertha's and there was a good possibility she might run into any one of them. She was willing to take that chance. I, too, had to make sure not to discuss her case in staff conferences, since the agency interns attended them. It made the whole process more complicated, but the client's privacy is paramount.

From her written work and her class comments, I could already see that Cheryl was very unhappy. Not that students are expected to be perpetually ecstatic. Many of them are eventually a bit ground down by the pressures of an academic load tacked onto an already full life of work and family. But Cheryl had been unusually distressed, sometimes tearful, quick to anger, and always late with her assignments.

By the time we finally started to work together, she was on the verge of collapse. Cheryl worked for the SSD, the Social Services Department, in protective services, or PS. Her job was to respond to complaints of abuse against children. The law required that all reports of suspected child abuse had to be checked out within twenty-four hours. It was well known that the department was perpetually understaffed and under siege. Each PS worker had an average caseload of seventy, and because of several widely publicized cases involving children dying in ugly ways, the public was up in arms and the Social Service Department was under scrutiny. Their solution to problems often seemed to be to cut bait in the form of some poor line worker.

Cheryl had spent most of the earlier sessions crying.

The latest one had started out in a similar way. She sat down heavily and pulled the tissue box toward her. "No sense leaving that 'til the last minute. I'm gonna need it."

I nodded. Her eyes were bloodshot and she sounded exhausted. "It's been horrible at work," she said. "One of my cases blew up last week and I've been working on it for days and I couldn't get to a couple of other cases that I needed to do something on. And my supervisor, as usual was for shit. The foster mother where I had placed Terrence, the blown case, called me on Tuesday—or was it Monday? Hell, I can't even remember. Anyway she tells me that Terrence had sexually abused one of her other foster kids and she says she can't keep him. When I get there, Terrence has a black eye and some angry welts across his back, which I know about because he yanks up his shirt to show me as soon as I'm at the front door. Then he starts to yell at me: fuck this and fuck that. The foster mother's boyfriend comes out on the porch and starts to yell at Terrence and threatens to call the police. I find out that the foster mother isn't even home, she's out at a PPT for one of her other kids." Cheryl practically spit out the initials, as if all parent, pupil, teacher conferences could account for the chaos.

Cheryl's volume increased as this all poured forth. She rubbed her face vigorously perhaps as a way to rid herself of the images. In any case, I remained the sympathetic ear.

"So anyway," she said, "I have to get between them and practically push the man back into his house so I can calm Terrence down. Now I've got to find him another temporary home, which as you know is a pain in the ass, and I've got to decide what to do with the child abuse. It means that we'll have one less foster home and I'll have to place all the other kids as well. I try to call my supervisor and I can't reach her." Cheryl pulled her face into a grimace and spoke in an exaggerated haughtiness. "Oh no. She's in one of her very important meetings and can't be disturbed. Shit."

I nodded sympathetically, but there was no need to do anything to encourage her to continue.

"So I spent the rest of the week talking with the cops, filing a report about this foster mother, dealing with her nasty phone calls, finding different placements for the three other kids she had, taking Terrence to the doctor and finally getting him settled in another home. In the meantime there are sixty-five other cases that I had to put on hold. Not to mention my schoolwork. Shit, I hate this."

"Yet it seems very important to you that you hang in there with this," I said.

"Oh, Addy, you know I couldn't leave. I know it's crazy, but I feel that I can do something here. Besides, I want to stay for the benefits and I still need to finish school." She shook her head slowly, "I'm not leaving."

"Yeah, I know. And you know the next question. What do you think you need to learn from this?"

She smiled for the first time. "You may not believe this, but it's already easier to work there because I can come in here and bitch about it. I'm less anxious and I have more energy."

I couldn't see it, but I had no reason not to believe her. Unless she just felt the need to reassure me.

"But I can't stand my supervisor. I can never get to her, and if I do she's no help at all." She laughed ruefully. "When she finally caught up with me this week, I'd gotten everything taken care of with this case. She says to me, 'I knew you could do it.' Can you believe that? I sweat and struggle on the phone, pleading and making deals to get this case put away and that's all she says. Shit."

"You wanted something more," I said.

"I wanted some recognition that this was a difficult case and that the work is hard and that it's really sad what some of these people have to deal with. I want her to be around when I'm trying to figure out what to do with some of my cases." Cheryl's volume rose again as she talked. "What the hell is a supervisor for? Just to say, 'I knew you could do it'?" Again the mincing words. "The place is a hellhole.

I know of eight PS workers who are seeing therapists. Most of the time, a bunch of us are out sick. I know two workers who can't stand their clients and yell at them on the phone. The rest of us pretend we don't hear them. Those two cases in the newspaper don't help. I know the workers who had kids die. They've been suspended and nobody can say their names out loud. And I know we are all secretly relieved that they weren't our cases. And when I go home, I have no energy for anything, including my husband." She seemed to sink down into the chair.

I felt her hopelessness. I've heard this story before. State social workers carry the weight of human sorrows caused by the social and economic system most of us benefit from. They are also often the ones who are assigned the blame if the rest of us are forced to know more than we want to about it. Granted, I only have one side of the story but it's always difficult to hear.

And it was probably time for the next chapter. "So, does this experience feel familiar?"

"It seems like I've been in this place for my whole life."

"Okay. Where have you felt hopeless and compelled to try to make it better?"

"Yes, I know—recreating family trauma. So I should be able to find a way out of this, at least this time. Right?"

I didn't respond. These kinds of questions, the client has to answer.

"I understand that theoretically," Cheryl said, "but ..."

"But?"

She paused, closing her eyes for a moment and then spoke slowly, "I heard about a project that the department has got going, where there's an opening coming up. At first, I ignored it but maybe I could look into it."

Her sadness subsided as she talked. She underwent a gradual transformation from despair to hope as she told me about this new possibility. It was an innovative pilot project, designed to help long-time welfare clients with children become self-sufficient. Cheryl was able to let herself be buoyed by the thought of doing this. She thought it might give her something challenging and different to do.

"What the hell," she said. "I'd be able to cut down on my caseload.

That would be reason enough to do it." She smiled thinly at this thought. "Maybe from sixty-five to forty-five."

I thought, *Small things for which to be grateful.* We wrapped up and agreed on a next appointment time. As soon as I could escape the office, I made my way to Rankin School to begin my second career as gumshoe.

CHAPTER 9

The school was quiet, as it should have been. The term had ended, and most students were pursuing anything but academic activities. Perhaps celebrating by sleeping in. While the students and the professors got a break, the non-faculty personnel were still working, so I headed to the room that housed the support staff for Kayson and several other professors.

The last time I had seen Marissa Dubov was when we had discovered David Kayson's body. I found her sitting at a desk peering into a computer monitor when I arrived. Several other women worked at desks nearby, or pawed through file cabinet drawers drawn out to take up even more precious space in the already cramped room. Each secretary answered to five or six faculty members and did much of the administrative paper shuffling that accompanies the work of a professor, as well as dealing with students or fielding phone calls that didn't land in the voice-mail boxes.

The women had been laughing about something, but stopped abruptly when I opened the door. Marissa turned toward me with a guilty start, and her worn face seemed to sag even further. I noticed that her dyed-brown hair, which she usually kept neatly coiffed, although in a style twenty years old, was now less controlled. This gave her a slightly wild look. Kayson's death must have had an unraveling impact on her. I thought she was in her fifties, maybe early sixties, and that day she looked every bit her age.

"It's okay," I said. "Life goes on, and we still gotta laugh sometimes."

And it only occurred to me then that maybe they thought I'd killed him. I had no idea how fast or far word of my interrogation had spread.

She shrugged and said, "What can I do for you, Addy?"

Apparently, it hadn't reached here yet, thank goodness.

Although I had timed our encounter to coincide with her break, I glanced at my watch, perhaps to suggest a disarming casualness, and asked Marissa if she had a few minutes to talk. She agreed and reached into her desk drawer for her purse; we walked down to the lunchroom, where she retrieved her paper bag from the refrigerator. I checked the adjunct faculty office and found it empty so we settled there.

I watched as she removed her salad, container of dressing, fork, and bottle of juice.

"So how are you doing?" I asked.

She took a bite of the salad, and as she chewed, her chin trembled. "I'm okay," she said in a tiny voice.

I was surprised at the depth of her feeling. I had imagined Kayson to be a difficult boss.

"It's been hard for you," I said almost automatically.

She nodded. "I can't believe that anyone would do that to him."

"You thought he was a good guy."

"I never had any trouble with him. I don't know. Maybe there are some people who didn't like him. But he always treated me good."

"How would he do that?"

She thought for a moment and looked down at her salad. "He would sometimes buy us girls lunch. I mean order a pizza, or take us out for no reason. And he always gave us something for Christmas, you know. Nothing big, but always something. Last year he gave me some pretty towels. Wasn't that nice?"

Okay. Despite the apparently rosy picture, I had my doubts. I develop them whenever I hear a mature woman refer to herself as a girl. "Really? I didn't know that about him."

"Yeah. And he was always giving extra help to students who were having trouble. And he was a very smart man. I mean all those books he wrote and he was always going around giving talks and stuff."

"How would he help the students out? What kind of extra help would he give them?"

"Well I didn't really know specifically, but he spent a lot of time with his students helping them."

"What do you mean by helping?"

"Well, you know, helping them with their work, or counseling them on what classes to take or where to apply for jobs. Sometimes he would ask me to get the phone number for this or that place, you know, like agencies or places that students might apply for work ..." She had been gazing around the room as she spoke. Now she turned to look straight at me. "Why? Why are you asking these questions?"

I took a breath. I have to acknowledge that I hadn't thought through how I would approach Marissa. I was hoping it would just flow. Now the flow had hit a snag. "I'm curious about why someone would kill him, and I thought ..."

She looked startled and blurted out, "You don't think I would ...?"

I waved my hands as if such an idea had so little weight I could just fan it away. "Of course not. Of course, he was important to you. I just thought since you know him—knew him pretty well—How long have you worked for him?"

"I worked for Professor Kayson for sixteen years." I could see water glistening on her eyelids and she looked away again.

"So you couldn't think of anybody who hated him enough to want him dead?"

She shook her head.

"Anyone who you saw get really angry at him and, say, stomp out or call to speak to him and sound pretty angry?"

"I don't ... wait. There was one time, but it was a while ago and I don't think it's what you're asking about."

"What came to mind just now?"

"There was one student who used to call, maybe a year ago, and when I wouldn't put her through, she would call me names. But most students are pretty good."

"Do you remember that student's name?"

"She never said. I remember that she made me very upset, when she would call. She called me a …" Marissa paused and looked around the empty office as if we were sitting in a crowd. "bitch. I couldn't believe it. And she called me a lackey. For a while, I didn't want to pick up the phone and Nora, another girl in the office, used to do it for me. She finally stopped."

"Why?"

"Why what?"

"Why did she stop calling?"

She seemed puzzled by the question. "I don't know, maybe she just got tired."

"Did she ever say what she was so upset about?"

"I don't really remember. I don't think she said. I know she was really mad at Professor Kayson, but I thought she was a weirdo."

"Did the professor ever say anything to you about her?"

"Only that he was sorry I had to go through that. He was very sweet about it. Oh yeah, and he also said that he would take care of it. Maybe that's why she stopped."

"In the sixteen years you worked for him, there was only one student who was that worked up about him?" I could have made a list.

"I didn't say that, but she's the one that stands out." She picked up the leavings of her lunch, packed them into the paper bag, and stood. "I need to get back to work."

"One more thing, please? Do you think I could just peek into Kayson's office?"

"Well, I don't know. I mean, it's locked and I don't think the police and Professor Kayson would want that. He was very particular about his office."

"I promise I won't touch anything," I said. "Just a quick look."

It felt like I was crossing a line. I could see she was one of those women who felt too guilty to say no to other people. Probably afraid of someone getting angry at her, something she could thank her parents for. If she had been a client, I would have tried to help her see it for herself. As a murder suspect, I was crossing a dangerous line, but I had no choice. We climbed to the second floor, where the faculty offices were.

Several office doors were open and heads turned as we passed by. After she nervously unlocked Kayson's office, Marissa told me to hurry and pull the door closed when I was done. That said, she practically ran back to the stairs.

Rankin School of Social Work was housed in a refurbished high school built in the 1930s. The narrow hallways had oak floors and mahogany paneling. The same was true for the faculty offices. Kayson had earned one of the more ornate and larger spaces, with a textured tin ceiling and a window overlooking the courtyard. I stood in the center of the office and looked around. One wall was completely covered by a floor-to-ceiling bookcase filled to capacity with journals, books, and neatly stacked folders and papers. An oversized desk sat at an angle so as to insure a good view of both the window and the door. The lamp, blotter, and penholder were primly arranged. A dark brown corduroy couch sat against the wall next to the door, matching throw pillows perfectly placed. There was nothing extraneous anywhere, nothing out of place, no books or papers carelessly left on the floor or chairs, no pictures askew. Although it had all the trappings of an academic office, the room somehow felt more like a window display than the real thing.

"Jeez, what a control freak," I muttered.

Unfortunately the unlocked desk drawers yielded more neatly ordered but unrevealing objects: pens corralled in a box, pads of paper arranged by size, and pushpins, paper clips, and other assorted office tools in little cubbyholes. The bottom drawer, however, wouldn't budge when I pulled. Neither did the file cabinet drawers. I decided to forgo actual breaking and just left it at entering. There would be no secrets uncovered in this search. On the way downstairs, I wondered if it were true that Kayson had more than a touch of compulsivity. What else this told me I wasn't sure. Need to control? Fear of chaos? Something.

There was one more person who might know something about Kayson. I couldn't find him on any of the floors so I headed to the basement where, among the storage spaces, old computers, and other discarded office machinery were kept, the janitor had made a space for himself. Mr. Olds was probably as ancient as the building itself. He could move throughout the school unnoticed—most people tend to ignore those who pick up after the rest of us—but I tried to make a point of at least acknowledging him as he transferred trash barrels and swept up after a week of traffic through the halls.

I found him sitting on a folding chair behind a scarred metal desk. He looked up and his expression suggested that he was torn between surprise and pleasure. He tried to drop a full ashtray into one of the desk drawers—smoking was officially prohibited anywhere in the building—but I told him he didn't have to worry about his secret. He screwed up his leathery face and created many more lines with his smile.

"'Ow can I 'elp you, Professor van den Bos?" he asked. This guy knew everybody's name. I wondered how many of the people who went in and out of this building even knew who he was.

"How's it going, Mr. Olds?"

"You can call me Jeremy."

"Well, only if you call me Addy."

"Okay, uh, Addy," he said, "so what brings you down 'ere to my little office?"

"I was thinking that you probably know a lot about what goes on in the school."

"Dat I do."

"Have the police questioned you about Kayson's murder?"

"As a matter of fact dey haven't."

"That's a surprise, isn't it?"

He nodded, his eyes glistening.

"I wondered if there was something you could tell me about Kayson. You must have seen a lot of him, just as you have about everybody who comes through here."

His smile was short, transforming his face into a blank mask. Best guess was, he was wondering how he could get into trouble if he answered my question.

"Mr. Olds …"

"Jeremy, remember."

"Okay, Jeremy. I won't tell anybody what you say to me."

He nodded and seemed to consider his next move. "Dat was an odd man," he said finally.

"How was he odd?"

He smiled "Dat man was always doing tings 'ere in the school."
He smiled again and nodded almost as if to himself.

"What kinds of things?"

"'E used to come down 'ere and talk with me. 'E was the only
one. 'E would be 'ere late and come down 'ere sometimes to talk, but
I know 'e also came 'ere when I wasn't 'ere."

"What do you mean?"

"Some days I came down 'ere and the place would be picked up,
like. I noticed 'ow tings were in different places than when I'd left
'em."

Kayson cleaned the janitor's room? "That was odd, all right.
You're sure it was him?"

"'E was the only one dat came down 'ere. Nobody else. And 'e
always left me gifts, for Christmas and stuff."

"Why do you think he did that, clean up down here?"

Olds shook his head and then seemed to make another decision.
"I'm sorry. I don't really know anyting. I'm just talking and dat don't
mean much. 'E was always nice to me."

"Yeah," I said, "there was more to him than I knew, that's for sure.
Is there anything else that you can tell me about him?"

Jeremy scratched his chin while slowly shaking his head. "I don't
tink so. As I said, 'e was always nice to me."

"Did he ever talk about anything when he came down here to
visit you?"

Jeremy took a breath and let it out slowly. "'E never talked much,
Addy. Mostly asked me 'ow I was doing, and if everything was going
all right. Nothing much else."

"Anything might be helpful."

"I don't know much about de man. But there was someting dat 'e
was pained about, dat I know."

"What makes you say that, Jeremy?"

"'E had a look in 'is eye sometimes when 'e didn't know I was
seeing 'im. Dere was deep pain. 'E used to be here late at night too,
you know, working in 'is office."

"Do you know what he was doing up there?"

"Nope. All I know is 'is light was on, and you could 'ear 'e was
in dere."

"Alone?"

He shrugged. "Don't know 'bout that." He swung his legs around and stood up. "Gotta get back to it."

It was pretty clear that he wasn't going to say anything else even if he knew more.

I thanked him, asked him to let me know if he thought of anything else, and climbed back into the end of the day's light.

I left the school asking myself what I'd actually accomplished. Kayson's secretary mourned him, and he often helped out his students. I also knew that at least one student was furious with him. So what else was new? What had he done, if anything, to convince the angry student to stop calling? After seeing his office, I knew that Kayson was a neat freak. He even used to tidy up the basement. What did this add to what I knew about him? The normally well-hidden pain that Jeremy saw wasn't unusual. We all had our share, and you could be pretty sure that someone as arrogant as Kayson had to have dirty secrets. The fact that Kayson stayed late and maybe not always alone was another piece of the puzzle. But what did it mean? And how did any of it add up to a reason to kill him?

Never before had I met with an attorney where I was the central player. In the course of my work, I have testified on behalf of clients and have had to meet with attorneys before court appearances. But sitting with Toni and Kris and talking about my situation had a dreamy, unreal quality to it. Toni seemed nice enough, and more important, she seemed to know what she was doing, so I had to go with that. However, despite her reassurances, I was determined to find the truth about Kayson's murder.

Toni had said she would get the prosecutor's evidence as well as the medical examiner's report. I was to keep doing what I would usually do and not worry. Not likely. Not worry, that is.

CHAPTER 10

Tuesday rolled around. It was normally my teaching day, but because we were on semester break I could stay in bed for a deliciously long time. The only thing I actually had to do that day was turn in my grades for the term. Lying in bed was spoiled by the low-level anxiety that had been with me since Kayson's murder and especially since my not very friendly meeting with Detectives Redstone and Kelly. At last I sat up on the edge of the bed trying to decide if I was up for a run.

After assessing my condition, I decided to forgo the run and instead had breakfast and headed out to the school. Traffic was light at this time of the morning, since rush hour had passed and the lunch hour was still some time away. Due to the break, I slid easily into a parking spot near the building. Had it been in the middle of the semester I'd have had to leave early and hope that I won the musical cars game for an empty space before I was too late for class.

Alice Major University was the brainchild of a group of forward-thinking citizens in the early twentieth century who wanted to give women a chance to go to college. Its primary mover and shaker had been Alice Major—and her husband's money. There was no central campus, and the school buildings were scattered around the city, a testament to the way the Boards of Trustees, over the years, had been able to raise money and gifts. Alums or other well-known, moneyed people had donated several structures, formerly serving other purposes, and it looked like no building had ever been turned down. Fortunately, Whitefield wasn't a large city, and the bus system was adequate, so students didn't have far to go between classes. Still, by the end of their years at AMU, most students could have taken jobs as city tour guides if their degrees didn't open other doors.

The old high school that housed the Rankin School of Social Work had been acquired in the sixties, around the same time that the university had gone coed. Although it had been renovated, you could still see the faint outlines of the words "girls" and "boys" on the bathroom doors. Rumor had it that the two staircases at the opposite ends of the building had been assigned to one gender or the other during the high school days. I wondered if that was because there were sections of the stairs that were not visible from certain vantage points. Perfect make-out spots.

I had planned to just drop off my grade sheets and check my mailbox, but when I reached the second floor and rounded the corner I nearly walked between Professors Brewer and Enriquez, which might have been dangerous. Professor Brewer stood planted in the center of the hall, screaming, spittle flying, arms shaking. Professor Martin Enriquez stood in an equally enraged stance at the other end of the hall. Between the two were ten or so faculty and staff offices. Some of the doors were closed, but those that were open suggested occupants who were lying low, out of the line of fire.

"It's a wonder that you can use toilet paper without instructions, let alone teach students how to function in the real world," Brewer screamed.

"You Neanderthal," Enriquez thundered back, "you use out-of-print texts from the fifties because you have no idea where the profession is now."

The insults slammed back and forth, overlapping each other and reverberating along the corridor, until words ran together into rumbling noise. Brewer actually began to bounce up and down on the balls of his feet, and I began to worry. These were short, middle-aged, well-paunched men, and I assumed that for each minute they kept it up, they increased the danger of heart attack or stroke.

"It's fifteen years beyond when you should have retired!" Brewer yelled.

"How you can think you could have any inkling of how to do that job tells me that you're delusional!" Enriquez shouted at the same decibel.

"You son of a bitch, don't ever call on me for help in any conceivable way," Brewer bellowed, "because you'll find yourself getting only a wrong number, you midget."

"Antique."

The door at the end of the hall behind Enriquez opened and two female students took a couple of steps in and stopped short. I also felt stuck to my place. The adjunct office was somewhere between them but I wanted to avoid getting anywhere near the two enraged educators.

Suddenly as Brewer took a breath, Enriquez yelled, "It's not enough that you sided with her, but you have the audacity to assume it's yours for the taking. God help us if you were in charge. It would soon be the disaster that the Field Office is," and disappeared into his office, slamming the door behind him.

Brewer stood a few seconds longer and then he mumbled something under his breath and retreated, but not before noticing me standing a few steps away. He tossed a scowl my way and disappeared behind his door.

I assumed there'd been a faculty meeting, since they were often preludes to these kinds of scream fests. This one must have featured a particularly polarized debate.

I shook my head and nodded and shrugged at the students. As we passed, one of them giggled while the other rolled her eyes. I felt an urge to join in, but as a professor, even an adjunct, I felt I should at least try to maintain some semblance of decorum.

I ducked into the adjunct faculty office. Georgia had been working at a computer and swiveled around as I entered. She seemed to be checking to see how I was taking the recent battle, because when I began to giggle she laughed hesitantly.

"Can you believe that?" I asked.

She shook her head, her short reddish hair bouncing. "That's what you have to aspire to, Addy."

"Do you know what that was about?"

She shrugged. "I heard this was a special meeting to discuss, you know, those important subjects that we mere mortal adjuncts should not be privy to. What I got was that Brewer really wants some position and Enriquez is siding with the Dean against him. But you know these guys have been at each other's throats for years. I think Brewer has trouble with all these 'foreigners' taking over, you know."

"Yeah," I said. "Foreigners who are citizens of the U.S., such a principled stance for a social worker. So what are you doing here?"

She told me she had come here for a quiet place to work on her syllabus for the substance abuse course she taught.

"Oh, by the way," she said, "I have a student placed at my agency, and she was asking around for a therapist. I gave her your name."

"Thanks for the referral," I said, and then took a seat facing her.

She eyed me warily and cocked her head. "What's up?"

"Georgia, I know you don't want to talk about it, but I have to ask. You know, they think I killed Kayson."

"What?"

"I know. I wish it was a joke. But it's not, and you may know something about him that can help me."

"I don't know what to say." I could see her reconsider. "It is hard to talk about, not just because he really hurt me, but because I still can't believe that I let myself get involved with him."

"Georgia, you know me. Anyone who wants to feel better about their relationship problems just has to compare themselves to my fiascoes." I laughed, not without ruefulness.

"Well, you probably would've picked up on the clues with him."

"Such as?"

"For one thing, he was a clean freak. He would scrub my bathroom, completely, before he would use it. Sometimes he would do it after I just cleaned it and I'm a pretty good housekeeper."

"Really? He was even more compulsive than I thought."

"What do you mean?"

I told her what I had discovered at the school.

"God, I didn't even know that." She shivered. "What the hell was I thinking?"

I shrugged, but my mind was elsewhere. Each person will inevitably recreate their dilemmas over and over. Hopefully some of us will work a bit out. I wondered what Kayson was trying to scrub away in those invisible bathroom stains.

"So what else besides his dirt phobia?" I said.

"He wouldn't ever stay over at my house."

"Did he say why?"

"Not really. Something lame, like he just felt more comfortable in his own place."

"That's not so unusual, is it?"

"No, but it was one more thing that I should have taken seriously. What makes me so mad is that I overlooked too much."

"Like what else?"

She shook her head as if to rid herself of an unpleasant image. "He used to bug me to talk about my background. You know, after he found out my mother abused me. For some reason he wanted to hear about it again and again."

Her rate of switching position in her chair went way up. She was uneasy even talking to me about it. "It looked like he was getting off on it. After a while I stopped telling him stuff, and that pissed him off." Georgia frowned. "Why did he like it so much? I started feeling creepy whenever he brought it up, sorta like I was being pressured. But it felt too weird, you know."

"So he had a thing for trauma stories," I said. "What do you think it meant?"

She shook her head and shifted again. "That's the last thing I want to think about."

"Did he ever talk about his own background?"

"Are you kidding? Whenever I tried to ask, he would get really sarcastic. That's part of what made me so mad and why I finally stopped seeing him. It was always a one-way street with him."

"Such a good social worker, don't you think?" I said. "Nothing like going through life psychologically blind to your own stuff."

Georgia nodded then, "Addy, I'm sorry about what's going on with you. Are you sure they think you had something to do with it?"

"According to my most recent conversation with the police, they do." I stood up and turned to go. "If you can think of anything else, let me know."

"Sure, Addy."

"Georgia," I said, "thanks for talking with me."

She shrugged and turned back to the computer.

I left the room feeling as if a lot had been left unsaid.

As I drove back to my apartment, I thought about how I was linked with Kayson in both life and death. Human beings have creative memories, with a grand capacity to forget the painful and rearrange what we do remember to fit the picture we have of the world. As often as I've seen this with my clients, I'm surprised every time I catch myself doing the same damn thing.

Scenes of a faculty party a couple of years ago, at the Dean's house, while David Kayson and Georgia had still been involved, came rushing back. A long-held pleasant and benign memory suddenly turned disturbing. Kayson had been waiting outside the bathroom and sidled in front of me when I tried to leave; then he pressed himself against me. And for an instant, I actually considered giving in to him. There was something alluring about his smoky good looks. I felt a flash of fury and embarrassment at the tickle of pleasure in my middle he had triggered back then. He had smiled slightly and kissed me on the cheek. When he reached to kiss my mouth, I pulled away, but only at the last minute.

I now remembered the shadow of anger sliding across his face as he realized that I wasn't going to succumb. I had walked away feeling flustered by the lingering scent of his cologne. During the whole incident neither of us said a word. I swore silently to avoid being alone with him again and not just because of what he might do.

I shuddered. "There's no accounting for taste," I said to myself as I pulled the car up to my apartment.

CHAPTER 11

Virginia Early's intake appointment had been set for 10:00 AM and I was surprised that she actually showed up. She was twenty-two but would probably be carded for years, with shoulder-length wispy brown hair and delicate, undernourished features. Her faded jeans and long-sleeved frayed green T-shirt hung loosely on her as if she'd recently lost weight. Her deep walnut-brown eyes were rimmed with dark circles that stood out against her pale skin.

"I'm not sure if I should even be here."

I've had worse starts to the therapeutic relationship. I waited to see if she needed prodding, and when she didn't say anything, I said, "It's hard to talk to a stranger about personal things."

"No. I mean, yes I guess, but ... well ..." She looked around nervously as if expecting someone else to enter my office at any moment.

I reassured her about the privacy of my office, although her fear was probably about other places and times in her life.

"Yes, I think I know that. But, I'm not sure this is going to work."

"Why don't you tell me why you called?"

"Well ... I ... People thought it might be good for me to come." Another pause while she scanned the office again.

"Others noticed that you might be having a hard time?" I said.

She paused and sighed and stared at the floor, her hair partially covering her face. "Um, yes. I sometimes can't concentrate. But it isn't all the time, and I'm not sure if it's anything that serious. I mean, I get down sometimes, but doesn't everybody? I'm dealing with a lot and I'm just stressed, that's all."

Was she inviting me not to take it seriously either? If so, I wasn't going to take her up on it. "How can you tell you're under stress?"

She told me she had trouble sleeping, with nightmares sometimes forcing her from her bed. When I asked her what they were about she went vague, although I had the sense that it wasn't because she'd forgotten them.

"So what do you think is causing your stressed-out feelings?" I said.

"I just have a lot to do. You know, everybody gets stressed. Maybe I just need some rest."

I shifted to less intrusive questions. It turned out that Virginia was a student at Janette Rankin. She was carrying a full credit load, doing a twenty-hour-a-week internship and working part time in a drugstore to help pay her bills. Her worry about her grades also kept her up at night. Before she went to college, all she ever knew was the family farm and the small town nearby.

"My parents don't say it much," she said, "but I know that they are very proud of being the fifth generation to work the farm."

"Tell me about your parents," I said.

She looked up at me warily. "Well, we've always been a really close family."

Ah. This little phrase is often code for "don't say anything bad about anybody no matter how much they might have hurt you." I wondered what she had to keep secret from them. Or me. Or herself.

"So how do your parents feel about your going to school?" I asked.

"They're very proud of me, even if they don't understand why I chose social work." She laughed weakly. "I don't think they really know what I'm doing, but I know my mom is always bragging to everybody that I'm getting my master's."

"And your dad?"

She paused before speaking, now even more subdued, "Well, he doesn't say much. But I know he's also very proud." I saw her begin to falter, and she hung her head to hide her face. The light glinted off the tears that had begun to flow down her cheeks.

"My parents are really good people. They work hard, my mom is active in the church. I have five brothers and sisters and there were usually one or two foster kids at the house too." She continued to cry quietly. "They give a lot, and I just want them to be proud of me."

She reached for a tissue and tried to sop up the evidence of her misery.

"Virginia," I asked, "why would your parents not be proud of you?"

She looked up finally, the tears having stopped. "You know, it's nothing. I'm just stressed. I just want some help with being less stressed."

We talked some more, but it was clear that Virginia wasn't ready to reveal what was troubling her. This wasn't unusual. It often took several sessions for people to overcome their fear or shame to tell a therapist what the real problem was. For some it took even longer. What was important at this point was that Virginia wanted to continue in therapy even though she was scared. I expected that it would be fine.

I was less sure of myself. For the rest of the day, each time a session ended, the reality of my situation would slam back at me with a fury and I found myself having a hard time doing the things I do between clients. Relief from my own anxiety came whenever I had to go back into a session with another client and concentrate on finding their hidden meanings. Then the ebb and flow ended and my day was over.

It had finally begun to snow when I stepped out of Bertha's to head home. Flakes landed wetly on my face as I tilted my head back to look up. I was reminded of childhood days of tobogganing down what seemed like huge hillsides onto the frozen lake. After hours of this, I'd trudge soggily home, cold cheeks, wet feet, feeling spent but completely satisfied. At that moment, staring straight up into the lead-gray sky dropping its crystalline load, I longed for those simple times.

Before I was considered a murderer.

Most of the next couple of days ran into each other. It became clear that I had much to learn about the private detective business, since I quickly ran out of ideas about where to go next. But, I couldn't put it out of my mind altogether and I found myself annoyed with the slowness of the legal system. My life was a rhythm of going to and from work and going in and out of sessions, my preoccupation with my predicament rising and falling with what was in front of me. It's true what they say; my work kept me grounded.

Cheryl Taylor was my last client of the day. Despite my feeling distracted, I noticed how drawn she looked. And subdued. She sat looking dejectedly at the floor.

I waited to see where she was going to start. Finally, she looked up and shrugged.

"You know that project that I wanted to join?" she said, "Well I've been working on it for two days now. I was actually starting to get excited about it. It was going to be something different. I don't know. It's supposed to help parents be better with their kids and help people make better choices in general. It felt like I might even be able to make a difference. I've been meeting with some of the clients and they seem to be pretty excited about what we were doing and I was so happy that it didn't involve taking kids away from their families or investigating burned babies."

She let out a sigh, searched for something in her purse and took out a pack of cigarettes. Before I could say anything, she waved a cigarette at me. "I know, I know, I can't smoke here. I just want to hold it."

I sat back, waiting.

"So anyway," she said, "yesterday I met with a young mom who has two kids and has been in the program for about six weeks. And man, she was tough. I mean, she wouldn't give me any room. She was so mad and there was no softening her. Normally I kinda like the angry ones, you know? I mean, it gets me going, and I like the challenge of turning them. Anyway, she has to be there because she's done some ugly stuff to her kids and the only way she can keep them is to finish the program. But boy, is she pissed."

Cheryl played with the unlit cigarette. A few shreds of tobacco fell to her lap. "So anyway, I'm trying to get her to talk with me, and she's getting more and more mad and foul mouthed and I'm thinking that I might have met the first one who I won't be able to reach. And then she says, 'At least they got rid of that asshole, Kayson.'"

At the mention of Kayson's name, I sat forward just enough that Cheryl took notice. She may have been thinking about her problem, but she was also a social worker.

"Then I ask her what she means," she said. "And she doesn't answer me but says, 'So what's your angle, bitch? You probably ain't no different from him. What is it you're gonna want?' And I'm thinking, what the hell is she saying? And I know I've got to go careful, here, because I don't want to scare her away before she tells me more. But after that, I can't get her to say another word. So then I talk to one of the other workers on the project and she shuts right up, too. She tells me to just focus on the work and never mind the stupid stuff that clients say. And I'm thinking, what the hell is going on here?" She gestured with the bedraggled cigarette. "And now I'm not sure what to do. I mean, doesn't it sound like she was saying that there was something not right?"

"You have an idea about what she meant?" Oh my, I had to tread carefully here. My heart rate definitely responded to Kayson's name. I was on the edge of making this about me and not Cheryl. "Are you sure she was talking about David Kayson?"

"What do you mean? Are you saying that she coulda been talking about some other guy? I don't think so. I mean everybody knows that he was the big boss on this project. Anyway, what the hell do I do?" She reached for a tissue and dropped the cigarette on to the table.

"What do you mean 'the big boss'?"

Cheryl paused and I assumed it meant that my questions had led her away from her train of thought and instead to what was important to me. Now I had stepped over the line.

"Oh, you know," she finally said, "he supposedly wrote most of the grants and got the whole thing started."

It was as if I couldn't stop myself. "So what does he do, or what did he do over there?"

"Well, I'm not really sure. I was supposed to meet with him this week, but of course ..."

"So what do you think she meant?"

"You mean my client?"

I nodded.

"I don't know, but doesn't it sound like she was saying that he was doing something he shouldn't have?"

I was about to suggest how to get more information from Cheryl's client but I caught myself. I had already gone way too far. I knew that I had to get us back on course, so I said, "You obviously think there's more to it. What are your options?"

She shook her head slowly. "Well, since I don't have a supervisor yet, I could ask about that." She rolled her eyes. "I'm not sure what good that would do. But I guess it's the right thing to do, isn't it? Since Kayson uh, left, the program is kinda in limbo, but I could be more up front with them about wanting a supervisor."

She seemed to be looking to me for approval and I didn't respond right away, giving her a chance to figure it out for herself. Finally, we were back onto her problems.

She smiled. "Of course, it's what I'm supposed to do, but I can't stand it if he somehow took advantage of clients." She paused. "Am I going off on this before I even know it's true? What if she's just doing a number? What if it's true? Damn it."

"You were hoping this project would let you get away from some of the ugly stuff people can do, and instead it might turn out to have brought you right back to it."

"Yes, yes. Shit. I'm not sure how much longer I can take this."

"Well, that's where we need to focus, isn't it?" I said as gently as I could, even as my mind was churning with this new piece of information.

For the first time in days, I couldn't wait for work to end.

CHAPTER 12

Juggling mail from my mailbox, I unlocked my apartment door and dumped coat, gloves, and mail on the table, and then I headed to the kitchen and made myself some tea. Before settling down, I listened to my phone messages almost not hearing them because I was so preoccupied with trying to fit what I had just heard about Kayson into the entirety of what I already knew. A picture of Kayson's psychology was beginning to take shape. He had a cleaning fetish, was obsessed with others' tragic backgrounds and probably denying his own. And he took advantage of his clients somehow. It suggested that he had been trying to rid himself of something painful in his past. As a child, Kayson might have seen something awful happen to someone he cared about, or that something awful had happened to him. Whatever it was, instead of facing it, he tried to master it through reliving it with others. But it was the end of the day and I felt frazzled.

I set my ponderings aside and turned to hear the messages again. Kris's was the first of three. She had called to confirm our dinner for that night. I made a mental note to call her back to arrange the where and when, although it was a safe bet we'd end up at Isadora's.

Mother van den Bos was the second caller. She was having a problem with her furnace and wanted my advice. This pretty much defined the extent of our relationship, in that whenever she had some mechanical or logistical problem of living, she consulted me. It was one of the only safe topics she and I could talk about. Anything else invited an argument. I tended to avoid talking to her about personal choices because it was hard to miss her unhappiness about the fact that I wasn't married and hadn't given her grandchildren yet. Her sadness about this hung in the background, behind every conversation. I didn't begrudge her her pain. With my father's eighteen-year-old murder remaining unsolved, she already held much sorrow, and she carried my childless and unmarried state as one more burden.

The third voice belonged to Betty, Toni Devonport's secretary, telling me to call Toni. Hearing this, my anxiety shot up. I fumbled the numbers twice before I got it right.

"Addy," Toni said, "I think I've made progress on your case, and I wanted to update you."

"What do you have?" I said.

"I've found out that they have some additional evidence ..."

"What is it?" I said quickly, climbing over her words.

"Give me a chance, Addy."

"Sorry. I'll try to control myself." I leaned to reach for the tea and instead knocked over the cup. A miniature steaming rivulet trickled across the table and formed a small, short-lived waterfall that splashed onto my floor creating a dark spreading stain on the carpet. I watched it with fascination as Toni talked.

"There are a couple of witnesses who say they've seen you with Kayson and you've got to explain this to me as well as to them"

"What? How could that be?" The tiny waterfall dripped making little thuds. "I never ... I mean, are you sure? That's not possible."

"So how do you think it happened that people saw you with him?"

"What are these people saying? I mean specifically?"

"Two students say they've seen you drive off with him several times; the last time was just before the murder."

"Toni, I have never gotten into the same car with that man. I swear." The denial sounded Clintonesque. "How could anyone have seen something that never happened?"

"Is it possible that somebody is trying to set you up for the murder?" She answered her own question, "I guess anything is possible." There was silence as she thought. "If this is true, Addy, you should be careful. The prosecutor needs a quick victory because this is a pretty high-profile case, but I'll go talk to her to find out if there's any wiggle room. So, keep your fingers crossed."

I let out a breath forcefully. "I still can't believe that they think I'm a murderer. I just hope you're persuasive with the prosecutor. I'm not sure I could get through an actual trial."

"Don't worry," Toni said. "We will get rid of this, sooner or later. If we can avoid a trial, we will. If you think of anything else, no matter how insignificant, you need to tell me. The more I know, the better position I'll be in to put on a good defense."

At the sound of that phrase, I felt cold. I was glad for her help, but I couldn't shake the slimy feeling that I had become somebody I had never imagined myself to be. We said our goodbyes and I dropped the phone into its cradle. I wanted to just avoid all thought or discussion of my situation, as if this would make it all disappear. It was a strategy I saw a lot in my clients, as well as in many politicians. The difference for me was that I knew it was just a way to try to feel better, and that it would never solve the problem. I had to keep facing this head on. It was my only way out.

It was time to call Kris, even if I didn't feel much like socializing. I needed a distraction and Kris would provide one. Besides, she might be able to help me work on a plan. Any plan.

Kris and I had gone through our undergraduate years together during the early eighties and had done things that brought blushes when I thought of them now. And I certainly couldn't see myself repeating what we had thought of as liberating experiences. While I went on to become a social worker, Kris attended law school, where she graduated second in her class. She often said to me that she would never be able run for office, given her forays into the wilder side during those years. She couldn't just say she never inhaled. We would laugh about that, but I thought I sensed sadness just below the surface. Although she never said it out loud, it made perfect sense that she would have wanted to throw her hat into the ring at some point. Kris had enough passion and energy to make an impact. But I suspected that she never really went after this dream, believing that it would not be possible because she had intimate relationships with women.

Kris was single. Again. Her most recent relationship had imploded last year. We had both hung out with each other during our relationship heartaches and now that we were both free, we sought out each other's company. She was a good friend, and as long as I didn't bring up Bonnie, she never mentioned Brody.

Just as I knew we would, we arranged to have dinner at Isadora's that evening.

CHAPTER 13

After changing my clothes, I drove through the frigid evening to meet Kris, arriving in time to watch Isadora brazenly flirting with her as she sat at a booth. I slid in next to Kris, flung my arm around her and said, "Hey, stay away from her. She's taken."

"I don't know about that," Isadora smiled. "It looked like she was really hot for this Italian mama." She winked and said she'd be back. Dean Martin warbled in the background. I caught a glimpse of furious activity in the kitchen as the door swung open.

Kris and I grinned at each other and I reseated myself across from her.

"What was that?" I said. "I know you're looking but I didn't know voluptuous brunettes were your type."

"I'm thinking of branching out." She indicated Isadora who was heading our way with water and menus in hand. "You think she actually does dance both ways?"

"The world is always surprising me." Isadora arrived and distributed her load.

"Say, Addy. Weren't you the one that found that dead professor?"

It was one of those rare times that Isadora wasn't being playful. I felt like I'd been found out, even though there was nothing to find.

"Yeah, and it set off a pretty wild ride."

"So," Kris asked, "what do you hear about it?"

Isadora stared at each of us and leaned toward the table. "That guy used to come in here sometime. Every time with somebody else."

"Man? Woman?"

"Either. I think his tastes were eclectic."

Kris assumed her attorney persona. "How do you know it wasn't business?"

"Hey, I can tell the difference, you know what I mean?"

"How the hell did I never see him?" I asked. "I practically live here."

"You guys usually only come here at night and the professor always brought his little ones during the day. Besides, they used to sit way in the back. I thought he was trying to hide something. Do you think one of those kids did him?"

"Kids?"

"The ones I remember were pretty much younger than he was. He may have thought he was fooling us into thinking he was just offering student advice, but that kind of advising isn't written in the student manual," she chuckled. "Anyway, you want to order?"

My head was buzzing. I'd come here to get away from the Kayson puzzle and just found another piece. We ordered and Isadora moved on to the next table.

"So," Kris began, "Your professor was a dandy."

"I'd heard that about him, but it's weird that he used to come here and we didn't know." I thought again about my encounter with him at that long-ago party.

"There's nothing new about a middle-aged man trying to recapture his youth through having younger lovers."

"Just because it's common doesn't make it right for a professor to use his students that way. And a social worker using others to fight his own personal demons. A serious no-no."

"I talked to Toni today," Kris said.

I nodded, swirling the burgundy elixir around the glass.

"She told me about the witnesses."

"And did she say it looked like somebody was trying to set me up?"

"Yes, and that's not a good sign. You need to be really careful about what you do and where you go until this is over."

I didn't like the sound of that and took a taste of wine. Its warmth spread smoothly around my mouth, easing down my throat.

"Anyway," Kris leaned forward. "We've got to be prepared for the worst."

"The worst? What worst?"

"Addy, we need to consider all contingencies. Like, if this should come to trial, we need to explore all possibilities for defense."

"You mean something other than I'm innocent?"

"I know, Addy. I know. But we have to think about promoting reasonable doubt. And one way to do that is to present an alternate scenario for Kayson's death. Like, who else had a motive to kill him?"

"What do you mean 'else?' This implies that I wanted him dead too."

"Look, the prosecution will argue you had a motive to kill him, whether the argument's nonsense or not. And since you don't have an alibi and your prints are on the weapon—and they now have two witnesses—we have to be ready with another explanation."

"They've made a mistake with the prints. I know I didn't touch the knife. I mean, why would I touch him at all? They must think I'm really stupid."

I didn't add the embarrassing fact that I have a strong—nearly bordering on the superstitious—fear of dead bodies. Any species of dead body. I have made it a point never to touch one if I can help it. My irrational self believes that as soon as life leaves the body, and decomposition begins, there is something toxic there. Touching it risks contamination. It's my secret phobia.

"What about the witnesses who saw you with him?"

"That's an outright lie."

"So who have you pissed off lately?"

"I have never done anything that would trigger murderous rage in another person." I was firm, not allowing any doubt to enter.

"Kayson triggered the rage. You were an afterthought."

Strains of Frankie Valli wove through our conversation. I took a drink and stared into the restaurant. Kris was uncharacteristically silent as she worked on her salad.

"Kris, I need you to do something for me," I said at last.

"What?"

"Look. It's something you can do more easily than I can. I mean, you know about this stuff. It's foreign territory to me." Was I wheedling?

"So out with it."

"I need more information. I think I can do some more digging about the witnesses, but I need more background information about Kayson and I don't have the kind of access that you do."

"What are you doing, Addy?"

"Don't ask me that. Just say you'll do it."

"You're looking into it, aren't you?" She paused, as if reflecting on her next sentence. "Okay. I'll see what I can do." Hints of a smile tugged at the edges of her mouth.

"I'm glad I've made your day."

"Hey, Addy, let's see where it goes." She was almost giddy.

"And I need the names of the so-called witnesses who claim to have seen me."

"You can thank me by being careful." She took another sip. "Why don't you just ask Toni for the names?"

"I'd rather that Toni didn't know about my little tangent." Another smile.

"Okay, I'll get them for you."

Operatic strains of The Three Tenors began to fill the spaces between the chatter and clatter of the restaurant.

After that, we ate in silence for a while. I know I was turning over my recently made decision, trying to settle the arguments against it running through my head. What clinched it was the murder charge hanging over me.

I went home and made it only as far as my couch.

CHAPTER 14

I wanted to sleep late, so the night before I had turned off the ringer on my phone. The answering machine was flashing a silent signal when I walked by en route to the bathroom.

"Damn early risers," I mumbled as I hit the play button.

"Hey, Addy," Kris's disembodied voice came out of the machine. "The two students who saw you with your professor friend are Julie Pigeon and Donna Blare. Hope that helps. Good hunting." Beep.

"What the hell?" Both Julie and Donna had been students of mine, although I couldn't remember exactly from when. Why would they lie?

After some wandering around the apartment, coffee in hand, I began looking through my teaching files. This was always a reminder of how long I had put off organizing the stuff. The search should have taken only a few minutes. It was half an hour before I actually got to the relevant files—those folders containing class lists and telephone numbers. I hoped the phone numbers were up to date, because they both had been in a class I had taught four terms ago. I noticed from my grade sheets that neither had been stellar students.

I could only leave messages at both numbers. Julie's answering machine message had been made by a child who encouraged me to leave my name and number while a chorus of children chanted some little jingle in the background. Blech. Too cute.

A digitalized male voice answered at Donna's, also inviting me to leave a message. I thought I remembered that Donna was a single woman living alone.

For the next several hours, I lost myself in writing and for the most part, successfully forgot everything else. I was drawn away from Burdy by the jangling of the phone. I was surprised to hear Natalie's voice.

"Hey, Addy. I decided that to wait for you to call was to wait forever, or nearly so. I'm an old lady and my days are numbered." She laughed.

I felt confused. Hadn't it only been a few days since her party? Or more like two weeks.

"Well, I … well, Natalie, I didn't want to bother you so soon after the end of the term, so I thought I'd give you a breather. Was I wrong?"

"So, Addy, afraid that you might get a bad rep hanging out with an old lady?" She chuckled.

"No. I … you know that's not it."

"I'm just toasting your tortilla, Addy, but, listen, I don't want you to stay away. We have so much to talk about, including what happened to dear old Kayson. And the pickle you're in. And Addy," she said in a conspiratorial voice, "there's something I have to tell you. The sooner the better. I think you'll really like it. Can you come over today?"

She sounded practically giddy. This was so like her. "What is it, Natalie? Can't you tell me over the phone?"

"Oh, Addie, you can't take this away from me. I want to see your face when I tell you, and besides, you never know who is listening."

"Who could be listening? What are you talking about?"

"Ah, trusting soul that you are. Don't you know that nothing is private or sacred anymore? It'll be worth your while. Anyway, it would be good to see you. I'll be here, because I'm not going anywhere. Please, Addy."

A mystery would certainly appeal to Natalie, but there also seemed to be a hint of what? Perhaps desperation? Or sadness at being out of the mainstream? I could only speculate. I imagined that Natalie was having a hard time adjusting to her new sedentary life.

Especially since her work had involved a lot of traveling and speaking or consulting with one group or another.

Natalie was most alive when she was engaging with other people. She loved to teach, although she expected her students to be as dedicated as she was to developing their skills. I'd heard of plenty of students who avoided signing up for her classes because they didn't want to have work so hard. They didn't know what they missed. I'd learned a lot from her about teaching and learning. On her office wall was an embroidered quote to which she often referred:

A student, like a plant, needs well-laid roots to flourish.

The teacher's job, like a gardener's, is to foster a strong foundation, through feeding the heart and mind so that wisdom can blossom. *-Anonymous*

Saturday afternoon felt like a perfect time for a drive and to get some physical distance. Natalie lived forty minutes away, on the outskirts of town, in a refurbished farmhouse she'd purchased thirty years ago. Although development from the city had crept out to meet her, she had defended her twenty-three acres from any incursion. Her house was surrounded by a combination of woods and meadow, through which we would often walk together. She also put in a large garden every year and supplied her friends with fresh vegetables throughout the summer. More recently, she had held summer retreats for therapists, where we would gather to seek perspective on our lives and work.

I felt the tension drain away during the drive. Going to Natalie's always felt like entering another country, like some secret haven. I turned into her long driveway, following the grooves left in the snow by another car. Driving between the parallel rows of mature maples lining the half-mile road always felt as if I was entering a Van Gogh painting. Although it was winter, there were faint earthy smells, and the only sounds were the rumble of the car engine and the crunching of tires on the semi-frozen ground. I parked the car next to her old maroon Volvo and shut off the motor. The stack of bricks next to the house that Natalie had collected had fallen over. For years she had been talking about building an outdoor barbecue, and any time someone had a few leftover bricks they would contribute them to her project. Perhaps she'd actually started it. I smiled at the thought. I sat for a moment to finish the psychological transition, and then got out of the car and walked to the front door.

Alarm bells started to sound inside my head when I saw that the front door was wide open like a gaping mouth held in a scream. I called out to Natalie, thinking that she'd just been standing there to greet me and perhaps had gone to answer the phone. There was no answer.

A ceramic vase lay shattered just inside the door.

Confusion blended with alarm. I glanced into the living room and dining room. Drawers were pulled out, their contents strewn. Tables were overturned; china smashed and chairs lay on their sides. It was shocking to see the things my friend loved treated so thoughtlessly.

My breath came in shallow gulps as I moved as quietly as I could. The house was bisected by the staircase with the den and afternoon room to the left, not visible from the hall. What if the intruders were still here?

I checked in the two rooms and found the same disarray but no person. Prickles of anxiety and fear made me shiver, but I kept walking. When I stepped into the kitchen, I was momentarily blinded by the afternoon sunlight. I frantically worked to get my eyes to focus and scanned the large kitchen, which ran the width of the house.

A set of feet were sticking out from behind the kitchen table, on the floor, at the far end of the room. I let out a cry as I ran toward them. Natalie was lying face down, her legs splayed at an unnatural angle. She was dressed as if she had been out working in the yard, in a pair of baggy, blue slacks and green quilted jacket. Clods of mud clung to her boots and in her left hand she was clasping a plant, roots and all. It lay limply, its yellow flower drooping, the pale roots exposed. On the table, an empty flowerpot on its side, spilling its earthen contents onto the white tablecloth.

I knelt next to her, repeating her name, looking for any sign of life. I touched her head lightly and I drew back my hand sticky with blood. There was an angry welt on her right temple and a pool of blood on the floor beneath her head. Her eyes were open, staring vacantly.

She was dead.

I had to fight to check for a pulse just in case I was wrong. I could feel the sweat forming on my forehead as I searched. She was dead, but I was touching her, but she was my friend. Her skin felt cool and dry, although the warmth had not completely drained away yet, but there was no heart rhythm on her neck or wrists. She was truly dead.

My stomach began to churn. Despite what I knew about not touching anything at a crime scene, I raced for the bathroom and threw up.

Afterward, I went through the motions of calling 911, but as I waited for the arrival of official personnel, I felt nothing. I was completely numb and only vaguely aware of the sour taste in my mouth. I wandered across the front yard, and after brushing off the snow I sat on an old chair, one that Natalie would often use to bid the day goodbye. I couldn't be in that house with my good friend lying lifelessly in her beloved kitchen.

CHAPTER 15

Sirens screamed from the direction of the city, and soon two official vehicles raced into Natalie's front yard, spraying stones and ice as they slid to a stop. Arnie Redstone and Fran Kelly stepped out of the unmarked car as the EMTs carried a stretcher into the house.

Arnie followed them in and Kelly walked around the outside of the house. I waited some more, idly surveying the small forlorn farm. It was hard to imagine Natalie not being around to tend to this little piece of territory. I jumped at the touch of Arnie's hand on my shoulder.

"So, Addy. Another body, eh?" The wry smile disappeared quickly when he saw my face.

"Oh, god, Arnie. This is unbelievable," I said to his familiar presence. At the moment, he wasn't a cop but a friend who, in the past, had shared some good times. I tried to stand up but my legs wouldn't hold me. Arnie grabbed my arm just before I fell and helped me sit back down. I started to shiver.

"Addy, let me take you into the house, out of the cold," he said.

I shook my head. "I can't go back in there, Arnie, I just can't. I just …"

"Okay." He became the cop and withdrew a notebook from his pocket. "Just tell me what happened."

"There's not much to tell. Natalie called me this afternoon. She said she had something to tell me, so I drove over and got here just a little while ago."

"Do you remember what time?"

I shrugged. "Probably less than an hour ago. I don't wear a watch so I don't know for sure."

"Yeah, I remember. So then what happened? You got here after she called you and …?"

"Nothing, really. The front door was open and I went in. I found the house like that with her lying in the kitchen. Dead." I could feel the tears starting, their heat burning grooves down my cheeks. "Oh, god, what's going on?"

Arnie drew another chair over and sat quietly for a few minutes while I struggled to pull it together.

"Addy, what would Natalie have that a robber would want?"

"I don't know."

"Did she keep money or anything valuable that somebody might have known about?"

"Arnie, I really can't do this now. Catch me in a few days. Or better, a few years."

I looked out over the land that Natalie had so fiercely defended and wondered what would become of it. Thoughts of developers devouring it brought yet another layer of sadness.

Then Detective Fran Kelly emerged from the house and strode toward us.

Arnie looked at her as she approached. "I've already questioned her. She doesn't know anything."

"She didn't see anything?"

Kelly seemed angry and I reacted to her tone, "Maybe you think I killed her. Since you're convinced I'm into killing professors."

"Did you?"

"That's enough, Kelly," Arnie said.

I caught Kelly's glare at both him and me. What had I done to get her so riled at me, I wondered. And why did I dislike her so much?

She seemed to regain her composure. "This looks like a straightforward burglary gone wrong."

"What about the fact that she wanted to tell me something? Doesn't that sound suspicious?" I said.

"What are you suggesting, Addy?" Arnie asked.

"I'm saying that there's a possibility that the two deaths are connected."

"Kayson's and Cruz's? Why? Based on the fact that Ms. Cruz called you to tell you something? That's pretty slim," Kelly looked straight at me. "Nope. It looks like a robbery. We'll get prints and probably find who did this pretty quickly."

"It's Dr. Cruz," I said. "She's a professor and should be addressed with the respect she deserves." When I had time, I'd figure out what I had against Kelly, but for now I needed to lash out at someone, and she was handy.

Arnie stepped between us and steered me away. "Addy, you should go home. I'll call you if we have more questions." He took a few steps toward the house, turned back to me, and said, "On second thought, stay right there."

I sat, taking shallow breaths. Had Natalie wanted to tell me something about Kayson's death? How had I jumped to that conclusion so fast? I tried to recreate the conversation with her before I left for her place, but without success. My head was swimming with images of scenes involving Natalie. Arnie walked over to confer with Kelly, one of the EMTs, and somebody from the medical examiner's office. He returned to offer me a ride home. I took him up on it.

The drive home from Natalie's remains hazy in my memory. The first clear recollection was that I hoped to avoid Mrs. Kaldione. I felt like I was a walking open sore, vulnerable to any poke, jab or stare. All I wanted to do was curl up and erase the last couple of hours.

I made it past Mrs. K's and was halfway up the stairs before she called to me from her door, "Addy, honey, how's it going? How would you like some homemade soup? *Zuppa de pomodoro*? I made it fresh today."

She held a bowl as an enticement. The aroma triggered visceral sensations from childhood of coming home, snow-covered and wet, the boggy smell of water-soaked woolen mittens, the hunger that follows vigorous snowball fights and construction of snow forts. I even felt the familiar ache of the cold faintly in my hands and cheeks. Coming home. Being comforted. Comfort food.

I stood for a moment on the stairs above the little Italian woman and then started toward her.

She sat me down in the kitchen and ladled up a bowl of the tomato broth, parsley floating. It was flat and bland, as I expected, but the warmth spread out from my stomach to melt my emotional leadenness.

"What is it, Addy?" she asked me kindly. I scooped and swallowed. My tears ran and mixed with the hot, red liquid. Mrs. Kaldione sat opposite me at her kitchen table crowded with ceramic figurines.

I told her about Natalie between mouthfuls. It started to feel as though I had to keep eating, as if something important would be lost if I didn't maintain the link between the soup, the rhythm, and me. She clucked and shook her head. Mrs. K had always been a good audience for gossip about the faculty. Although I got the impression that she didn't catch the nuances of all the stories, she liked to be kept informed. So she had heard me talk plenty about Natalie, among others.

I knew, however, that I would never be able to make her understand what this loss meant to me, no matter how intensely I slurped and ladled and talked. Or cried. Suddenly I felt panicky at the possibility that I had somehow caused the death of my friend and mentor. It felt like a secret thought that was too awful to share with anyone. So I just kept talking and ladling. But the awful question lingered.

Then, abruptly, I was worn out by it all, so I thanked Mrs. K and climbed the stairs to my apartment. I would deal with the secret question later.

CHAPTER 16

Natalie was laughing, dancing with excitement in front of a classroom, passionately arguing a point in a meeting, standing amid the garden greenery, a smudge of dirt on her face. She held a plant she'd just pulled from her garden, an unripe tomato plant she shook in my face. I was wearing a mortarboard hat. Then she was crying and laid the plant down on the ground, where it withered and disappeared into dust. When I looked up again, Natalie was gone. I felt afraid.

The feeling stayed on after I awoke, as much as I tried to shake it off. My eyelids were puffed up like little marshmallow pillows from crying on and off throughout Sunday. That sense of unreality, the disbelief in my own experience followed me throughout the day. My denial wasn't complete, but I knew that my mind was trying to assert it in all its grand capacity to distort reality. I fought to avoid thinking about Natalie's death because I had a full schedule of clients, as was usually the case on Mondays.

That's where I focused, and I was mostly successful for the morning. However, after lunch, just as I steeled myself enough to tackle the rest of the day, I got a message that Toni had called and everything came rushing back. When I called her office, Betty told me she was going to be in and out all day but she would get back to me during one of the stops back at the office.

I try not to arrange for calls to come into my office because it's too easy to have the phone ring in the middle of a sensitive moment during a session. I had no cancellations that day, so I had no chance to call Toni until late in the afternoon. I grew more and more impatient as the day wore on. And my fear grew in proportion. What did she have to tell me?

"Hey, Addy," she said when we finally connected. "You'll be happy with my news."

"That'll be a change. What is it?"

"The medical examiner's report on Kayson came out and the knife they found in him was not the weapon that killed him."

"I don't get it."

"What it means is that your fingerprints on the knife don't automatically make you the killer. Somebody stuck him with a double-bladed knife and then removed it and put in the knife with your prints. They also found chocolate cake in the wound. Any ideas about that?"

"What the hell? Wait, there was chocolate cake at Natalie's lunch." The scene with the knife and Ralph Brewer came to mind. "I did handle that knife, but I dropped it into the sink. Do you think it was the same knife? That's weird and scary."

"It's a good bet that somebody's trying to set you up. Anyway, the charges against you were dropped as of ten o'clock this morning."

"Great. A whole day of worry wasted."

"What?"

"Never mind. What about the other evidence? You know, the witnesses and my so-called motive?"

"They didn't think it was enough."

"That's good, isn't it?"

"If you mean, will they open up the case again, I couldn't say for sure. But I think they will need a lot more than what they have. Especially since there's now evidence that somebody deliberately tried to set you up. So take it easy. I'm pretty sure it's over."

"Thank you for the good word and for all you've done." I felt a twinge. "Oh, did you hear about Natalie Cruz?"

Toni made all the appropriate sympathetic noises.

"Will this affect my case?" I said.

"It shouldn't, unless you actually did kill her."

"What?"

"Sorry. Bad joke. As far as I know, they are two separate cases and it was just a coincidence that you discovered both bodies. However, you can stop doing that anytime because the police are not that forgiving."

"I had nothing to do with Natalie's murder."

"I know. It was a burglary and it was too bad that she was home at the time."

"I'm not so sure it was a random burglary, but the police won't listen to me about it."

"Addy," Toni said, "don't get involved. It's best to keep your head down for a while. I gotta go."

"Okay. Can you tell Kris about the charges being dropped? And thanks again."

"Sure. You're welcome. But Addy, you should still be careful. If somebody is trying to set you up, it may not be over."

CHAPTER 17

I tried taking a shower and then I made myself a cup of tea. Neither of these helped much with my grief. If it had been anyone else, I would have gone to Natalie for comfort since she was the closest I had ever gotten to a motherly person in my life. It was Natalie who would reassure me when I started to doubt myself, especially when something would happen at the school. She helped me make sense of the politics so that I could maneuver around the mines. She felt like my safety net. Now she wouldn't ever be there again, for anything I might need from her.

And then, one of those conveniently forgotten memories surfaced. The one time Natalie and I had argued heatedly was around a decision she had supported in one of those faculty meetings she liked to tell me about. She had been describing one of Brewer's tirades against a proposed change. "So he stands up, rocks up and down on his heels, turns beet red and begins to scream that he's not going to allow the faculty to railroad him into 'this stupid idea.'"

"What stupid idea was that?" I asked.

"Oh, some proposal to require students to do an antiracism project as part of their internships."

"Sounds like an interesting idea," I said. "What happened to it?"

"We were concerned about Brewer's heart, so we rejected the idea." She had said it lightly, but it still meant she had sided with

Brewer. I gaped at her. She smiled. "It wasn't such a good idea. Anyway, then ..."

"Wait a minute. How did you vote on it, Natalie?"

"Addy, you don't understand all of the politics. We decided against it."

This didn't fit with what I knew about Natalie. "I don't get it. Why isn't it a good idea for social work students to focus on the issue of racism?"

"It just wasn't."

"Explain it to me."

"Addy, I will not be interrogated by you or anyone else. This is a question of academic freedom."

"I'm not asking you to answer to anyone else. I'm asking you to explain a position that, from what I thought I knew, is not like you."

"I had my reasons. Do you want to hear the rest of the story or not?" She set her jaw firmly as if to dare me to try again. This was a side of her that I had really only heard about.

"You have a right to your reasons," I said, "and if you don't want to talk about it it's your choice. But it's not like you to just reject something that might have had possibilities."

"Let's just drop it."

Thereafter we didn't talk about it, but I was left feeling puzzled by how out of character this was. She finished telling the story of how the issue had triggered yet another screaming match between Martin Enriquez and Ralph Brewer, while the rest of the faculty tried various strategies to get them to stop. Because of what else I knew about Natalie, I let it slide.

And I still didn't know what it meant. Although she could be irascible at times, my overall picture of her was as someone generous, compassionate, and thoughtful about the plight of others. And despite that specific memory, the picture still held.

My relief at hearing Toni's news only slightly lessened the heaviness I had been feeling. To have the last impression of Natalie be that dreadful scene at the farm, and to be left with the thought that someone could have killed her, continued to plague me. I still didn't know if it had been murder as part of a burglary or if her death was related to Kayson's murder and I couldn't let it go. It was all mixed up with the thought that I might have been responsible for her death in some way. Should I have known that what she wanted to tell me was about Kayson's death? Did I unknowingly lead the killer to Natalie? But how could that be, since the killer, if there was one, had gotten there before me?

I went back and forth until I felt like jumping out of my skin. After a few hours of this brooding and sitting and more crying I decided that I needed a distraction and that the best way to do this was to get out of my apartment. I thought briefly that I might stop at Mrs. Kaldione's just to make contact, but it wasn't going to do it. No, there was something else I needed to do. I called a cab to take me back to Natalie's to retrieve my car.

Natalie's farm sat as if waiting, and for some reason I didn't want to break the silence. Another round of snow had begun as if the sky was weeping frozen tears. Yellow police tape hung draped across the front door. As I walked to the house, I saw the detritus from the crowd of official people who had been there. There were footprints in the muddy snow and everything seemed just a little out of place. The two outdoor chairs lay toppled over, one of the doors to a small outbuilding was ajar and the maroon Volvo was now parked on the lawn. A vehicle had driven over a couple of baskets that had been lying next to the porch. They looked like bird nests crushed into the snow. I could almost see Natalie wandering around her lot setting things back the way they should have been.

No yellow tape was going to stop me from entering. I searched for Natalie's extra key, which she kept hidden for her friends. It was in a small hole that had been created by wood-gnawing insects at the base of a windowsill. The police had either overlooked it or decided to leave it there.

The house was cool and dark and smelled musty. Not like it was when Natalie had been there to greet you. The life of the house had ebbed away. I wandered through the rooms taking it all in, feeling very little. The mess left first by the murderer and then by the police made it necessary to tread carefully. Arriving at the foyer after having been upstairs, I glanced at the embroidered work hanging in the hall. It was the same saying that she had in her office:

A student, like a plant, needs well-laid roots to flourish.

The teacher's job, like a gardener's, is to foster a strong foundation, through feeding the heart and mind so that wisdom can blossom.
-Anonymous

Tangles of green embroidered vines bordered the words, their tendrils weaving through some of them. I noticed, as if seeing it for the first time, that the wooden frame had become slightly warped.

And then it struck me.

I walked quickly back to the kitchen to orient myself. I stood looking down at the spot where Natalie had been lying, now outlined with white tape. It was a flattened representation of a person who had just recently been fully multidimensional. Three dark blots of blood lay where her head had been and there were crumbles of dirt left by the plant she'd been holding in her right hand. On the table was more blood, now darkened. The small splats were in the middle of the table, appearing smudged as if something had been laid on top of them while they were still wet.

She had been holding a plant. At that moment, I felt sure that I knew more about Natalie's death than anyone else did. I was scared and angry and mostly mystified, wondering what I should do with the awful reality of what I thought I knew.

When there was no more reason to stay, I reluctantly left. I felt sad at the thought that I would probably never come back there again.

I drove on autopilot back to my apartment. There was a lot to figure out. I had to consider my job and make sure not to jeopardize it, but more importantly, I had to do something with the information that would help catch Natalie's killer. I didn't know who had murdered her, but I was pretty sure where to look. It also seemed clear that my own recent forensic situation was linked with hers. I might have been off the hook, but her death was not unrelated to Kayson's murder. Through her death, Kayson and I would stay joined together.

Once home, I called Kris. She didn't answer, but I left a message with the receptionist. She buzzed an okay with her smoke-coated voice.

My next move was to take a drive over to the local police station.

It would help me feel as if I was doing something and give me the simple task of driving to focus on. It took fifteen minutes to get to the station and I was glad it wasn't any farther. Snow had been falling with a fury for a couple of hours. As I turned down a small dip in the road, the car slid around like a wheeled toboggan and I slowed gradually to a crawl. I hated feeling out of control.

The police were housed in a building that was long past its glory days. It stood overseeing a dilapidated neighborhood where people who belonged to the easily-disposed-of class lived out their lives. Years of seepage and dirty rain had stained the granite blocks of the walls. The department had a reputation for toughness, perhaps in an attempt to compensate for their less-than-respectable housing. I climbed the crumbling steps and decided to take the stairs to the third floor where Arnie's office was.

I found him leaning over his desk, the phone clamped to his ear, while he struggled to either put on or take off a jacket. When he looked up, he was not happy to see me at all.

I stood waiting. When the conversation ended, he seemed to want to slam down the receiver but instead set it firmly with a controlled irritation.

"I'm on my way out, Addy. Whatever it is, it'll have to wait."

"I have some information that might interest you and the good detective."

"Addy, leave police work to us."

"Just call her in here so I don't have to repeat myself."

He stood for a moment and I waited while he engaged in his internal debate. Then he picked up the phone. Soon after that, Detective Fran Kelly arrived. She scowled as she saw me. I gave my most innocent look of puzzlement. "Sorry to disappoint you detective. I know you had your heart set on my being guilty." If I was in no mood to suffer her gladly yesterday, I felt even less well disposed today.

Kelly tossed a look at Redstone. "We could reopen at any time."

She glared in my direction. I glared back, sensing the growing tension between us. This woman was out for blood. Well, so was I. "What's with you, Kelly? You sore because I slipped your noose?"

"Your type always wiggles out of tight spots."

"Yeah? What's my type?"

"You're soft and privileged, and people like you never seem to have to pay for stuff, including your crimes."

"Must be nice to be able to make up your mind like that. Just leap to a conclusion and stick with it, no matter what. Saves time."

"Detective Kelly," Arnie said, "Addy here says she's got information about the case. Don't you, Addy?"

Kelly smirked. "Oh, do tell."

"What do you have against me, Detective Kelly?" I challenged her. "I don't get your attitude,"

I was being bold or stupid but I forged on. "Think what you want, Detective Kelly, but I would appreciate it if you would concentrate on finding the person who actually did this. I mean killed both Kayson and Natalie. I think your best lead would be to look for a student."

"So, a big mouth and an amateur detective?"

Arnie said, "What makes you so sure it was a student, Addy?"

"I don't know the why, but I do know that Natalie left a clue."

"What clue?" Arnie asked.

"She was found holding a plant. Natalie had a quote on her wall at home and the same quote in her office at school. It compares students to plants. That's why I think it wasn't an accident that she grabbed the flower. She was telling us something."

The two detectives looked at each other and then back at me. Kelly spoke first, "If that's all you got, I'll stick with the original theory, that it was a murder committed during a burglary." She held up her hands as I began my protest. "Look, the old lady probably reached for anything to throw at the intruder, you know, to try to defend herself. But instead, the plant came out of the pot and she didn't get her shot off. Maybe if she had, she wouldn't be dead. Anyway, that's what we're going on." She looked at Arnie again.

He shrugged. "Addy, I'll keep it in mind."

"Arnie, I know I'm right, no matter what your sidekick says. And if you guys don't look into this from that angle, then maybe somebody else should."

At that, Arnie beckoned to Kelly and they talked quietly together, turning away to shield their conversation. From her body language, I thought I could see the reason for her dislike of me. Kelly seemed to soften and look at him with what might be affection. Perhaps she had a thing for him and felt threatened by me? Had Arnie told her about us? Or, rather, that there used to be an us?

They finished kibitzing and Kelly tossed me one last scowl before leaving. "Addy," Arnie said, "you've got to admit it's not much. I'll look into how it might fit, but in the meantime, don't you dare do anything stupid like trying to play detective. Leave that to us."

His words stung a little, but as I began to formulate my next volley, I caught his look and instead threw him a lob. "I'm sure that you guys will find out what happened to Natalie. Just remember that she isn't just another nameless murder victim. She's … she was somebody very important to me."

I wasn't sure if he nodded just to pacify me or if he really got it, but I was not going to let them shove this into some dusty unsolved case file. During my ride home, I made a pact with myself that Natalie's murder was going to be top priority for me even if it wasn't for Detectives Kelly and Redstone.

CHAPTER 18

Now that I had decided to go ahead with my plan, I felt like a kid who'd been promised a trip to the zoo. So when Edith, my boss, wasn't available when I first called, I had a hard time changing direction. As I stood over the phone debating my next move, it rang and I jumped a mile.

"Addy, I'm glad I caught you," Georgia said at the sound of my voice. "You'll never guess what happened. I just got off the phone with the Chair of the Clinical Sequence, you know, Dr. Andrews? She asked me if I could temporarily take over Kayson's supervisory slash advisory spot over at the Social Services Department until they worked out a permanent replacement."

I smiled, thinking about trying to talk to the professor. "How long did that take?"

"A good twenty minutes," Georgia laughed. "She kept forgetting what she was saying. I mean the woman has some kind of senility thing going, I think. She led me around, and it was a real act of concentration on my part to stay with her."

I thought about Professor Andrews with her reputation as a very soft-spoken, kindly, extremely confused older woman. More than a few times, I had seen her in the hall in an earnest conversation with a very bewildered looking student. Dr. Andrews could carry five or six unrelated threads of thought, sort of knotting them together as she went, leaving the listener baffled. It was rumored that she was a secret tippler. Maybe alcohol-induced dementia was in full swing.

"So what do you think of that, Addy?" Georgia said. "I mean, I've got a chance to see what he was up to now and I bet it isn't pretty."

"He was a piece of work." I was still sorting out what this latest piece of news meant.

"I know you're in trouble, Addy. I'm not sure what all's going on, but I want to do what I can. Maybe this could help?"

"They've dropped the charges," I said.

"Really? I thought there was an article in the *Whitefield Chronicle* announcing your arrest."

"What? How come I didn't know about this?"

"I swear it was in there. I'll dig it out for you."

Great, my phantom crime aired for all the world to see. I'm sure they wouldn't be as quick to print a retraction proclaiming my innocence.

I had a sudden inspiration. "Georgia, are you going to need any help with this? You know, consultation or something?"

"But you're in the clear. Why would you need to know anything more about Kayson?"

"Georgia, I think there's a connection between Kayson's and Natalie's deaths. And doesn't it make sense that the more I find out about Kayson, the more I'll know about who killed Natalie?"

There was a long pause. What was she thinking?

"Addie," she finally said, "I'm not so sure about this, but if I can help you out, maybe you can help me in the process. They think that I'll only have to do this for a month or two, but I've been worried about convincing my board to go along with me dropping to part time and giving my assistant director some of the load. The client pools of the two programs overlap so it makes sense, but you know boards. I hadn't thought of having an assistant. And who would be better than my good friend and colleague, Addy van den Bos?"

I smiled at the idea and at her characterization of our relationship as a good friendship, since I wasn't sure I would have described it that way. "Well I was thinking of taking some time off so I could focus all my energy on my case. Even though I'm not a suspect anymore, there's still somebody out there who tried to jam me up. Besides, I want … I need to find out who killed Natalie. And I believe finding out what I can about good old Kayson could lead me to Natalie's murderer as well."

"How do you know there's a connection?"

"Well, I don't. But I'm sure Natalie was going to tell me something about Kayson. It would be great if I could snoop around over there."

"Okay, let's see what we can do."

"Talk to Dr. Andrews and whoever else you need to. I think I can work something out with Edith."

"Do I have to? Talk to Andrews again, I mean? For something like this it'll mean setting aside an entire afternoon."

"Take her out for a drink. Maybe that'll help."

"God, Addy, great idea. Being in a bar with a drunk old Andrews. Who could ask for a nicer time?"

"Give the girl a break. She's had a hard-drinkin' life. And it ain't no picnic having to deal with the other faculty for your entire adult life."

"Not to mention students," Georgia said.

"Right," I said. "Anyway, thanks for thinking of me. If you can pull this off, it might open up some possibilities."

"It's okay, Addy. Actually, I can't think of anybody else I'd rather work with on this. I'll give you a call when I get something, okay?"

Next I tried Edith again, and this time she was available. She was curious about the status of my case, so I filled her in and then I brought up the reason for my call. "Listen, Edith. I need to take some time off."

She sighed, "I was afraid that might be coming. Addy, you know this is a bad time. We have a waiting list longer than I can remember, and the board is putting pressure on us to improve our productivity. I'm not sure I can spare you."

My stomach started to churn. "Edith, I know this is a lot to ask, but I won't be at my best until all of this is settled. I'll get my clients ready for the break."

There was silence on the other end. As I waited for her response, I mustered up another round of arguments.

"I'm under a lot of pressure here," she finally said. "How long are you thinking?"

"Maybe a couple of weeks, maybe a month." How much time does it take to find a murderer?

"I can't just have your slot unfilled, so the best I can offer is a leave of absence, without pay. And it has to be for a set length of time so I can hire somebody to fill in. If I can find anyone. We're down too many workers now, with one on pregnancy leave and another taking care of her mother half time. I'm sorry, Addy. I know this might put you in a bind, but ..."

I knew I could hold out for a while, but being without pay would make it tight, especially if it were for a month or longer. Anger flickered briefly because I had expected something different from Edith, but it wouldn't help to snap at her, although she didn't know how close she came. My job situation was already precarious, and after all, snapping wasn't professional.

"Okay," I said. "That will have to do. I'll come in on Wednesday and start the process of transferring people."

"I'm sorry, Addy. I'll see you on Wednesday."

That conversation did nothing to improve my mood. It took me some time, but I finally settled on going for another run. Afterward, I tried to focus on Burdy but my heart wasn't in it, so I gave up and went downstairs to visit with Mrs. K. We sat in her front room, drinking tea and watching the snow fall. We talked about her family and she asked me how things were going. I brought her up to date.

"How could they think that of you, Addy? Social workers don't go around killing people. And you're such a nice person. They should have known it from the start that you weren't guilty. You tell them to talk to me. I'll tell them."

"It would have taken more than that, Mrs. Kaldione."

"Give me a break, Addy. I'm just saying what an old lady is supposed to say. But it's a ridiculous idea, you a murderer. From what you've told me about those folks over at the school, there are plenty of crazy people they could pin it on. And now that other one being killed. If there's anything I can do ..."

"Thanks, Mrs. K."

I left when the gloom deepened enough to blur Mrs. Kaldione's features beyond my ability to make them out.

CHAPTER 19

There was no way to protect my clients from the shock. I had mentally gone down the list trying to gauge how each client might react to my temporary leave. I needed to meet with each of them at least once to help them adjust to this major tear in our relationship. There would be a few who might need more than one session.

During a break, I walked to the coffee room and ran into Edith pouring herself a cup. We stood quietly for a moment and then she said, "How is it going with your clients? I mean with the transition." A first year intern could have picked up on her coolness.

"Okay, you know. It's hard. It stirs up a lot of stuff, for me and them."

"Addy," she said, "do you have to do this?"

"Natalie was very important to me."

Edith stirred her coffee and took a sip. She spoke to the wall, "Are you sure you aren't confusing her murder with someone else's'"

"I don't give a damn about Kayson."

"I didn't mean him, I meant—"

"Shit. It has nothing to do with that." Or did it? "This is something I need to do for her and for me. I know the police are not taking this seriously. After all a dead, little, old Mexican woman isn't a high-profile case."

"You were never one to trust others to do it better than you could."

That stung. She may have been right, but at that moment it felt like a slap, and not the affectionate chiding I expected from her.

"What's the deal, Edith?" I said.

She shook her head. "Sorry. You know, sometimes I spew when I should keep my silence. But still, this seems sorta radical."

"I know. But I'm not sure I can even concentrate on the work, I'm so preoccupied with this. And it's not just Natalie. Somebody tried to set me up as well."

She put away the milk, and walked back down the hall. "Come in to my office."

I followed, my stomach tightening. What else was coming?

She didn't speak again until the door was firmly closed behind us. "Addy. There are those who are interested in putting as much distance between you and the agency as possible."

I stared at her. When she didn't say anything I found my voice. "What does that mean?"

She waited a beat. "It means that if you leave this agency, you might not be able to come back."

There was a rushing sound and pressure in my head. I loved this place. Of course, there were the usual frustrations with weird decisions that came down from above, and the ongoing conflict with the insurance companies, but I had long ago decided that Bertha's Place was my home away from home. I loved the clients for the most part, and most of us on staff had been drawn close together just by virtue of the work. It hadn't occurred to me that this decision would jeopardize my position. Stupid, I guess.

"God, Edith, what are you saying? Who? Can you tell me who wants me out?"

"No, I can't, you know that. But, they weren't all that happy with that incident last year and the negative exposure that it brought." She was referring to a spot of trouble I had gotten myself into while Kris and I had tracked down another mysterious death.

"What the hell …? That worked out all right. Besides, the charges have been dropped, so why are they being so unreasonable?"

"You know the board has become more conservative over time,

and they are very skittish about anything that could be seen as bad publicity. Actually it's only a couple of people, but they seem able to sway others to their side. I'll try to shield you, but I get the feeling it won't be enough. They're nervous about having an alleged murderer working with our clients."

"The operative word is 'alleged.' And now it's 'exonerated.' Or do they think I did it but have some sway with the police? Maybe I should talk to them."

She shrugged and took a sip of her coffee. "I can talk to the president, but there's no guarantee. In the meantime, if you go through with this, you might start looking for something else."

Over the years, I had ruffled some feathers on the Board of Trustees who oversaw Bertha's. After all, it was hard to keep quiet when some of the board's decisions seemed less about social work values and more about the bottom line. Was my tendency to open my big mouth coming back to bite me?

I left her office with a vague worry about what was coming. But I held on to the idea that my friendship with Natalie had been based on more than playing it safe. Natalie would not have sat back if anything had happened to someone she cared about. Someone had to stand up for her. And, as reluctant as I may have felt at times, that someone was me. And there was no way I could concentrate on finding Natalie's killer while trying to cover all my work hours. And I also wanted to know who had been out to get me. If there was one more reason for trying to find her killer hanging around the edges of my consciousness, I couldn't or wouldn't let it take center stage.

I finished out the day, although I wasn't really at my best. It didn't make sense, but I was feeling irritated with Edith, too. She had just been the messenger. It wasn't her fault. I was in pursuit of a murderer and had been hung out to dry.

CHAPTER 20

C hurches, no matter what the denomination, always made me nervous, especially when there was a funeral going on. So I opted out of going to Natalie's funeral at Our Lady of Sorrows, a fitting moniker. But I did decide to attend the reception at the home of the Dean. I really needed to be with others, to be with people who had known her.

Snow had begun falling lightly around sunrise, and by noon it had developed into a full-fledged storm. Mounds of new snow on top of old plow drifts along the edges of the street made parking a challenge, especially since the road was already lined with vehicles by the time I arrived. Cars had been eased into any place that could pass for a parking space, looking rather like the haphazard arrangements of neurons in certain mental illnesses. I had to trudge for two blocks over hidden sidewalks through the driving flurries. By the time I got to the house, my fingers and feet buzzed with the cold.

Dean Forsythe's majestic five-bedroom home was set back from the elegant curving street lined with expensive but uninspired colonials. I found it full of somberly clothed people when I arrived. The crowd spilled into several rooms on the first floor. I knew that the Dean had only one child, now an adolescent, whose separation struggles had left the family exhausted and fragmented. At least they had plenty of room to keep as far away from each other as possible.

Everybody appeared to glide rather than walk, as if the ordinary act of moving from one place to another wasn't appropriate to such an occasion. Somewhere from the back of the house, laughter tinkled briefly, and then was snuffed out. It was impossible to avoid the thick scent of perfumes and colognes blending with the cloying smell of flower arrangements.

At first, I couldn't focus on anyone, and wondered if I'd been right to come. I concentrated on the furnishings and colors of things. Attending to inanimate objects gave me some psychological distance and a place to anchor myself. I planted myself against a wall out of the way until I could ease into being there.

From my observation point, I watched Brewer hoisting canapés and cold shrimp onto his plate while holding forth with a small cluster of students and faculty members, including Professor Anderson. It struck me as odd since it was well known that he usually didn't bother with her. But there she was in rapt attention, head slightly cocked, as words of wisdom mixed with food fell from his lips. His nemesis, Martin, stood near the front door deep in conversation with two other faculty members. I wondered if they had placed themselves within sight of one another like two elderly male lions too tired to fight but still needing to keep the enemy in view.

Somebody was waving from across the crowd. I hoped they were gesturing to somebody else since I still felt too vulnerable to deal with somebody who wanted to actually talk. But the person kept it up so I felt forced to see who it was.

Georgia nodded when she caught my attention and beckoned me to join her. Reluctantly, I wove my way through the thickly packed crowd, exchanging solemn looks with several students as well as faculty members from the school. A picture of Natalie, smiling subtly, stared out at us from the mantel, flanked by two vases of flowers. Her expression suggested that only she knew what the joke was. I wondered what she would think of this scene of mourning. Probably not much.

I tried to have a conversation in my head with her about this being for the people left behind and not for her, but I wasn't sure who I was trying to convince. What was I seeking there?

Images of another funeral flashed on my inner screen like a

determined mosquito buzzing around my head. I gave it a mental swat.

I felt as if I was walking in slow motion. Brewer looked over at me as I passed him and I felt his disdain. I knew that he and Natalie had not liked each other at all, and I had heard that he and the Dean had been at odds about who would head the new International Institute at the school. I thought ungenerously about his reputation for showing up for the free meal, no matter what the event, and almost said something, but I squelched my indignation. It wouldn't do to make a scene. Instead, I waved and smiled in his direction and he scowled and looked away. Perhaps he was still miffed about my cakey encounter with his shirt. I couldn't help but smile at the thought.

Georgia pulled me into a hug as I joined her and when I turned to her companion, I found myself staring at Roz. She gave me a brief acknowledgement and then turned to Georgia. "I can't believe she's gone, can you?" From her expression, it was clear that Roz didn't want much to do with me. I tried to recall our recent conversation to see if I had made some faux pas that warranted the snub. We had talked about how Kayson had helped her get an adjunct position. Had I said something? Was I missing something? I imagine it could have made her mildly uneasy, at worst, but I sensed something more. There was a tinge of what? Fear?

Or was I just projecting? I wasn't at my most perceptive at the moment.

Somebody came by with a tray of plastic wine glasses, red and white. I didn't feel much like drinking. Roz took one and Georgia declined. I thought I detected an exchange of looks between them. I felt like I was standing with people who were speaking in Farsi.

And when you don't speak the language, the best bet is to withdraw, which is what I did. I shrugged and looked out again at the crowd. In the background, sounds of a new group being let in through the front door folded in with the murmuring conversations in the room. I recognized many people from the school but wanted just to be among them without effort or without too much intimacy. I scanned the room and whenever my gaze landed on a teary face I looked away quickly so as to keep my own tears in check. How was

I going to do this? I knew the theory for managing the large feelings of grief but I didn't have much patience doing it for myself.

Beside me, Georgia, Roz, and another woman I didn't recognize chatted. I wondered how they could. Chatting didn't seem to fit.

Amy Arnold's face suddenly stood out from the crowd as she turned my way. I remembered our last phone conversation on that late evening, when she'd accused me of being a bad social worker for not looking up her grade. I hadn't heard from her since then. By her expression when she spotted me, I guessed that her poor opinion of me had solidified into pure hatred. Maybe I should just leave.

I excused myself from Georgia and her group and headed into the center of the house in search of a quiet place. My dislike of crowds was being reconfirmed, as this one was growing more unpleasant by the minute. The kitchen was also full of people who were much livelier than the ones in the front room. Food preparation and being of use to others can buffer some people from the reasons for such a gathering. Perhaps it's a way to feel less helpless and it certainly offers a distraction from the hard feelings of loss.

Somebody, in a rush to get by, bumped me, and I turned to see that it was Julie Pigeon, who had fingered me to the police. She wasn't too pleased to see me either. Her lip curled briefly into a smile—or was it a grimace—and she hurried away. I watched her blend into the crowd behind me, a hardness growing in my stomach.

Her crony in my betrayal, Donna Blare, was leaning over the sink when I walked to the back of the kitchen.

The crowd noise seemed to swell and I ducked quickly into an adjoining room to find a place to sit down.

You might expect that students would be at the funeral of a professor, but something about those three together, being here, bothered me. And there was no misinterpreting Amy's fury. Apparently, to her I was a demon.

Not knowing where I was headed, I walked back toward the front of the house. Then, yes, I knew where I was headed. I would just say good-bye to Georgia, locate the Dean and say something, anything, and get out.

Back in the living room I felt like a molecule in a sea of other molecules, bumping and being jostled around while trying to make my way to where I'd last seen Georgia. With a screen of people between her and me, I was surprised to find her deep in conversation with Amy Arnold.

Another quick change in plans as I tried to melt back into the crowd that a moment ago I'd wanted to escape. When someone tapped me on the shoulder I whirled around, knocking against several people, and found myself face to face with Kris Connor.

"What the hell are you doing here?" I said sharply. Several people turned to look at us.

She was holding a half-empty plate and a plastic flute of white wine. "It's okay, Addy. I thought you might want some support. I know how much Natalie meant to you." She winked. "And more to the point, I know how much you hate this kind of thing."

My two worlds, which had been comfortably apart before this moment, now crashed together. I stood staring stupidly at her grinning face until she punched me lightly on the shoulder and pulled me into an alcove off the kitchen. "It's worse than I thought," she said. "Addy, you of all people ought to know you're not yourself. You walked right by me in the living room."

"Kris, you wouldn't believe it. You remember the student I told you about? The one who called and went off on me when I wouldn't look up her grade at eleven o'clock at night? Amy Arnold. I saw her talking to Georgia."

"So?"

"Don't you think it's odd? I mean, I do."

"People get together and talk at these things. That's what makes it a *social* gathering. As a social worker, you ought to know that. Don't you think you might be making something out of nothing? Anyway, how long do you need to stay here?"

Maybe she was right. Maybe I was being paranoid. We caught up with the Dean, although it took several minutes to find her, since she had been leading a tour of the house. Dean Forsythe acknowledged my friendship with Natalie and said that she assumed I felt the loss as deeply as anyone. I nodded and mumbled something. Then we said our good-byes in a way that would have made our mothers proud.

It had become a comfortingly familiar ritual for Kris and me to spend Christmas Eve day together. We would work all day preparing a great meal, often with other wayward souls we'd invited, and end the evening by the fireplace with a group of friends singing off key. My mother was usually on some cruise or another, and since she was my only relative, that left me free to do what I wanted. Actually I wasn't sure that I would do it differently even if I had family living nearby. For several years, Brody and I had created our own little holiday celebrations, but those had fallen by the wayside as our relationship soured. Close to the end of our time together, we had spent a Christmas Eve with Kris and Bonnie. After both of our relationships imploded, Kris and I decided to resurrect our old regimen and cook for our friends.

I joined Mrs. Kaldione and her son's family on Christmas day for the feast and exchanging of gifts. I felt lucky to have been included in her family. I was almost able to let my troubles fade into the background.

CHAPTER 21

As expected, Cheryl didn't react well to my news that we would have to stop working together, especially when I told her that it might be a permanent arrangement.

"What am I gonna do?" she said. "I don't think I can start over with somebody else. It's too much to tell it all again. It's hard enough to do it the first time."

I kept quiet to stay out of her way.

"This sucks. I waited to work with you and now you're telling me this. Can't you see me in some other office?"

"You must feel like I'm betraying you." I thought about my own sense of betrayal. There would be time later to explore another option with Cheryl as well as my own reactions to Edith's not-so-subtle warning.

"Aren't you? I mean, I spill my heart out to you and it feels like we're getting somewhere, and …," she paused, her eyes glistening with tears of rage. "I'm sorry. I just wasn't expecting this." She reached for a tissue.

"I know." I felt a twist of guilt in my middle. Premature termination with clients was never a good idea, although sometimes it couldn't be helped. I wondered briefly, for the hundredth time, if I was doing the right thing.

Cheryl blew her nose and pulled out several more tissues. "Ah, fuck it. There was something that I really wanted to tell you." She looked at me as if to gauge whether it was okay to change the subject.

"Since we will only have one more time, at most, to meet," I said, "I want to make sure that you get a chance to talk about our ending, and about where you'll go from here. What do you think?"

She waved her hand at me. "I'll find somebody else when I'm ready. Damn. I don't like this, but there's something I really wanted to talk about today. I've been waiting all week."

"It's up to you how you want to use this time."

"Okay." She leaned forward. "Do you remember that client I told you about who said she was glad that Kayson was dead?"

I nodded and tried to remain impassive. I felt anything but.

"Anyway, I saw her this week and she was as tough as ever. I mean, we were talking—or, I guess, we were arguing. That's the only way she'll talk. I'm having a hard time not being angry with her. She was mad because I'd just told her she had to go through the program again because she missed too many sessions. She got so pissed at me. At one point she stood up and I really thought she was really going to hit me. She got in my face and then she spit at me and said something like, 'That's what I think of you social workers. And you all sure don't think much more of me.' Then she stomped out. Can you believe it? She got me all over my face. I'm not sure I can work with her anymore."

"Did she say anything more about Kayson?" Dear God, what was I doing? Last session, not much time, serious emotional revelation and I'm talking about my stuff?

My question stopped her. "No. She booked. But I did hear somebody else in the hall mention his name. I think it was one of the other supervisors." Cheryl looked puzzled, which I could certainly understand. What I was doing was nothing like a responsible therapist would do.

But I couldn't stop myself. "Why do you suppose people would still be talking about him?"

"He used to be the boss and he's been murdered? I don't think it's all that unusual."

"I guess you're right."

I paused and she looked at me expectantly. The thought flickered through my head that I was right. I was too preoccupied with this to be able to do my job.

I had to try and salvage this while I could.

"Cheryl," I said, "I've been preoccupied and I led us away from what was important for you."

"What is it, Addy? Is there something that I can help you with?"

I laughed. "Look at us. I've just brought my own stuff into this and you were more than willing to help me with it. We helping types give ourselves over to others so easily sometimes. And we have a hard time seeing when we are both doing it to others and letting them do it to us."

"What do you mean?"

"Take your client, for example." This was the way back. "She was telling you how it felt to be mistreated and devalued and then she does the same to you. We work with people who have been used and abused, and who often turn around and do the same to us. And you know we do this partly because we're trying to repair something in our own histories. So let's go back to what you were saying. There's something about that client that has really hit you hard."

"It's … it's the spitting. I can't take somebody spitting on me. I don't deserve that. It's disgusting. But I don't think that I can leave the agency yet." She started to cry again. "I don't know what to do."

I noted the link between my telling her that I had to withdraw from my agency and her struggle with staying at hers. It can be hell to turn your back on people in trouble, especially if you share the social worker's save-the-world Achilles heel. "So, have you ever felt this kind of conflict before?"

She nodded wearily, "Shit, Addy, I've had these feelings all my life. I'm stuck. What do I do?"

"What do you mean, you've had them all your life?" I asked as gently as I could.

Tears streamed down her face. "I remember when my dad and mom would fight." There were echoes of the small girl in her words. "He would scream and she would cry, and they would throw things at each other, and he would go out and drink and come back and yell some more. My brother and I would talk with her while my dad was out and tell her that we would be okay if she just left, but she would just cry while she cooked dinner for him. I remember a couple of nights, he came home really late and he would explode. I guess me and my brother were in bed, but I got up because they were yelling downstairs and it was so loud and he was throwing stuff around. So I went downstairs and there was food all over the first floor. He had taken a couple of pots of food and just dumped it everywhere and my mother was down on her hands and knees cleaning and crying. He was standing over her, screaming at her. It was horrible."

She sighed and looked away. Perhaps the scene was playing itself out in her mind. Then suddenly she chuckled, "In fact, I remember seeing his spit spraying as he yelled in her face."

I nodded. She didn't need any help from me. She was in the home stretch.

"I got so angry that I ran at him, yelling at him to stop hurting her." Cheryl wept, sniffling and wiping her face as the fluids flowed. "That bastard picked me up and threw me." She started to sob and talk simultaneously. "Umpl, ee idntcare, at wazhe thningning?" She cried hard for a while, her face hidden in her hands. I sat and waited.

"I was seven years old," she said quietly, the river of tears ebbing to a trickle. "I vowed that I would never let myself do what she did. I mean, I would never, never," she pounded her fist on her thigh, "never, let some asshole hold me hostage."

Okay, time for the next hurdle. "You must have been angry at her for not doing something."

Cheryl stared at me. "Angry? I mean, why would I be angry at her? I mean she was so weak. It was him. It was him. He was the bastard." She almost yelled. "She was so ..."

"Passive? Pathetic?"

"Why didn't she leave him? Why didn't she take us away from that?" The tears ran.

"We want so much for our parents to be perfect," I said presently. "To be good, no, ideal, parents." Images of my own parents locked in their tortuous dance flitted briefly through my mind. "It's painful when we watch them be incompetent over and over again."

"God, Addy. Why was she so weak? What was she thinking?"

Normally, I would hear this question as a signal about how much work there was yet to be done. But because we were terminating, I couldn't encourage her to go there. I had to redirect her. Damn.

"Cheryl, this is important and normally we could begin to explore this further. But because our relationship will be ending, either for a while or permanently, we need to think about where you might want to go from here."

"This just sucks."

Cheryl stood up and I tensed, wondering if she would or could live this out with violence just as her father did. I relaxed when I saw she was moving toward the wastebasket to toss out her handful of used tissues. It was a common way to get a break from the emotional intensity, although I sensed a layer of rage just below the surface. An image intruded on my thoughts. My father, his face contorted with fury, as he pulled his hand back to strike me. I felt impatience with myself that I was not able to keep the images more tucked away.

When she settled back down, she had composed herself enough to refocus. "So what do you suggest, Addy?"

I took a breath and concentrated on Cheryl.

For the rest of the session, we talked over her feelings about our ending and where she might go from there. Although I knew that any decision she made was open to reconsideration, she was firm about not wanting to start with another therapist. I couldn't go into the details about why I was taking this break and could only say that I was having some personal problems I had to take care of. If she knew about the murder accusation and the dropped charges, she never mentioned either. I could only guess what her thoughts were.

At the end of the session, Cheryl told me that she didn't want to set up one more appointment "just so we can wallow around in this ending stuff." Instead, she wanted me to let her know if and when I could see her at Bertha's or some other office.

Variations of this session took place all day, and I felt like I'd been emptied by the end, like a sandbag with a small hole, its contents pouring steadily out. The next time I was at Bertha's, I would be meeting with those clients who were going to continue with someone else, with the social worker who would be picking them up. Edith had left me a brief note telling me that she'd hired a per-diem worker who would be ready to start with my clients on Monday. I called the social worker to talk about the transitions. It all felt like some kind of slow-motion movie, in which I felt compelled to be a bit player.

I called Martha, a long-time friend from graduate school, and asked her about an idea that had been rolling around in my mind. She agreed to think about and get back to me. One more call to my client, Cheryl. That done, I picked up my briefcase and headed home, feeling the weight of exhaustion descend as I went.

I practically lurched through the front door of my apartment and landed on the couch. As I settled into the cushions, I decided that I would just stay there for the rest of my short life. I started wondering how long it would take Mrs. K. to smell eau de corpse before she came up to investigate. She'd probably have her son break down the door and they'd find me ...

I sat up and shook my head. A sure sign of depression, this rumination about gory endings.

Hoisting myself up against the inertia, I went into the back, threw off my clothes, and ran the shower as hot as I could stand it. After a while, it made me feel like singing, and so I did. My rendition of "Oh Baby It's You" was for my ears only, but that and the shower helped me refocus. My thoughts were on Natalie's death scene, not my own.

CHAPTER 22

Later that evening, I discovered, several phone messages waiting for me. The first one was from a Mr. Enrico Garza, saying he was an attorney representing Natalie's estate who wanted to discuss something with me. I couldn't imagine what that might be and I wasn't sure I wanted to know, so I made a note and went on.

My mother's voice came next.

"Adrienne. Adrienne! Oh. I, do I have the right number? Are you there? Is this …? Oh well, I hope so. Anyway, Addy, my God! I read something in the paper today. It was inside the paper, somewhere in section D or E or whatever, but I was looking for the obits, and there was this story about a social worker who had been arrested for killing somebody. I forget who. Where is that article?" There were sounds of paper rustling and then a pause. Then three beeps, because my voice-activated machine had stopped recording.

She continued in the next message as if there had been no interruption. "I have it here. It says that Adrienne van den Bos, an adjunct faculty member at the Rankin School of Social Work, was accused of stabbing a professor David Kayson. Adrienne? You stabbed somebody? Why would you do that? What's going on? Is this about you? Who else could it be about? How is it possible that you do these things? You have to call me. Today. I just got home and this is what I find. Oh, Adrienne, what have you done this time?" She kept up in this vein until the machine cut her off at the four-minute mark.

As my mother's voice emanated from the machine, I thought about how I would talk to her, because I knew that if I didn't prepare myself, I might say something that would set off another tirade. Thanks to some eager reporter who had written what he thought was a breaking story, my worst fear had come true. My mother had acquired some personally difficult information about me and we would actually have to discuss it. My mother didn't discuss. She had two general strategies for approaching a subject. Either she dismissed it with a roll of the eyes as too unimportant to squander precious time on or she found a way to make it something that was a direct affront to her personally. She could run with it then. It sounded as though this was tending toward the latter.

To be fair, she wasn't all bad. There were moments when I had felt a flicker of her kindness. Such as when we had traveled to Canada together, after my father's murder. She told me it was to get away. For a brief time, she seemed actually aware that I might need something from her. She had tried to comfort me by telling me about him, saying that it was important to keep him alive in us. But the timing had been bad. I had hated it. What fifteen-year-old wouldn't? Much later, I could understand how hard it must have been for her to be totally responsible for a sullen adolescent while grieving the violent murder of her husband. A murder that remained unsolved.

Despite my father's brutishness when he drank, in his sober periods you could see what had once been between my parents. I carried one precious image, from my childhood, of a late evening well after I was supposed to be in bed. I'd had a bad dream, long since forgotten, that compelled me to creep downstairs looking for some comfort. Strains of "Stardust" came from the living room, and when I peeked around the corner, I saw my parents swaying in each other's arms. I watched them from my hidden post. As the song ended, my father leaned to kiss my mother, who reached passionately for him as well. At that moment I retreated, feeling as if I had violated a sanctity, but that scene stayed with me like a secret treasure.

I shook off those images and decided to put off calling my mother.

The next message was a short one from Kris, asking me to call her. Then there were two hang-ups. It sounded as if the person had held the receiver for a while, because I thought I heard breathing before the calls were disconnected. It could have been the metallic buzzing of the machine, but it was certainly enough to make me take note.

Then a message from one of those computerized spiels promising a fabulous deal at a bargain price. I hit the delete button while grumbling about this downside to our techno-dependent world and moved on.

Georgia had called to catch me up on the latest developments on her appointment over at the Social Services Department. She wanted me to call her work number at the shelter. I glanced at the clock and saw that it was late, perhaps too late to catch her, but it couldn't hurt to try. Fortunately she was in, although I had to wait a while before she picked up the line. She sounded breathless.

"Addy. I was inches from making a clean getaway, but then all hell broke loose here. I think it must be the full moon. We had a husband who was stalking his wife show up and he was standing outside waving a gun and screaming for fifteen minutes before the police got here. We're absolutely full and everybody went crazy, women and children racing around as if they had someplace to go. The guy's wife got hysterical and tried to run out to stop him. Kids crying, staff trying to calm everybody. You know, same old pandemonium."

"Did this just happen?" I asked. "Do you need to get back to it?"

"Oh, hell, they took him away 'bout two hours ago, but people are still all riled up, and a couple of women are thinking they have to leave without having anyplace to go to. So we've been working to settle everyone down." She laughed dryly. "I'm for the chance to focus on something else. So what's up?"

"You called me, remember?"

She paused. "Oh, yeah. Let me see. Where did I put that?" I could hear her shuffling around the top of her desk in search of something. "I had another ... well call it a conversation with Professor Andrews and I think she agreed to the idea of hiring you as my assistant."

"You think?"

"Well, I'm pretty sure, but I thought we should start before she had a chance to realize what she actually agreed to. I'm at the Social

Services Department main office as of tomorrow and I think you should get over there as soon as you can so we can fill out all this paperwork—" she rattled the papers for emphasis "—and make it official. Okay?"

I agreed, though I was only partially successful at ignoring the little doubts that were taking shape. It felt like I was jumping in with both feet without knowing there was a bottom. And my mother's message nagged me. Although I knew I should call her back, there was something else I wanted to check out first. I went in search of my newspaper, which I had left lying in a drift in the front yard. When I couldn't find it, I knocked on Mrs. K's door. She opened it wearing her apron, stretch jeans, Mickey Mouse sweatshirt, and white tennis shoes. She was short but ample, so Mickey had a slightly sardonic look as his smile was stretched across her breasts.

"Good, Addy, come in. I've got your paper in the kitchen, and I was just about to stop and have some tea. Aldo and the family are coming over tonight for dinner and I've been working like a madwoman. I need a break."

Despite the promise of tea and conversation, I declined and retrieved my paper. Back in my apartment I found the story on the local news page—"Adjunct Suspected in Murder of Full Professor." There was my name in the first sentence. I felt everything inside me sink as I stared at the story. There wasn't anything new in it, but that it actually was there in black and white made it harder to erase. Now my alleged crime was exposed for all to see.

The last time my family's name landed in a newspaper linked to a murder had been over my father's homicide, more than twenty years ago. Long enough, I'd thought, to remain buried. But now I was disgracing the family name with an accusation that it was I who had taken somebody's life. Although it had gotten increasingly difficult over the years, I could still call up my father's face if I really worked at it. I didn't remember him in clear snapshots. More like vague images attached to the strong emotional colors of fear and sadness. How I mostly remembered him was either sleeping or drinking and raging. I always thought of him as an explosive device set to blow at any vibration. Sometimes I thought I could still feel the stinging sensation where one of his blows had landed.

He had been found lying in an alley in a decaying neighborhood, one bullet lodged in what was left of his brain, another in his back. The investigation had turned up his secret life of gambling and numerous dalliances with women, some of who had made a living at the sex trade. Looking back, I could see that my mother must have felt humiliated by these revelations, but at the time I just didn't care how she felt. Even knowing this and with the time that had passed, it wasn't any easier for me to be around her. After our trip together, she refused to talk about the murder, giving that familiar line about it being in the past and no longer important. I knew differently. It enveloped us whenever we were together, suffocating us into superficiality.

But it was only right that I call her back. After all, when you read that your only daughter, unmarried and childless though she may be, is suspected of murder, you do deserve a return call.

"Hi, Mom."

"Adrienne, what the heck is happening? What have you gotten yourself into now? I don't understand why you don't just settle down and …"

"Mom," I interrupted her, because I knew where that was headed, "do you want to know what happened, or do you want to lecture me?"

"Well, no need to get snippy. Okay, so tell me what happened."

I gave her a thumbnail sketch, since I was racing against a pretty short attention span. I knew she was staying with me by her "really's" and "oh no's."

"So it's all a misunderstanding," she said.

"Yes, the story got printed before the charges were dropped."

"Then we don't need to worry. They'll find the real murderer."

It's not often I'm handed an entrée that nice, so I decided to use it. "Well you know, Mom, they don't always find the murderer."

"Oh, Adrienne, sure they will. Don't be such a spoilsport. Just keep your chin up, and if you hope for the best, the best will come. Adrienne, these things usually work out."

Was this a record for platitudes?

"Okay, Mom." I toyed with the idea of telling her about Natalie, but only briefly. Instead I told her I would try to get the paper to print a retraction.

"Good, Adrienne. Try to get it taken care of quickly, okay?" There was a distinct lack of invitation for me to keep her apprised of my situation. She had enough information, and had already convinced herself that it would resolve itself favorably. She couldn't stay long with distressing thoughts. It was her way of protecting herself against facing some deeper and more troubling subjects.

But at least the conversation was behind me.

I thought back on that night when the police came to the door to tell us that they had found my father's body. The doorbell rang at 2:38 in the morning and my mother and I had stumbled from our sleep. We both shivered in the cold air as the uniformed officer stood in the doorway, silhouetted by the moonlight. He gave us the news gravely and then asked my mother to come to the police station in the morning. Afterward, we were left to our shock and I retreated to my room. The last thing I wanted was to witness my mother's grief, or to have her see mine.

The memory sent me in search of something. The file, which I had lugged around for the last eighteen years, had been jammed into the bottom of a bureau drawer. Leafing through old newspaper clippings I saved, I came upon the one that announced my father's murder. He had been killed on the evening of December 9, twenty years ago to the day that David Kayson had died. This fact had faded from my memory until I saw the date again. I shivered at the thought that this meant more than some coincidence of timing.

I was so absorbed in trying to sort it out that I nearly leapt across the room at the sound of the door buzzer.

CHAPTER 23

"You are not going to believe what I've found, or perhaps more to the point, what I didn't find." Kris raced up the stairs and practically leapt into the room.

I stepped back quickly to get out of her way. It was that or be trampled. "What the hell?"

She grabbed me by the arms and spun me to face her. "You asked me to look into Kayson's background. The thing is, I couldn't find anything about him before he was in graduate school. The man has no history."

"How can that be? There has to be biographical information about him. He's written several books."

"That's just it. One of the leads I followed was the publisher's bio. It says that he was born and raised in a New England small town by parents who were teachers at the local high school. But people in Durnsbury, Vermont have never heard of the Kayson family. There is no history of his family ever living in that state. No official records, no nothing." She paused. Leave it to Kris to reach for the suspense. "And get this. I couldn't find any record of him or his family anywhere in the United States."

"Are you sure? Those things should be pretty straightforward to find."

"They usually are, and I checked and rechecked several ways. I found a lot of Kaysons, but none of them related to David E. Kayson.

The man did not exist before he entered graduate school at Mansek College in Wisconsin."

"What about social security numbers and all that? Don't you have to have that stuff to even exist?"

"Yes, he has everything that a good, compliant citizen should have. Credit history, genealogy, academic records back to graduate school, and job history. But David Kayson's social security number actually belonged to a Jeremiah Acre."

"Oh, so he really was this Jeremiah?"

"Jeremiah Acre was born in 1960 and died in 1975."

"He stole somebody else's number?"

"Looks like it."

"Genealogy?"

"According to his bio, he was an only child with an idyllic childhood. He even writes about how his father was an inspiration to him and how both parents supported him through school. His father supposedly came from a family that helped establish the town he grew up in. He even went so far as saying that his mother's family was descended from one of the Mayflower families. But those people existed in some other realm known only to him."

I noted the comment about the idyllic childhood. It always raises a red flag when a client tells me how wonderful his or her parents were.

"So what does all of this mean?" I said.

"Well, for one, it means he went to great lengths to hide his real past. I'm really dry. Can I have something to drink?"

I nodded and headed to the kitchen. It gave me time to think as I busied myself with the mundane. When I returned to the living room carrying a tray with tea and an added treat of stale cookies, Kris was pacing. I knew she'd been at it the whole time I had been gone.

"Listen, Addy, I know some people who can do a more in-depth search. I'm sure that they could turn something up. But it's gonna cost you." She reached for a cup.

"Hold off on that. I've got another idea. You know that program he was involved with at SSD?"

"What program?"

I gave her as much information as I could, leaving out what my client had told me. I couldn't violate my client's confidentiality, and I wasn't sure what to believe about what she'd said.

"So you think you might find something over there?" Kris asked.

"Doesn't that make sense? Anyway, I wasn't sure about it until you told me what you found out about Kayson. I mean, why would a guy go to such lengths to separate himself from his past?"

"Wasn't sure about what?"

"Whether I should go sneaking around there, but this has decided it for me."

"What were you worried about?" Kris asked.

"At the very least it could be awkward for others to have me be there. And it felt voyeuristic, you know like a vulture diving for the corpse."

Kris laughed. "Tell me again why you need to follow up on this guy?"

"It's not Kayson, really, but I thought looking into his murder would lead me to why Natalie was killed and maybe I'd find out who did it. I don't think the police believe the two are connected and I'm worried that they'll never find out who killed her." I felt the twinge of sorrow again as her final scene flashed through my mind.

Kris sat looking at me for a while, but seemed to decide to keep her thoughts to herself.

CHAPTER 24

I was not going to get a break from this. Many of my clients had seen the article about my alleged crime. Some of them brought it up or alluded to it indirectly. We ended up talking about me, and how knowing this affected them.

One client was a man who had spent some time behind bars. I got him because his most recent probation mandated being in therapy for his violent tendencies.

"So now you're gonna be a con like me," he said. "Hey, Addy, I hear it's pretty intense in those women's prisons. You're gonna need to hook up with somebody."

"You're worried about me," I said.

He furrowed his brow. "This ain't a joke. I seen some things in there. And you don't want to ever be by yourself, at least if the women's prisons are at all like the men's."

"Thanks for the warning, but I'll be okay. I'm not going to prison."

"Yeah, I heard that before. I never thought of you as somebody who could kill somebody."

I looked at him for a moment. This was interesting. "I believe you're almost admiring me."

"I know you ain't gonna tell me. That's okay. But just be careful."

Another client summed it up when she said, "I didn't think I would ever be getting psychotherapy from a murderer."

Nothing like a murder accusation to stir up the imagination and heat up the therapy. This, on top of the task of ending with everybody, gave it an odd twist. Were they afraid I was going to kill them off psychologically if not corporeally?

Between appointments, I made phone calls. Kris had seen the newspaper story. "God, Kris. Now it's all over that I'm a murderer."

"Are you going to get in touch with the paper and have them write an update?"

"I guess I have to."

"Yes, you have to. And let me know if they cooperate or not."

"Okay." Kayson was going to stay with me longer than I had ever wanted or anticipated.

Later, I checked my messages and saw one was from Martha, so I gave her a quick ring. Because she was in private practice, we could only talk in the ten minutes between sessions, when everything else has to get done. Martha and I planned a meeting, and then I went back to work.

At the end of the day, I made two more phone calls. First I called the newspaper and could only leave a message for the reporter who had given me such nice exposure. Then I called my client Cheryl and left a message telling her I had found an office where we could meet. I told her I would try her again later. It would take a little while to get up to speed. I needed to arrange for a phone and message service, not to mention some kind of billing system. Just the reason I went to social work school.

Now I had to juggle private practice hours with those I was going to put in at the Social Services Department. I hoped it would lead me to what I wanted, which was flexibility so that I could focus on finding Natalie's murderer.

CHAPTER 25

Nancy Barton and Martha Winter had their offices along a quiet street known around town as couch canyon. Among the large, converted Victorian homes, built back from the street, there were more than a dozen shingles hung up on both sides. You could get the Gestalt approach to explore your "death layer" or select a therapist who would encourage you to create soothing patterns in a sand tray. Somebody offered biofeedback and her office mate did cognitive-behavioral therapy. I knew of one analyst who actually still used psychoanalysis, his clients reclining on his couch and discovering their forbidden sexual fantasies.

In the past, the only reasons that I had to come through this neighborhood were to meet up with a colleague for lunch or just to pass through on the way to somewhere else. A lot of social workers consider private practice the pinnacle of their careers, but I had never imagined it as something I wanted to do. I'd always thought of myself as staying in the trenches, working with people who couldn't get service anywhere else but from such agencies as Bertha's. Bertha Reynolds was a hero in our profession. She had challenged social work to return to our mandate, which was to work with the poor and disenfranchised and to be politically active. I imagined that she would probably frown on this modern turn toward private practice. I felt a little like I was letting her down at the act of pulling into the parking lot of Nancy and Martha's building.

They were both there when I walked into the waiting room furnished with graceful Danish modern furniture of light wood and dark blue upholstery. A curtain of plants hung from the ceiling by the windows. It was an airy, pleasant room, unlike the functional, windowless, scuffed up waiting area at Bertha's. The offices were equally stylish and comfortable, easily places where people could feel cradled and safe. I was introduced to the receptionist, who murmured quietly into the telephone. The whole setting had an understated elegance.

It took us a couple of hours but we worked out the details, so when I walked out of the building, I was officially in private practice. I thought about the relaxed manner with which Martha and Nancy talked about the business they were in. It was obvious that they were sure of themselves, much more so than I was. Was it arrogance on their part? Or insecurity on mine? And was it ethical to begin such a thing using clients I'd gotten at the agency?

No. I had to have more control over my time, and this was the only way I knew to do that.

Mrs. Kaldione met me in the hall as I started to climb to my apartment.

"Addy. Somebody left this for you just inside the front door." She handed me a plain white legal sized envelope. It was sealed and had my name typed neatly in the center of the front. No return address. No stamp.

"Oh, by the way," she said, "Aldo got a letter from his father. First in years."

It was an invitation to join her for a further discussion of family drama. Although I was curious about it, I felt my reclusiveness kicking in, so I asked her if we could do it later. It was hard to miss the look of disappointment, but I was able to resist.

Once upstairs, while on the phone arranging for business cards, I picked up the envelope and turned it over to look more closely at it. There was nothing unusual about it so I tore off the end. It contained a single piece of paper with a terse message:

SOMEBODY IS OUT TO GET YOU

I stared at the words and struggled to make sense of them. The trembling started in my middle and spread to my hands, so that the paper shook as I again turned it over searching for some clue as to the sender. After my futile investigation of the envelope, I slowly set it and the sheet of paper down on my table. I had always felt perfectly safe in my little abode, but suddenly it had been invaded by this ominous message. Was there no end to how my life would change?

Just then, a voice on the other end of the line asked how she might help me. I stuttered that I would have to call her back and set down the receiver. Was I getting close to something? After all, why send this warning now? All I had been doing is asking questions.

The phone made me jump. The damn thing was getting on my nerves. It was Jerry.

"Jesus, Addy, what's going on?"

"Why? Why do you ask?"

"You answered the phone as if somebody was after you."

"You must be psychic. I just got a friendly unsigned note and I'm a little spooked."

He pressed me for details, and after I filled him in, he said, "Maybe this is getting too serious."

"You were the one who encouraged me to try amateur sleuthing," I shot back.

"Hey, Addy, doesn't this tell you something?"

"Not really. If this is from the murderer, it wouldn't bother them to try to scare me."

"At least you could tell the police about this."

"It was probably just a prank." I didn't like his suggestion, but if I did decide to go to the police, I would only want to talk to Redstone. "I don't have the best of relationships with them now, but if it gets more serious I'll get them involved. Anyway, what's up, Jerry?"

"Oh, yeah. Listen. Nothing specific, but the buzz is that whoever did in Kayson was either a member of the fellowship or somehow connected."

"Really? But I thought you said it was somebody connected with the school."

"They aren't mutually exclusive groups. I can't give you more than that, but you said you wanted me to keep my ears open, and this is what's being whispered. Nobody is actually owning up to knowing

119

anything more than that. And if I did know something more, it would be hard for me to tell you. I mean I couldn't give you names, even if I knew them. Still, I thought you should know this much."

"Thanks, Jerry." I told him about my plans to work for the Social Services Department and about Natalie's murder.

"Addy, you have to be careful. Two murders linked to the school, and now somebody is sending you a warning."

"Yeah and somebody at the school told the police that I spent time with Kayson, when that's impossible."

"Somebody has it in for you, Addy. Let me know if there's something else I can help with."

"Just keep your ears open."

Since I hadn't heard back from either Julie or Donna, I decided to try again. I started with Julie. This time she answered and sounded startled, as if I was the last person she wanted to talk to. Or did I imagine it? Probably not. I remembered how she scurried away at the reception for Natalie at the Dean's house.

I got straight to the point. "Julie, what is this about you telling the police that I was with Dr. Kayson?" I probably sounded too accusatory but what the heck, this wasn't a session.

She stuttered and stumbled over her words. "I only told them what I saw."

"Well, you couldn't have seen what you think you saw, because I've never gone anywhere with Kayson."

"I was sure it was you. I saw you. I know I did."

"I don't know why you're doing this."

There was a pause. "So you are saying I made a mistake? If that's true, then I'm really sorry. But both me and Donna saw you."

"When?"

"Maybe three or four times. We saw you get into his car and we saw you and him at Isadora's a couple of times. And we aren't the only ones. Everybody's talking about it at the school. So ..."

"Maybe there's somebody who looks like me." I was trying to get myself back under control. It wasn't going to help matters if I just got angrier.

"Maybe," she said. "But we both were sure it was you. We couldn't lie, could we?"

Well yes, but I wasn't getting anywhere with that tack. I took another. "Assume that this woman you saw wasn't me. If you see her again, could you let me know? It would help me a lot. Maybe you could find out what her name is."

"I don't know. How could this help you, anyway?"

"Believe me, it would. Whatever you can do for me."

I was treading on thinning ice. Technically I was her professor and she could easily react to this request as if it was an order. Damn, here I was, again, imposing my own needs on someone with whom I had an unequal relationship. One more no-no. But I could justify it because she had made life more difficult for me. Maybe all bets were off.

"It's okay, Julie. If you don't want to, that's fine." Give her an out.

"I guess it wouldn't hurt to keep my eyes open for her."

It was time to end our fruitless conversation. I gave her my office number just in case. Was this meddling with the prosecution? No, there was no prosecution.

Fortunately, Donna Blare wasn't around, because I wasn't really up to another conversation trying to shake somebody off a lie. I could do it with clients, but they were lying to themselves and wanted to stop. That's why they came to me. I guess I wouldn't make a very good interrogator.

CHAPTER 26

Virginia Early was my last appointment of the day. She looked gaunt and nervous as she sat playing with her coat sleeve. Although, I'd shown her where the coat hook was at our first meeting, she held her coat in front of her like a shield. I made some relaxing small talk about how it was for her to come back here. Although some anxiety is necessary for this talking relationship to work—you can't get close to working it through without tolerating what some see as unbearable—too much can paralyze the person or simply make them bolt and run. So for Virginia, who was so jittery that she looked like she was going to end up on the ceiling, it was important to create a less-threatening atmosphere. She also wouldn't be comforted by my silence.

"I don't know if I should even be here," she said slowly, without meeting my eyes. "I was thinking that I wouldn't come anymore and not even come today."

"What made you come, anyway?" I asked.

"I don't know. I thought that I should at least tell you that I wouldn't be back. It didn't seem right that I just leave you in the lurch."

"You were worried about how I might feel if you didn't come?"

"Well, I didn't want you to think that it was anything about you." She shook herself as if to get rid of a disturbing idea. "I don't know what to do. I don't know what I want. I only know that I'm feeling lousy all the time and I need to feel better."

"You told me about how full your life is, and you had taken on so much, it was creating stress. Is that right?" There was clearly a lot more than that happening, but I thought I should take the easy approach.

She nodded quietly although she seemed to be only half listening. I waited. She sat quietly for some time.

"I've been having weird dreams that make it hard for me to get to sleep," she said finally. "I mean, that I'm having trouble going to sleep. Well, more that I … I'm avoiding going to sleep until I can't stay awake anymore. When I do sleep, I have these dreams that wake me up in a sweat. My heart is racing and I feel like I'm going to die. I haven't slept well in I don't know how long."

I was having one major dilemma at this moment. In any normal therapy, I would encourage her to describe the dreams, and then explore her other symptoms to get clear about how to help her. But there was this little issue of my leaving. I had to introduce it. I knew she wouldn't take it well, but there was no way around it.

"Virginia. There is something that I need to talk about."

She looked up at me with alarm. Great. "Unfortunately," I said, "things have happened in my life so that I have to leave the agency. However, I also think it's very important that you continue in your therapy. I believe we can find a solution."

Virginia seemed to shrink away from me. Almost trying to disappear into the chair.

"I know that this is poor timing," I said gently, "since we've just begun." Actually, I was feeling downright surprised that she'd even come back.

She didn't say anything but grabbed a handful of tissues into which she blew quietly. I could see her try to hold her shaking in check. I'd seen few clients over the years who became overwhelmed so easily.

"We can talk about how we might solve this," I said. "Are you up for that?"

She looked up, gazing anxiously at me, and nodded for me to go on.

"Actually, I was going to offer you the chance to continue with me, but in another setting."

She seemed confused and finally ventured to say, "So you're going to work somewhere else?"

"Look. I know this comes as a big shock to you, and there isn't any way for you not to feel disjointed. But I have access to an office where we can continue to work together if you want to. It's a private-practice setting."

"Oh." Her expression changed gradually as understanding washed over her like a wave. "Private practice?" Her hands shook and she clasped them together in an attempt to hold them still. "Well I know I'm not going to be able to afford that for sure." I could barely hear her, as her voice seemed to recede at the same rate as she was disappearing into the cushions of the chair.

"I think that we could work something out around the fee. What I wanted to know was that, if the money issue was resolved, would you be interested in continuing with me?"

"Well," she said, "I was so happy that I could see somebody who I heard was good, at a fee that I could pay ..." She wound down and we sat in silence. I was wondering if she was trying to formulate another sentence, or if I should say something, when she spoke again. "I know I can't afford your fee." She seemed to have decided that this was an unsolvable problem.

"Virginia, I believe that we can work out something."

"What do you mean?" She was wary.

We talked then about how we might solve this problem. I had already decided that I would drop my fee to whatever she could afford. Clearly I knew I wasn't going to make any money from this case, but what the hell. She needed help and was willing to trust me for it. I didn't want to let her down.

She was only somewhat relieved and seemed to be waiting for some other terrible thing to befall her, but she agreed to try, so we arranged another session, the first at the new site, and I gave her directions. After she'd left, I sat for a few minutes again, wondering if she'd actually show up. The way she had been instantly suspicious led me to wonder what had convinced her to believe that people would take advantage of her. And further, that she couldn't defend herself against whatever came. If she made a commitment to the therapy, we would probably get to the bottom of it so she could finally start to live. At least that was the hope.

I took the last part of the day to finish making notes and picking up my office. Although the official story was that I would be coming back, it was probably better to assume that I wouldn't be, at least as a regular employee. I fought off the sadness as I went through the routine motions of cleaning out and preparing for a long absence. Several colleagues stopped by to wish me good luck, including Jerry.

"Addy, don't worry too much about Edith," he said as he leaned in the door way of my office. "I think that as she calms down, she'll come around."

"Don't be too sure of that, Jerry," I shook my head and finished filling another box. "I think she'll be happy when I'm gone, because I'm a reminder of her own fall from grace."

We talked then about a case that I had transferred to him, as much to stay away from the subject of my leaving as to answer any questions that Jerry had. I was going to miss him. I was going to miss being able to check in with him after an especially grueling session, or to get his input on some case that had me baffled. His forte was his alcoholism—Jerry was a long-standing recovering alcoholic as well as a child of alcoholic parents, and so had the insight. But he also had a special way with kids.

I'll always remember coming across him in the coffee room, wiry frame crouched down in the corner, peering into the space between the refrigerator and the wall. A six-year-old had hidden himself there and Jerry was talking to him softly, about how he could understand how scary it was to be in this strange place. A woman who I assumed was the mother was angrily pacing in the room and the boy, who was not in my line of vision, was whimpering. The woman reeked of the demon gin.

I had watched as Jerry gently coaxed the child to come out from his hiding place while occasionally turning to say something equally soothing to the agitated mom. She seemed to quiet at the same time that the boy eased himself into Jerry's waiting embrace. By the time the crisis had passed, both mother and son were walking quietly down the hall led by this kind man.

God, we human beings can be hurtful. Or kind. A painful past can lead us to create pain for others, or try to alleviate it. Or both. Jerry was one of the good ones.

This memory and others brought me dangerously close to tearing up, so I continued to work on my office and avoided looking at him standing in the doorway.

"I'm going to miss you, Addy," he said at last. "I mean, who will I be able to gossip with? And, more to the point, who will keep me supplied with tissues?" I smiled at this. Because the agency hovered forever on the financial edge, supplies often ran low. Once, I found the supply cabinet empty of boxes of tissues, and had gone into a small panic. I scrounged to get enough to last me until the end of that day. Then, to stave off a repetition of that crisis, I had developed a reputation as a hoarder of tissues. I made it a habit to buy a case at a time and kept my closet stocked with them. Soon everybody knew where to come if they ran out. People chuckled about my little compulsion even if I had the last laugh. Actually, it was kind of funny. There was little room for anything else in my closet.

"So, Jerry," I said solemnly, "I suppose that it will now fall to you to watch over the stash, to keep it full, and to distribute it as you see fit." I opened the closet and handed him a box to close the deal.

He laughed as he took it and gave me a salute. Then he bowed his way out and I was left alone, with my closetful of tissues.

CHAPTER 27

I left Bertha's and headed over to the school. There weren't any students in the halls since the term hadn't yet started. However, the staff was all there preparing for the onslaught of students and taking care of other tasks associated with running an academic institution. I had decided to throw myself on the mercy of Marissa, Kayson's secretary-in-mourning. I found her staring into the same computer monitor while several other women worked at desks crammed into the crowded office. The walls were festooned with holiday decorations representing every religion possible, including a couple of solstice greetings for the office pagans.

"Hey, Marissa," I said cheerily and, I hoped with a hint of intimacy, as if we were good friends.

She looked at me as if I had just jumped out of a cake and perhaps was still covered with crumbles of chocolate. "Oh. Hi."

"Marissa, how about a late lunch? I'm paying."

"I've already had mine."

I walked over to her and lowered my voice. "Okay, but I need to talk to you in private."

Marissa agreed, but I could tell she felt reluctant. I led her out into the hall and down to an alcove where we could have some privacy.

"Marissa, listen, I need your help. It will only take a few minutes of your time."

"I don't know how I could help you."

I felt bad for her. Again, I had to play on her tendency to avoid other people's anger and watch her anxiety grow as she felt more and more worried.

"You wouldn't want anything to stain David Kayson's reputation would you?" I said.

"Of course not. He was a fine man."

I hurried on when I saw her begin to tear up. "There are students who are saying negative things about him. And about me as well."

"Like what?" Now she looked indignant, a dog growling to defend its master.

"I couldn't repeat any of it, but it would damage the memory of the professor if it continues. I would like to talk confidentially to those who are responsible, so that I could nip it in the bud. If they knew that one of the faculty could identify them, then maybe they'd stop. That makes sense doesn't it?" This was a stretch, but Marissa was psychologically disposed to giving people the benefit of the doubt. I felt a twinge of guilt when she nodded and said, "How can I help?"

"Well I assume that the culprits probably had him for classes, so if I could just see some of his recent class lists, perhaps I could identify some of them."

I could see her feeling puzzled and then frightened as my suggestion washed over her.

Before she could say anything, I said, "All you would have to do is get me copies of class lists that go back only three or four terms. And I would keep quiet about where I got them. No one would ever know and we'd be protecting Kayson's reputation. You'd be doing something important for the professor."

"I don't know."

"Look, I only need the names. And nothing else. How long do you think it would take you get that together?" I didn't want to give her a chance to say no.

"I could do it in about a half hour, but ..."

"Good. I'll come by tomorrow to pick them up. Thanks so much for your help, and I know if the professor was around, he'd be very grateful."

I left quickly, feeling ever worse about strong-arming this woman into doing something that probably wasn't above board. Fortunately, I had another stop to make that would take my attention off the guilt.

CHAPTER 28

I t was late. The sun was nothing but a pale purple glow on the horizon, and I felt worn out. But I'd promised Georgia I would meet her at the Social Services Department, so there I would go. Crusty remnants of the recent snow clung to the sidewalks, roofs, and a few tree branches. In the space of a day, the temperature had inched upward enough to soften the snow, and then plummeted to refreeze it into crunchy ruts on the road. The tires made the sound of driving over glass.

The Social Services Department was housed in a four-story building shaped like two half circles backed up to each other. From the air it must have looked like a drooping x. X marks the spot. Each arm arched gracefully away from the center where the front and back entrances were. Wearing a laminated visitor's card, I trotted behind a young assistant who showed me the way to Georgia's office through a maze of tiny half-walled cubicles. Here and there were people on phones, working at computers or reading files. A few of the nooks had two people crammed in, deep in discussion. Perhaps it was over a case, or maybe there was a more interesting topic, such as department policy or some piece of gossip. The air buzzed with electronic and human noises.

Georgia's office, it turned out, was on the front of the building, with windows overlooking a courtyard. It would have been considered almost roomy had it not been for the walls of bookcases brimming with binders and books as well as the piles of material leaning against them. Georgia sat at a small clear space on which to work in the middle of her desk, flanked by a computer and more stacks of papers and files. I heard rather than saw that she was on the phone, since I could only partially see her from the doorway.

I cleared off the other chair and sat so that I could catch her eye between heaps. She nodded and held up her hand signaling that she'd be finished in a moment. I waited and stared out through the open door. If I leaned and looked down the hall, I could just catch a corner of one of the cubicles. A face was looking back in my direction.

Of course, people were going to be curious about the comings and goings in the boss's office. I sat back.

"So, Addy, here we are. Can you believe this mess?" Georgia stood and looked over the piles, like a giant peering over the castle walls. It made me feel hemmed in. "Apparently, Kayson rarely hung out here."

I surveyed the boxes and mountains of paper. "Georgia, it looks as if he used this as a storage and dumping zone." It struck me that this did not fit the image of the obsessively neat Kayson, This office was anything but. It must represent a serious dichotomy in him. Anyone who would clean the janitor's room could not have tolerated being in such a space for long.

She snorted as she came around to the other side of the desk. "That's what I've gathered. I'm not sure I'll ever get to all of this. I have an urge to toss it all and start over. So let's go down the hall to your space. It's a peach, too."

She leaned back over the desk and pawed through some files until she found the one she wanted; then we headed out. As we walked out along one side of the maze of offices, I sensed that our progress was being followed over the low walls. The room that would be my office was not as large or as full but looked as if it had been used for storage as well. It, too, opened onto the large cubicle forest, and it too had a small window overlooking the front courtyard. At least the walls went all the way to the ceiling. I was going to be the new kid, with a bona fide office, certainly a subject for discussion and grumbling.

We sat amid the accumulation of a dead administration talking about how to orient ourselves.

"You're not gonna believe the disorganization," Georgia said. "I can't even find the most recent budget anywhere. There are notes for the one from three years ago, but that's all I could locate so far. The computer has the original grant on the hard drive, but there's nothing else in there, and there are plenty of disks but none are labeled. People are asking me questions I can't answer because everything is so jumbled. I'm going to need an army to straighten this out." She paused. "Sorry to dump this on you but I've been sitting here—I mean there—getting more and more angry at that guy for leaving it like this. I'm glad you're here, Addy."

That made me worry. Georgia was telling me that she was going to rely on me in a way I wasn't sure I was ready for.

She read my expression and smiled.

"It's okay, Addy," she said. "I just needed somebody to vent with. Anything you can do would help." She turned to the file she'd set on the desk. "Oh yeah, here are the forms that you need to fill out and sign." As she handed them over, she looked directly at me. "I hope that being here will help you with your, uh, situation."

"I hope so, too."

"I was thinking about setting up a staff meeting. This might shed some light for us. There is literally no way to know what's actually going on because there are no coherent records anywhere, at least that I've found so far. In the meantime, I'm going to read the grant to find out what we're supposed to be doing and try to find the actual goddamned budget."

"Do you know who your staff are?" I asked.

"Fortunately, I did find a list of unit supervisors. Which may even be accurate."

"So what do you want me to do?"

"I need you to bounce things off of. And I thought that you might talk to all of the supervisors individually to get to know them and find out how their units are going. Maybe sit in on some of their group sessions with clients. Also, you might look at some files I found … monthly and semi-annual reports from the supervisors about their programs. At least I think that's what they are. I didn't actually read them. I just haven't had time." She looked as if she would actually throw up her hands, letting papers and discs fly. "I'm amazed that this project has even continued. I think the staff must be pretty good if they can maintain in such chaos."

I don't think I'd ever seen Georgia so flustered. And I wasn't sure I was up to this. I mean, could I be fair to her, given my own agenda?

Another thought occurred. Georgia was asking me to assume a consultation role with the staff that included a client. Cheryl had talked about joining this project and I was obligated to protect the confidentiality of the clinical relationship. How to approach this?

"Um," I said, "there's something I need to clarify and this is awkward, because I can't really say why." Georgia's forehead creased with concern.

"No, I'm not backing out," I said and she seemed to relax. "But, there's one person who I think is in the project, a worker, who I should probably not be supervising. Can we discuss making other arrangements?"

"Who is it?"

"Well, I can't really say until I discuss it with the person. I'll let you know."

"Okay." She seemed to dismiss it as soon as it was clear that there wasn't anything she had to do at the moment. "So why don't I introduce you to whoever's around? Come on. All the project supervisors are in one area." She led me out into Cubicle City to the corner farthest from our offices and I wondered what that meant. I was also aware that I felt a little nervous in case I ran into Cheryl. This was one of those times that I should have done more preparation. I was certainly not at my best.

Two of the five supervisors were in their cubes. Janice Wolf, a tall, round woman with round glasses and long brown hair rose as we stood in her doorway. There wasn't any way we could all fit, so Georgia introduced me while I looked around and over the wall. Janice and I awkwardly shook hands.

"So, hey, Janice. How's it going?" Georgia asked.

"Everything's fine."

I asked, "Which program are you with, Janice?"

She looked startled at my question. "I supervise two units."

"Oh? Can you tell me something about them?"

She paused and looked at her watch, "Well, actually, I have a meeting that I'm already late for. So, maybe we can have this chat some other time."

"Okay. Sure," I said. "I'll check with you later."

Janice's expression told me that she wanted to meet as much as she wanted to be dipped in acid. I smiled as warmly as I could, not wanting to reveal my surprise at her chilliness.

When we approached Kenneth, the other supervisor, it seemed he had to rush off to an important rendezvous as well.

Georgia and I exchanged glances but waited until we got back to her office. I pulled the door closed. I considered the message that would send, but I felt it was important that we not be overheard.

"That was interesting," I said.

"I thought that you would find it so."

"You knew it would be that way."

"Well that's what I've gotten from anybody related to the project. I'm sorry that I didn't tell you. I wanted to see if they would be any different with you. I guess not," she said.

"Wow," I said, "hostility and paranoia inches deep around here. It's going to be interesting to get to know that group. Have you met the others yet?"

"Yes, and they're all the same. It's not just that they're playing their cards close to their chests. It's as if I'm, and now probably you're, the enemy."

"This doesn't bode well for a staff meeting. Do you think it's even worth it to hold one?"

We discussed this further and decided to play it by ear. And I mulled over how the staff's curious behavior might be related to what I already knew about Kayson. He had certainly selected a sullen crew to work on the project. The question was, what were they hiding?

As I was gathering up the files that Georgia had so kindly selected for me to review, I knew I had to clear the air. Georgia was again on the phone so I signaled that I needed to ask her something and waited.

She looked puzzled, as if she had dismissed me earlier and wasn't expecting that we would talk again that day. "What's up, Addy?"

"How do you know Amy Arnold?"

She paused and frowned. "Why?" Paused again and, "She was a student of mine. Why?"

"I wondered, since I saw you talking with her at the Dean's house after Natalie's funeral."

"Yeah, so I was." She was becoming testy, as if I was probing too deeply, or accusing her of something. "Why do you ask, Addy?"

"I was curious because I had a very unpleasant conversation with her one night, and it just surprised me to see you two talking together." What was I doing? Was I accusing her of something?

"So? She was a student of mine and she came up to me to talk about Natalie, that's all." I felt her irritation rise. What was she doing?

"That's it?"

"What are you asking, Addy? What's the problem? I know Amy can get worked up pretty quickly, but that day she was just looking to talk with somebody familiar about a professor we all cared about. That's what you do at those things. Not slink off somewhere."

Zap. "You know me, Georgia, I can't stand those kinds of group get-togethers. I'm sorry if I did something that offended you."

"Forget it. I'm sorry, Addy. I'm kinda overwhelmed here, and one more thing to deal with, well …"

I waved away the last part of her sentence, "It's okay." I turned to go and then had the sudden urge to warn her to be careful. I didn't.

I took the files and left her amid the carcasses of many long-dead trees. The world I drove through seemed cleansed by a layer of new snow that, by the look of it, had been falling for a while. My car rolled along in the storm, as if tearing through a lace wedding veil. I barely noticed, because I was concentrating on how I was going to juggle all this. What an irony, that I had left my nice, safe, predictable, job to focus on a search for a murderer, and now it felt like I had more than ever on my plate. And that last conversation with Georgia hung on, like a flu that insists on staying.

No I couldn't go there. I had to remind myself that I was going to help out Georgia, but I was also hoping to get some answers about Kayson.

"This shall set you free, Ms. van den Bos," I said aloud. "Or at least it should. "Time to go home."

I went directly there. I was in no mood to talk to a real person and was happy that I got Eduardo Garza's computerized voice-mail system so that I could tell him that I had received his message and when and where he could call back.

CHAPTER 29

"I'm a mess, I'm so tired, if I could only get some rest but I'm afraid to go to sleep. My mind is going so fast I just can't."

Tears began to roll down Virginia's face, forming shimmering ribbons along her cheeks. Her voice quivered and her hands shook as she reached for the tissues. At times it looked like her whole small body was taken over by the trembling. I also thought she hadn't eaten in awhile, and purple half moons under her eyes gave her a haunted appearance.

"I need help. I can't go on like this. I'm having these dreams that wake me up and then I can't get back to sleep, and when I do, the dreams come back. I've never felt like this before. I feel like I'm going crazy. Am I?" Her question hit me almost physically.

"No, you're not going crazy." Clients often ask this. My usual response is no. Even though I'm not really sure what's crazy and what's not and my clients are certainly troubled, how could it ever be helpful to tell someone else that they were crazy?

"So what's happening to me?" Virginia asked, pleadingly. "Why can't I sleep? Or eat? I'm afraid of everything. Yesterday, somebody came up behind me at the agency, and I was so jumpy that I fell down. I just lost my balance and knocked over a stack of files and fell on the floor of the main office. I was so embarrassed." She cried and quivered with anxiety. I could see her working to get the quaking under control. Tears streamed down her face and liquid ran out of her nose. She waged a tissue war against the flow. "You have no idea how embarrassing that was. Everybody was looking at me like I was crazy. God, I can't stop crying."

"If you were to just go with it," I asked, "instead of fighting it, where would it take you?"

"God," she whispered, "you're telling me to just accept this?"

"It may sound like that's what I mean. But, try to let it happen and keep talking. Tell me how it feels."

Panic lit up her face and I thought she wasn't going to let me lead her there. But she was apparently finding her courage. She took a shallow breath and said, "I feel it all over. It's like I've gone for a long run, and I'm totally exhausted. My legs and arms are shaking. My stomach is in a ball. I feel weak, and scared. And I don't know what I'm scared of."

I watched her shivering increase as she spoke. She bent over with her head in her hands and began to rock. "Oh, God. I hate this."

"So keep telling me what you feel," I said soothingly, "and where you feel it."

She sighed again. "I'm going to shake apart. I wonder if that's possible." I thought I heard the sound of a small smile, but since her face was still hidden I couldn't really see. "I'm afraid and I think I'm going to die. It's the end of the world."

"Go on."

"My heart is racing. I think it's going to beat a hole in my chest."

"Take a deep breath and keep talking," I tell her in a slow calm voice.

"It's like death is looming over me. When I try to sleep, somebody who I can't see is chasing me. I feel terrified and I wake in a sweat, my heart thumping, and I'm breathing hard as if I've actually been running." She cries and hides her face in her hands. "I can't get away from it."

I noticed that she was beginning to slow down, both her speech and the shaking. She was facing her demons and they were backing down.

"Tell me about the person chasing you," I said.

137

Her breathing was shallow but still slowing. "It was bad. Not so much what I dreamed, but how it felt. I felt so, so, helpless."

"You're not helpless now," I said. "It's okay. They are images from your unconscious. Tell me about them."

"I'm running down some hall. It's long and dark and it feels like a church or some office building. I'm scared. There are rooms off to both sides, and I can see into them as I'm running. They're full of people sitting in rows, like in churches, and there are preachers standing in front of them. It goes on and on. Room after room. It felt like it would never end."

"How did you feel as you ran?"

"Scared. Really scared. Somebody is chasing me, something wanting to hurt me. I turn and see a huge man carrying a sword. He fills the space behind me. Then suddenly, the halls begin to flood with rushing water, like a river. It comes so hard that I get thrown around. I feel like I'm drowning. Everybody else seems only mildly interested. But I'm really scared and I feel drugged. I can hardly run and the water is rising and the man is getting closer." In between short pauses where her crying overwhelms her, she continues. "I can smell his breath. It's alcohol breath. But there's something terrifying about that smell. I'm running and then the hall just ends. There's nowhere to go and I turn to see the man raising his sword. I know he's going to shove it right through me. It's as if I can see it happening before it happens. Just as the tip of the sword touches my clothes—I look down and see it begin to penetrate my shirt—there's another person. I can't tell if it's a man or a woman, and the person is wearing a gold chain around his or her neck."

She paused and shook her head as if to rid herself of the image. I nodded to encourage her.

"Anyway, this person grabs the sword and stabs the other guy who was chasing me. His blood gushes out and turns the water around us red, so that now I'm standing waist deep in bloody water. The person with the necklace is standing behind me and I know they're smiling even though I can't see their face. I see the dead man floating in the bloody water coming toward me, and then I wake up."

By the time Virginia finished, she had stopped crying. She sat quietly and I asked how she was feeling. I could see her trying to figure out how I was reacting to what she had just said.

She gave another sigh, "I don't know, but I think I feel less shaky. I've had that dream a couple of times, with some differences. You're the only person I've told."

"Oh? There was no one else you could tell?"

"I don't know, but I felt kinda embarrassed about it. It's pretty weird."

"What kind of thoughts come to mind, when you talk about it here?"

There was a long pause and I could see her anxiety begin to increase. Her rate of fidgeting went up and her breath came more shallowly.

"Virginia, I have the feeling that you're trying to decide about telling me something, but you're not sure it's okay."

"I ... don't know if I can. I don't know if I can live with myself about it." Virginia got up and walked around Martha's office. We had been sitting across from each other in two dark blue swivel armchairs. A small table was set to one side between us, with a box of tissues and a clock turned toward me. Sunlight came in through two large windows, feeding the greenery that Martha nurtured on the windowsills. When Virginia returned to her chair, I noticed that the shadows from the plants created geometric patterns on her face.

She sat without speaking. It was obvious that she was in turmoil over whether to reveal her misery. Finally she took a breath and said in one fast breath, "I was forced to have sex with a man I didn't love."

I waited. There was no sense mentioning that her dream had already told me this much and more.

"It was ... God ... I can't say this."

When she looked down at her shoes, it gave me a chance to glance at the clock and I saw that we were running out of time. The end of a session was never the best time to start a new topic, especially one like this.

"Virginia, we have only a few minutes left, and I see that you're having a hard time telling me about it. I'm concerned that we won't have enough time to give it the attention that it deserves. I don't want to discourage you, but …"

She was faced away from me, and her words came out in a flurry. I had to strain to hear her, since she spoke in a whisper. "That's okay. I just want to say it and then I don't want to talk about it again. One of my professors told me that I had to have sex with him in order to pass his class." She paused, and I saw her chin and lower lip quiver. "So I did. And I hate myself for it. God, it was awful."

Yep. The office building that was like a church, with people sitting in rows listening to preachers. She'd described the school without recognizing it herself.

I leaned toward her. "Virginia, when you say you were forced, are you saying you were raped?"

"That's what somebody else said it was, but I don't know. That seems too strong. It was so horrible. But I just couldn't flunk that class. I mean, my parents think my education is the most important thing, and I couldn't let them down. I don't know. Every time I think about it, I just want to die."

Now we had even less time left. I had to help her get ready to go back into her life without her feeling that I wasn't taking her seriously.

She appeared to be on the verge of tears again. Then she shook herself and took in a deep breath. "I'm glad I said it. I'm glad you know. I feel so …"

I nodded. "That's a hard thing to keep to yourself. It will help if we can talk more about it."

"I don't want to ever think about it again," she said, more strongly than she had ever spoken.

"I understand that, but I'm not sure it's possible. Yet. You may need to talk about it at times."

Virginia had an almost-vacant expression and she nodded wordlessly. We set a time for our next meeting and I asked her what the rest of her week would look like. She told me it would be a full one, which would serve to distract her and provide some structure. I hoped that despite the fact that she might have some emotional fallout from her revelation, Virginia would be able to attend to the necessary tasks of her life and get some sleep.

At the door, Virginia turned to me and held out her arm. "Look. I've stopped shaking." She smiled weakly. "I'll see you next week."

I closed the door and sagged against it. Of course, it was Kayson who had taken advantage of his power and forced himself on her. Her dream was a reflection of her helplessness and rage about it. Is that what happened behind Kayson's closed office door? Who was this man that he could treat another human being in this way? Had he been exploiting her vulnerability? Subduing her naïve enthusiasm? Maybe it had been something else altogether. Did she remind him of someone or was it her promise that he had to kill? This kind of hatred of women seemed to be as common as dust. Over the years, I had heard so many stories of what one human being could do to another that I was pretty much convinced that this was one stain on our species that would never be eradicated. We would never rid ourselves of power used cruelly. The irony for me was that it was precisely this kind of cruelty that provided me my livelihood.

Then the thought hit me. Who was the figure with the gold chain? The one who had stabbed Kayson with his own sword?

CHAPTER 30

Virginia was my last client of the day. I drove home through plow-narrowed streets and then spent some time futzing around the apartment. I knew I had to follow up on Garza's call, but each time I thought of it, I was also reminded of Natalie. And each time I felt the wound in my gut from knowing that I would never see what she could have yet done. Natalie had told me several times that she wanted to finish writing three different books, which she had started but had put off until her retirement. I could still see her telling me with a mixture of relief and sadness that she was finally able to put down the load of responsibilities that go along with being a professor. She had had plans to start a day camp, at her home, for kids from the city. It had been really important to her to give kids a chance to tend a garden. Her excitement about this had been as fresh as it ever had been about anything, including some of the strategies we had devised together to screw up some of the plans laid by the "other camp" on the faculty.

God. At times, it had felt like guerrilla warfare waged in the halls of the Rankin School of Social Work. Nothing was easy or straightforward as people jockeyed for the best position. Natalie had been my guide through the minefields and she had stood up for me more than once.

And more than once I had witnessed conversations, heavy with code, between Natalie and Kayson. The two of them had been on opposite sides of a debate about the direction the school was going to take, through endless committee meetings on how the curriculum was to be revised, and who was going to teach what, and which core theories every student would be required to learn. Natalie wanted to make sure that psychodynamic theories would be included ... theories that said your past influences your present and often in unconscious ways. Kayson fought for his view that those theories were unsubstantiated hokum. What were those two really fighting about?

On a day when I was on my way to meet Natalie, I rounded the corner and found Kayson standing in her office doorway. I couldn't see her, but I heard her voice finishing a sentence when he leaned in to the room.

"You know that it's not really social work," he said, "to use that stuff. I mean, the Freudian approach is only for the titillation of the worker, and social workers have no business getting off from their client's sexual fantasies."

"David, that's such a narrow view of a whole body of theory." I heard Natalie's irritation controlled yet still evident. And you know that social workers have been successfully treating clients using psychodynamic approaches, besides ..."

"Treatment. See, that's what I mean. That's no word for social workers to use. You people put yourself above the client when you talk of treatment. We have the obligation to make sure students know what their professional history is. You just want to turn us into a psychoanalytical institute."

I thought I heard Natalie sigh. "This is old, David, and you know it's not going anywhere. I think that this material is important so that students are exposed to the whole array of possibilities for helping people. It borders on unethical to keep it from them."

He snorted, "Your type always resorts to the unethical argument when you know you don't have a leg to stand on. But let me tell you what's really unethical. It's telling students that they're being trained as social workers and then telling them that it's social work to sit in some cozy office for fifty minutes a session. That's not social work, and there's nothing you can tell me to change my mind. If they want to be psychologists, we shouldn't let them take a short cut by getting an MSW."

His words stung a little as I stood listening. After all, he was talking about me.

There was a pause, and then Natalie said, "You certainly wouldn't want students to learn how to control their urges to avoid acting them out with their clients. I mean, that's your forte, isn't it, David?"

His chuckle took a menacing tone, "You giving your specialty lecture today? The one on repression?"

"That one comes after sexual deviance."

It seemed a good time to clear my throat.

"Oh, your little sidekick is here." His words were weighted with ice. "I'll leave you to whatever you two do … interpret each other's dreams or massage each other's ids … or whatever you do. Oh, by the way, Natalie, can you recommend a good attorney? I seem to have need for one."

There was a long pause, and then I heard Natalie say, "I'll let you know, David."

When he turned to go, he smiled and winked at me before heading in the direction of his office. I felt both slimed and a twinge of something else in my middle, as if we two had a secret between us.

Natalie was shaking her head when I walked through her door. I thought she seemed sad, but that was quickly replaced by a smile.

"He really doesn't like the idea of the unconscious, does he?" I said.

"The unconscious is his nemesis. He's gonna stamp it out wherever he finds it. Makes me wonder what he's trying to keep covered up."

"I'm not sure that I want to spend too much time contemplating Kayson's unconscious," I said. "I wouldn't want to get any on me."

"Oh, it might be pretty juicy at that. But he does all he can to make sure that he keeps it at arm's length and his fear, of course, is that somebody else is going to peek under his psychological skirt. Little does he know that none of us care what's up there."

"I certainly wouldn't want to get that close to him." I did an exaggerated shudder. I didn't mention the fact that that I had once been close enough to count his pores.

We were planning a new class together, so we had turned to that work and I was glad that Kayson didn't take up any more of our energy that day.

Thinking about her and the way we worked together intensified the sorrow of losing her. I tried to sweep the memory away by concentrating on what I had to do next. Mourning for Natalie would go on for a while, and I had something more pressing to deal with. Finding her killer would help me feel less helpless.

I had been thinking for a while that there were answers at SSD. The way the two supervisors had responded told me that they didn't want anybody poking around the project. So I was convinced that I had no choice but to return to the SSD offices. The question was, what to do with what I'd learned—or at least guessed—from my session with Virginia. It was a tricky ethical call. Of course, I couldn't reveal names or details, but I was obligated in Natalie's memory to reveal what it said about Kayson's character. But how?

In the end, I could only see one possible way. I made a phone call and then picked up Georgia's files and began to study in earnest. Janice was running a session that evening, and I intended to be there.

CHAPTER 31

The evening session consisted of eight clients sitting in a circle on orange plastic chairs, dwarfed by the huge, high-ceilinged classroom. Even though I was on time, it looked like they were just finishing up. As people turned at my entrance, I saw that Janice was with them. She scowled perceptibly in my direction and then turned back to the little group.

"Okay," she said. "We can stop at this point, and we'll meet back here on Thursday."

They all rose, gathering up their coats. Amid the sounds of chatting and scraping chairs, I walked toward Janice, who was packing up.

"Hi, Janice. Since we haven't been able to talk, I decided to drop by to see how things are going. Am I late?"

"Oh, I'm sorry. I changed the times of my sessions. I must have forgotten to give you an updated schedule."

She seemed torn between maintaining a certain professional air for the clients still lingering, and screaming something pretty unflattering at me. There wasn't anything overt, but it just felt that way.

It was time to go on the offensive.

"Look, Janice. I left you several messages that you were too busy to answer, so this seemed the best way for us to talk."

She was piling things into a cardboard box and drawing on her coat when the last client filed out of the room.

"I don't like it when people interfere with my work with clients," she practically spat at me.

I walked slowly toward her until we were only a couple of feet apart. Her hands were shaking. With rage? Or fear?

"How is this interference? Frankly, I don't know what's going on. You race away on the day we are first introduced, and then you don't respond to any messages that I leave. I've stopped by your desk at least a half a dozen times and you weren't there. Why are you avoiding me?"

She began to take on the aura of a trapped animal. "I wasn't avoiding you. I've been very busy. And besides, I just want to be left alone to do my work."

Although I felt quite cool in the cavernous space, Janice had developed a sheen of perspiration. She was not enjoying our chat. Good.

"Janice. I've been asked by the acting director to do a job, and that includes getting some idea from the staff about how the program is going. I'm not sure what's going on with you, but I am not the enemy."

"I ... I never said you were. I've, just, been busy, that's all."

"I certainly understand that, but I assume you can find an hour or so for us to get together."

She nodded. What choice did she have?

"Oh, by the way, is this a subgroup of some kind?"

I had read in the description of the program that each group, or unit as they were called, had about two dozen members. They were required to meet regularly to discuss their progress, to get support and help with problem solving. This was in addition to meeting individually with the unit coordinator and other group meetings focused on specific tasks.

She looked startled at my question. "Oh. Yes, well. There's flu going around. So a lot of them are home sick."

"Okay," I said. "So, can we plan for a time to meet?"

We worked out a day with some difficulty, since Janice seemed to have a very full schedule. But I wasn't going to let her slip out of it before I prevailed. As we were leaving, I asked, "You look familiar. Have we met in another setting?"

She shrugged.

"I know we've met before. Perhaps at the school? You know, Rankin."

"Maybe. I graduated from there. I know that you teach there. But I never took any of your classes. I really gotta go."

Janice hurried toward her car as if trying to lose a bad smell. And I had one more stop to make before I could go home.

CHAPTER 32

The clock over my car radio glowed 10:30 mutely in its neon green as I pulled into the dark shopping center parking lot. I shivered involuntarily. It was too late for me to be out. My headlights threw a splash of light on the slick pavement ahead as they made an arc across the empty lot. Overhead lights reflected their sparkle in the icy pools of water gathered in the dips and small, steamy clouds rose lazily from several grates. My tires made sloshing sounds rolling across the asphalt. As soon as I rounded a corner, into a side section, I saw the unmarked cruiser, idling in a shadow at the edge of the lot. I could just make out a figure sitting in the driver's seat and the glow of a cigarette.

He'd taken up smoking again.

I drew up to the police car, driver side to driver and rolled down my window. Redstone nodded and motioned to me to join him, which I did.

The heater was blasting and I soon felt myself begin to smother in my heavy coat. "Jeez, Arnie. You running a sauna here?"

"Sorry. Keep it going full because I'm in and out so much." Redstone leaned forward to adjust it, the leather on his gun harness squeaking.

"I see you started smoking again."

He laughed. "Yeah. Don't tell my wife."

"I wouldn't think of it." Arnie Redstone had never been married.

In fact, once when we'd been out together, he had confessed to me that he thought he'd drive any woman who agreed to marry him crazy.

"So," he said, "this is your party. What's going on?"

We'd been facing the front, and at that I turned to look at him. I could barely make him out in the gloom. "Arnie, I know I don't have the right to expect to draw on our personal relationship ..."

"What personal relationship? We went out a couple of times, a long time ago. And now we're, I dunno, you tell me."

Did I detect the sound of hurt in his voice?

"Arnie, look, I know it's unusual for you to talk about an ongoing case. But this was my good friend who got killed." I waited, giving him a chance to respond but he only shifted position again. "The reason I wanted to see you was because I have some information that I think you should know about, but I wanted to bypass your very charming sidekick."

At that, I heard him chuckle quietly from the semi-darkness. He inhaled from his cigarette, the glow illuminating his face.

"I'm not sure how to tell you because I'm really not supposed to say any of this, but I think it gives a new wrinkle to the cases. Both Kayson's and Natalie's cases. A client of mine, a student, told me that Kayson had raped her. She said that he was threatening to flunk her if she didn't go along with it."

"Who was that?"

"You know I can't tell you. But she told me that ..."

"I can't use it unless I have a name. For all I know, it's some crazy person who saw the story in the paper and now wants a piece of the publicity."

"Oh, come on, Arnie. Don't you think I can tell the difference between a delusion and the real thing?"

"You have to give me something solid or this is a no-go." He tapped the steering wheel, his face hidden in the gloom.

"This Kayson was a real piece of work. I run into that everywhere I go. How many other students was he forcing to have sex for grades? Poke around a little, and I'm sure you'll find it. Arnie, I'm asking you to trust me."

He didn't respond right away. I suddenly felt like I wanted a cigarette, although I hadn't smoked in years. A pack lay on the seat between us and I almost reached for it before I stopped myself.

"Addy," he said at last, "I'll ask around. But, I can't do much without names."

I shrugged. It was the best I could hope for.

"Anything else?"

"Yes. Besides the fact that whoever killed Natalie was a student, Kayson was involved in something fishy over at the Social Services Department."

"What do you mean?"

When I was finished telling him about what I had heard from Cheryl and learned on my own, we sat silently for a few minutes.

"What are you doing over there?" he asked sharply.

"Arnie, I'm consulting on a project which just happens to be the one Kayson was in charge of." Before he could say anything else, I said, "Here's something else. This was delivered the other day." I handed him the paper with the warning on it.

He took it and snapped on his flashlight. I watched his profile as he studied the note. "Damn it, Addy, you should have told me about his right away. We might have gotten prints off it. But now you've probably screwed up any possibility of getting anything from this."

"That's good. Yes, very helpful if we start yelling at each other. How long do you think you need to feel superior to me before we can continue?"

He sighed and I realized I was being a little too defensive.

"This is getting dangerous," he said. "You're obviously riling somebody up."

"Don't worry about me. I've got a friend on the police force."

His chuckle let me know that we were past the friction for the moment.

I ventured another question, which I expected would get another rise. "So, how is it partnering with someone who has the hots for you?"

He shifted to look at me. "One of the drawbacks of your profession is that you tend to read too much into things. This is one of those times."

I had been told. I fact, he was right, but for a different reason than he thought. I knew I was right about Kelly, but it's not a good idea to offer unsolicited interpretations. People don't tend to like them.

The radio crackled and Arnie reached for it. "I have to go. But I'll think about what you said. About the Social Services Department. Also, watch yourself."

"Thanks, Arnie. And thanks for meeting me."

I watched him drive off from the cooled-down interior of my car, my breath fogging up the windows. The smell of tobacco smoke lingered.

CHAPTER 33

The following morning, I sat in my SSD office waiting and looking again at the big-faced clock on the wall. It told me that Janice was fifteen minutes late. A couple of workers had walked by my open door during my vigil and glanced in without saying anything. Some would add a nod and slight smile, while others merely swiveled their eyes away. The Social Services Department office was always busy with activity, and that day wasn't any different, except that the specific activity I had been expecting wasn't happening. Janice just didn't show up and I developed a slow burn. What did she think she could accomplish with this tactic? And what was she hiding? After another fifteen minutes I decided that she wasn't coming.

Of course, when I checked with the office staff, they informed me that Janice had called in sick that morning. A sudden convenient flu attack, like her clients. Interesting. After I called Janice's home and left a message on her machine, I wandered over to Georgia's office and found her glaring into the computer monitor.

"This is shit," she spat. "This is such a mess that I'm going to have to just rewrite almost everything. It looks as though the grant promised to do certain things, but I think they're not the things that are actually being done. And it's not clear what was actually going on, but I do know it's using a lot of money. This is one big grant and there seems to be money oozing out everywhere."

She appeared to be gathering steam, so I put up my hands to

indicate that she slow down. "You starting to have second thoughts about taking this on?"

She shrugged. "Well, it's a little more complicated than I expected. How are you doing?"

"Before I knew it, I was in a duel with one of the workers, but I don't know what the stakes are. Janice has been avoiding me for several days. So, what do you think about me just bypassing her and going straight into the program files for her unit?"

"That's okay by me. We need to get on top of this project, and if the workers aren't cooperating, then we need do what we need to do. You might even talk with some of the clients as well, just to get an idea of how the project is going."

"Really? I had been thinking about doing that but it felt a little sneaky."

"Look, there are millions of dollars at stake here, not to mention the integrity of the department. There's an audit planned for two months from now, and the boss wants us to be ready for it."

"This sounds like more of a commitment than you first made. Or than I first made for that matter."

"I know, but the boss is very nervous and even if we aren't the ones to finish this, at least we can begin to identify the issues. Do what you think's best. I trust your judgment."

That was kind of her, but I wondered if I deserved such trust. After all, part of my reason for being here was to get something on Kayson. I knew it was enough to cloud my judgment.

Janice's cubicle had no lock, because there was no door, but the file cabinet was locked, as was her desk. I gave all the drawers a tug, knowing that they wouldn't budge. The secretary of the unit had no idea where the keys were, but she did know that Janice's group would be meeting tonight with another social worker sitting in as the group facilitator. I decided that there would be two social workers attending that night.

Kenneth Braden, the other unit supervisor I'd met on my first day, turned out to be the substitute group leader and his welcome to me was anything but warm. He stood wordlessly as I approached him. Kenneth was actually tall—about 6'2"—and dark, as though his family came from the Mediterranean area. But he wasn't what I'd call handsome. He sported a goatee and closely cropped hair. I gave him a big smile and an outstretched hand, which he took less than enthusiastically. Before he could speak, I told him that I was just here to observe and offer any support that I could. I also asked him for the group membership list, which I told him I assumed Janice had given him.

His dark eyes seemed to narrow at the question. "Janice seems to have overlooked that item."

"So, where can I get it?"

"I suppose Janice has one."

"Well, she and I have been having difficulty connecting, so I thought you could help me out. And, by the way, you and I should set up some time to meet as well."

At that he demonstrated how a person could actually blanch. What the hell were these people hiding? Whatever it was, I was certain that Kayson had orchestrated it. These people weren't in decision-making positions. It had to come from higher up.

"I'll check with you tomorrow," I said, "but now, I want to sit in on the group, so you can introduce me as another social worker who's trying to learn about the project. Is that okay?"

He nodded and seemed to droop in resignation.

We sat in a circle in the center of a room designed to hold four times as many people. There were ten of us, counting both social workers. It was a paltry group. In fact it seemed to be the same group I'd seen with Janice. We all introduced ourselves and Kenneth gave them the story about my attendance. Our voices rebounded off the hard surfaces of the walls and floor. A fluorescent light hummed and flickered.

Darlene, a large, sad faced woman talked about her struggle with her boss at the fast food restaurant where she worked. She felt he was too rigid in his expectations of her since she had three small children, one of whom was often sick. She was in danger of being fired for missing too much work. This would put her on probation in the project and threaten her housing as well. She cried as she talked, exuding despair. Another group member tried to comfort her while several others rolled their eyes. So far, it seemed like a normal group. I waited and watched.

Finally Lucinda, one of the eye-rollers, said, "How many times do we gotta listen to this? She's been blubbering about this every time we meet, and me and some others are tired of it."

She addressed her question to Kenneth, who turned to Darlene. "So what do you say to Lucinda, Darlene?"

Darlene looked up from her sodden tissue, tears streaming. "I don't know. All I know is I'm gonna lose everything because of my boss."

"It ain't because of your boss, honey. We all got kids," Lucinda swept her arm to indicate the others in the group, "and we don't sit here week after week crying about how mean our bosses are and how hard it is to take care of our children. You gotta stop feeling so sorry for yourself and get up off your dead ass and go to work. You put your kids in the day care or you get somebody from your family to watch 'em and you go to work."

I could see Kenneth nodding. Advice that blunt could only come from someone else who'd been there.

"That's great coming from you, Lucinda," a small woman sitting across from me said. "Who was it who cried and moaned for months in our meetings, and who we all worked to help out? Now you're attacking Darlene for doing something that you did too, so shut up."

"What right you got to talk to me like that?" Lucinda leaped up with fists clenched.

Kenneth also stood up, knocking over his chair, which clattered on the hard floor. "Remember the rule: Just words, no fists."

The rest of the group sat in silence. I could feel my body tense.

Lucinda took a step back. "I've had enough of that bitch. Who is she to sit all high and mighty like that?" She turned to Kenneth. "And what do you know about it? You ain't never been poor, and been forced to go through this silly shit, just so you can have a home for your kids. I gotta check in here, and I gotta get permission to do that, and I gotta go to them AA meetings. I'm sick of being treated like I'm some kind of child. And I'm sick of sitting here and listening to her snivel about how hard her life is."

She turned to Darlene. "Your life ain't no harder than ours, sister, and you got to attend to business and stop bothering us with your sad ol' story. I heard it. I lived it. I don't need to hear yours or anyone else's." She stood breathing deeply, waited for a few seconds and then jerked her coat off the back of her chair. "I'm outta here," she declared as she strode toward the door.

Okay, this kind of venting was also part of group, and wasn't necessarily a bad thing, handled properly. But Kenneth seemed unsure about what to do. I wondered if he wanted my help, but since there was no obvious signal from him, I sat quietly and waited. Finally, he turned to me and said, "I'm going to see if I can catch her. Can you take over the group?"

I nodded and he hurried away. Good choice, Ken.

"That was something, wasn't it?" I said.

There was a shifting of positions and uneasy laughter from a couple of women.

"That was nothing compared to what you see sometimes," one woman said. "Lucinda's got one major temper."

"Uh-huh," another said. "But she was showing off. She don't usually blow so soon."

"So it was for my benefit, you think?" I asked.

More nodding and uh-huhing.

I turned to Darlene. "How are you doing with what went on?"

Her tears had dried, and I could see anger in her glower. "She's always going off. I've heard it before and it don't bother me. I got more things to worry about than that fool. I'm lookin' for help with my problems and I don't see it happening. So I guess I got to do it for myself."

"Uh-huh." Several women nodded their agreement.

"What would that be like, Darlene?" I asked. "I mean, to do it for yourself?"

She sat with a frown, and then shook her head. "So what else is new? I don't even know what I come to these meetings for. I mean, ain't this program supposed to help us? But at least we don't got to deal with that fucker Kayson no more."

More nodding.

"Oh? How's that?" I asked this as casually as I could, but even so, I suspect some eagerness got through because nobody replied.

"Did you have problems with Kayson?" I said.

There was a shuffling and adjusting of positions, and finally Mona Sonoria, a woman who'd been pretty quiet, said slowly, "He didn't make many friends here. But we put up with him, because we knew he had the power."

"The power?"

"He could decide if you stayed or went. So, what do you expect?"

That was all I got. I floated several different invitations for them to tell me about Kayson, but it seemed they had decided that was all they would say, so I redirected our focus to how to manage several problems of living that these women were contending with.

Kenneth's absence gave me a chance to subtly check out some things. I asked about the complete membership of the group and was surprised to learn that nobody had ever seen the group be larger than nine members. This from a group that ought to have at least two dozen people in it.

I also asked them to tell me about how the program worked. At least what they said pretty much jibed with what I understood from the grants. Each woman had a long history of being involved with the law—on charges ranging from shoplifting to child abuse and drug use. Some had done a few years in prison. Some had been homeless and had gone through bouts of knocking on doors begging to be allowed to sleep in a family's or a neighbor's living room on frigid nights. Each woman had, on at least one occasion, not been able to feed her children, and some had flirted with, or resorted to, prostitution.

These were exactly the kinds of women the program had been designed to help, the hard cases who couldn't be helped by something more incomplete or piecemeal. It was an expensive and comprehensive pilot project. The women and their children were assigned to a unit comprised of about two dozen families. Each group was given housing in a single apartment complex, which was governed by a board of residents who had experience in the program. The board was also assigned a team of social workers and each family was assigned a caseworker who acted as coach, mentor, or whatever was needed. Everyone in each family was required to attend a set schedule of groups focused on various skill-developing tasks. In short, this was a last-ditch effort at integrating these families finally into society.

Every step of the way, each woman had extensive access to social workers and other professionals connected with the program, as well as to necessary resources. It was truly a wrap-around service. In the group, there was quite a bit of complaining about how little time they actually had to themselves, but I sensed that if I were to scratch a little deeper, I'd find a lot of relief and gratitude beneath the dissatisfaction. Perhaps at some level, many of them knew that this was their last chance.

Only two things gnawed at me, the discrepancy in the numbers and their silence about Kayson.

Kenneth didn't return until the group was almost over, having spent the whole time trying to convince Lucinda to come back. When he finally showed up, alone, we were breaking up. He announced a reminder to the room about the next meeting. As they dispersed, he told me that Lucinda had agreed to come back to the next meeting but was adamant that she wouldn't return to this one. Was he suggesting it had to do with my presence? I wanted to talk further but he picked up his supplies and left faster than a race car at the green flag. I had no choice but to leave as well.

CHAPTER 34

The sound of tires screeching punctuated the crashing of shattering glass.

From a dead-to-the-world sleep, I bolted upright in bed and sprinted into the living room, where the sound had come from. I stopped when I hit a blast of frigid air and I felt a sharp stab of pain in my left foot. I stood rooted to the spot, half-asleep in the dark, trembling in my usual night gear of an old oversized T-shirt and a pair of underpants. It took a minute to shake the fog of sleep from my brain enough to put the cold together with the sound of breaking glass. Someone had broken a window. I still had no idea what to do next.

What roused me was a pounding on my door and Mrs. Kaldione's high-pitched voice calling my name. I limped over to let her in and flipped on the light.

Mrs. Kaldione stepped gingerly into the room, at least as gingerly as an older woman can move. Standing there in her bathrobe, her hair askew, she surveyed the wreckage with her mouth open, breathing hard from climbing the stairs. Then she pointed at me. "Addy, you're bleeding."

"I am?" I looked around to see what she meant and finally saw the smudged bloody tracks that led to the door. "Oh, yeah. I guess I am." It was then I became aware of the warm liquid oozing from my slashed foot and the stabbing pain.

"We need to get you fixed up, but we also need to get you out of this freezing apartment."

The culprit appeared to be an ordinary building brick. It had landed at the far end of the room leaving a spreading trail of glass. I went toward it to pick it up.

"Addy," Mrs. K. screamed," leave it, leave it. We have to call the police and let them deal with it."

She was right, of course, and I wondered why it hadn't occurred to me. In fact I felt numb. Being yanked from a deep sleep can do that, or perhaps it was the cold. Or something else?

"Addy, come downstairs and we'll call the police from there. I'm also calling Aldo to come and block up this window. Let's go."

She practically pushed me along and I walked awkwardly on my left heel to avoid grinding the crystal splinter further into my foot.

Once I was ensconced in Mrs. Kaldione's apartment, under a blanket and with my foot loosely bandaged, she called the police and we waited. We waited some more while they went over my apartment and an officer took my statement. When he saw my foot he urged me to go to the emergency room. After Mrs. Kaldione had retrieved some of my clothing, I drove to the hospital with her riding shotgun. Mrs. Kaldione didn't drive, but she provided the reassuring presence of another person, which I needed just then. We made a peculiar couple. Mrs. Kaldione had thrown a long green woolen coat over her nightgown and pulled on a pair of scuffed up, fake-furred, ankle-high boots. I wore what she'd selected for me, a heavy red plaid shirt coat that I normally only use to work outside, a pair of stained blue jeans and one work boot. She held its mate on her lap. I could feel blood oozing from my foot into the gauze bandage.

The visit to the emergency room was like old home week. It felt odd to be on the other side of the treatment team, but it was a good thing that we went. They had to dig several pieces of glass out of my foot and actually had to stitch up the wound. So by the time we got back to the apartment, it was 8:30 in the morning. I must have slept for eight hours in Mrs. Kaldione's guest room, which, of course, was made up for such an emergency.

CHAPTER 35

The sheet of plywood covering the hole in my front window gave my apartment a late-afternoon gloom no matter what time of the day it was. Mrs. Kaldione had ordered a new windowpane, but because it had to be a special order to fit the antique windows of the house, I would have to live with the darkness for a while. Even though I thought I had done a thorough job of cleaning up the shards and splinters, I still felt nervous walking through the room, and made sure to wear shoes whenever I did. I also found myself checking the furniture every time I was about to sit. I wondered if I would ever again be able to feel comfortable hanging out in my apartment with my tootsies flapping in the breeze.

I had finally settled myself on my couch, with a big bowl of vegetable soup and a chunk of whole-grain bread from the bakery around the corner, with my poor throbbing foot propped on a pillow. The pain reminded me of the doctor's orders to stay off the foot, which I had thus far been ignoring. And of course, that's when the phone rang. I waited for it to stop, but the caller was insistent. In setting the soup down, I sloshed a good portion of it onto my lap.

When I picked up, I was conscious of my soggy front and the hot, greasy liquid seeping down my legs. "What?"

"Addy?"

"Yes. Who is this?"

"It's Kris, and what crawled up your butt?"

"What do you want, Kris? I'm tired and my foot hurts and I've just poured a bowl of soup all over myself."

"Is that some new religious ritual you've picked up?"

"Yeah, and the timing of what comes after is crucial to the spell actually working. It's designed to rid the world of lawyers."

"Things haven't been going well, I take it." Her tone was serious.

"I'm sorry. You should probably stay away from me for a while. I think I'm in danger of losing control of my foul mood and unleashing it on any poor unsuspecting soul who happens by."

"I heard what happened. Are you okay?"

"Sure, I'm fine. I don't have a job. There's a big hole in my window. Somebody is out to get me and my foot is on fire. And all I want is to know who killed Natalie."

"It's all catching up to you, Addy. Do you think you should maybe talk to somebody?" It took me a moment to recognize what she was saying, even though I'd used the phrase myself more times than I could remember. She was telling me that I should see a therapist. Now that was a twist.

"No, I'm really okay," I said shortly, and then recanted slightly. "I'll think about it."

"Addy, I know I'm not going to talk you into it, but you should see somebody."

She was right about not talking me into it. Helpers can make the most reluctant clients. Still … "Thanks for your concern, Kris. You're a good friend."

"So what do you think this attack is about?"

"Hell if I know. It's funny that whoever it was threw a brick. It got me thinking about the bricks at Natalie's. She was going to build a …"

"What are you saying? That the brick tosser was linked to Natalie's death?"

"Why not? Natalie had a pile of them next to her house. Why else would someone throw a brick through my window in the middle of winter? Where could you possibly get a brick, even, at this time of year?"

"Interesting point. But what would push somebody to kill Natalie and then come after you?" Kris seemed to be thinking out loud.

"I wonder if it was what Natalie wanted to tell me. Somebody wanted to keep her quiet and ..."

"and wants to do the same to you."

"That's stretching it. I don't know anything."

"Yeah, well. This thug doesn't know that, does he?"

"Why do you say 'he'?"

"Probability. Besides, even if you don't know anything, you could always find something out."

"Actually, I've been thinking about that." My foot throbbed and I just wanted to curl up somewhere warm and safe. Instead I told Kris the idea that had been brewing.

CHAPTER 36

At her next session, Cheryl Taylor was as angry as ever. She paced around the office and swung the ubiquitous unlit cigarette for emphasis. "I don't know what I'm doing. I can't even see if I'm doing any good at all. It all seems so complicated and their lives are so bogged down in problems." She threw herself into the chair facing mine. "You remember that client I told you about who was so angry at me?"

I nodded.

"I'm still trying to work with her. She doesn't come to the meetings and when she does show up for our individual sessions, she's angry and insulting. She's close to being thrown out of the program and there's nothing I can do to stop it. She's so goddamned stubborn."

"You are very angry today," I said.

Cheryl let out a loud sigh. "I'm not angry, I'm, I'm …" She searched for a word and then sat silently. "All right, I'm angry. And actually, I felt okay before I got here today."

"So you weren't aware of being angry before you came in? What do you think happened?"

"I don't know. I'm always coming in here and feeling so awful about that pit of a place. Maybe it's just a conditioned response."

"Maybe. I wonder if it might be something else as well."

"What else could it be? In fact, this project isn't all I thought it would be, but I'm much less stressed and I'm actually able to go home at a decent hour." She stared straight at me, her eyes flashing. "So what are you getting at?"

Yeah, I'd thought so. "I wonder if you might be angry at me?"

"Why the hell would I be?"

I just shrugged. She'd get there.

She stood up again. I had to look up at her as she hovered over me. "Well, maybe I don't need to come here anymore. I mean, things aren't so bad now. I think I can probably manage on my own."

"So right after you strongly deny being angry with me, you talk about ending our relationship. What do you think that means?"

"Give me a break. Why would I be angry at you?"

"You're under a lot of pressure, what with this difficult job and going to school. And we haven't even touched on other stuff that might be going on. All of this, it would seem to me, could make you feel on edge."

"So? Why would that make me angry at you?"

"Well, I wonder if it has something to do with my also working at your office. We've never had a chance to talk about it." I had given her several chances to say it, but I just didn't want to dance anymore.

She sat down and screwed up her face, scowling at me. "Interesting technique. I mean, sneaking into your client's workplace without telling them."

"So it feels as if I snuck in. Do you believe that I wanted to hide it from you?"

"Of course. Why else would you have conveniently left it out of our talks? I couldn't believe it when they told me. I didn't know what to say. The last thing I want is for anyone there to know that I'm in therapy."

"No one will. That fact is absolutely confidential, you know. But I understand how you might have felt ambushed by it."

"So why didn't you tell me?" There was a plaintive quality to her question.

"I made a mistake in that. The timing of all of this wasn't good, but I should have been more thoughtful about it." I never like it when I blow it with a client, but it's all "grist for the therapeutic mill," as they say.

Cheryl started to tear up, sniffling slightly. "I just couldn't believe it."

"Yes?" I waited. We were on to something else.

"I felt like a little kid finding out that her mom was having an affair with her teacher."

"Oh? What happened when you found out about your mom and the teacher?"

"What? I never …"

"Didn't you?"

She paused a long moment; then the words spilled out as if under pressure, "Kids at school were all talking about it, is how I found out. I couldn't believe it, and I couldn't believe that those kids were talking about my mom that way. I was furious. They teased me, and I even beat one of them up. When I told my mom what they said, she denied it completely. She got so mad at me. She started yelling and crying. I don't think I ever saw her that mad at me before. Shit."

"That must have felt really horrible, because I know how much you loved her."

"I was so scared that my dad would find out. I thought he would kill her."

"You believed he could do that."

She nodded and said, "And then I saw them together. One day I skipped school and went to the mall with a bunch of friends and we saw them there. They didn't see me because they were in a restaurant laughing and stuff. I was mortified and it made me sick."

"You felt betrayed and perhaps it showed you that people you care about will let you down."

"It felt like I lost both my parents that day. My dad was already lost to alcohol, and now my mom was a … a liar and cheat." She slumped low in the chair. "I don't think you can trust anybody."

"Even me."

She didn't answer but instead looked down at the soggy cigarette in her hands.

"I think that people we love let us down at times, because they're human. And then we have to decide if the break in the relationship can be fixed or if the disappointment is too great to come back from. The mistakes your parents made were doozies, which hurt you deeply.

The question is, do you want to find a way to live with those realities so they don't hurt you so much?"

She didn't seem to be listening, so I waited.

Cheryl raised her head as she spoke, eyeing me, "I've heard some more stuff about Kayson, speaking of people disappointing you."

I tried to stay calm but felt my heart jump. "Oh?"

"I don't have any proof, but I get the feeling that there are other clients who had reasons to not like him. But it's hard to get anyone to talk about it. My spitting client is still fuming about him."

"Did she say why she's so angry at him?"

"No, but she can't talk about him without getting really pissed. And when I ask her point blank she says, 'What do you care?' But she doesn't go any further than that. She won't talk about him and acts as if she's scared of something." Cheryl sat up straighter in the chair as a signal that she wanted to change the subject. "Which reminds me. You're now a part of the project."

She'd handed me the ball. "Yes. And you're right, we should talk about how we're going to handle that."

We explored her feelings about my being at her workplace and discussed how we would deal with it if our paths crossed. Cheryl wasn't happy about that possibility, but we gave it as much attention as we could. We were all talked out about it when the session ended, but I assumed that it would come up again. By the time we made an appointment for our next session, all thoughts of ending therapy had dissipated.

CHAPTER 37

The morning after I'd talked to her, I realized that Kris had been way too excited about my idea. I should have anticipated that from her. Maybe I was slipping.

She showed up at my apartment around 2:00 AM and we drove through the silent city of Whitefield. Thankfully, it was not snowing. Street lamps illuminated the empty streets and snow was piled so high that sometimes the buildings were hidden from view. I listened to the squeaking sound of the tires rolling along on the powdery dry snow and watched the stillness of a sleeping city slip by us. There was an occasional taxi, sitting with parking lights glowing, and nothing much else. Most of my focus was on keeping myself from getting too nervous about what we were about to do. Kris was uncharacteristically quiet.

We left the car parked among others on a nearby street and walked the two blocks to the building. My heart was knocking against my chest as we approached the Social Services Department, where I had been earlier that day. Entering was a cinch, since Georgia had given me the codes for the electronic locks. Still, my hand shook as I read the numbers from the piece of paper. Georgia had also told me that the codes were changed once a month on random days. So I hoped today wasn't one of the random days.

Glancing at Kris, I barely suppressed a smile at how we looked. Without planning it, we had each chosen dark clothing and black tennis shoes. All we need were black ski masks. It took me two tries to get the key code to work and we let ourselves into the building. I had hoped that the moon would light our way, but she had not made an appearance, so we clicked on our flashlights and I led the way back to Kayson's domain.

This break-in was starting to seem like cheap melodrama, but I still thought it was necessary. Although I had access to the building, it wasn't clear how I would explain Kris's presence, and I wanted her along. Besides, Georgia might tolerate my keeping my eyes open for information on Kayson while I worked, but she wouldn't welcome my rooting around in her files. It had just seemed better to circumvent any official system and sneak in on the off hours.

I had noticed earlier in the day that uniformed people roaming the halls guarded the place. I had made a point of talking to a couple of them and found out that the guards were there mostly to protect the employees from any angry client who might want to express his or her frustration. The night crew was made up of two guards who made spot checks but mostly holed up in a small office in one of the wings. Fortunately we didn't need to go near that area and I hoped we could just avoid any run-ins with them. I had recently been exonerated for a crime. I didn't want to call attention to myself for another possible criminal activity. At least not so soon.

We had traversed nearly the entire length of the building when Kris said, "Jeez. How far do we have to go?"

"Keep it together," I hissed at her, "and keep it down."

I started to see things moving in the shadows in every corner. At one point, I stopped quickly, and Kris ran right into me. We were becoming a comedy act.

"Addy, if I knew where we were headed, I'd lead." She wasn't as cool about this as she'd let on when we discussed this plan earlier that day. "Just keep going."

"I think it's just around this last corner."

"You think?"

I let it go and started our little procession again. My foot hurt and I limped to avoid aggravating it.

We stopped in front of the office that Georgia was using. "This used to be Kayson's office," I said. "I assume if there's something to be found it'll be in here."

"Okay," Kris said.

I pushed open the door.

"By the way, it's a mess."

The scene was just like I'd seen it that afternoon. Cardboard cartons, files, and books piled everywhere, now cast in shadow.

"Jeez, how can anybody work like this?" Kris asked.

"It's really weird. His office at the school is meticulous, almost as if nobody ever worked in it. And did I tell you that he used to go down to the basement over there and clean it up? So this is really strange."

"What do you think it means?"

"Extreme neatness and compulsivity sometimes have to do with fears or anxieties about internal threats."

"What does that mean?"

"If you keep the world around you under control, you think it helps you control the inner world ... to keep certain thoughts or desires out of consciousness. On the other hand, some people think compulsivity is just a chemical imbalance."

"But he didn't do it here."

"That's what's strange. People who are compulsive are usually consistent. On the other hand, there are no rules about this stuff. Maybe the clutter was just another strategy to hide ... something."

"Well, I'll leave Kayson's ghost to you. Let's get to it," Kris said.

It was the computer that we'd come to examine, which was why I'd asked Kris to come along. She was the computer whiz, while I avoided the things as much as I could. Kris settled in behind the desk and I concentrated on the other stuff in the office.

"Keep me posted on your progress," I whispered. We kept the lights off and I swept the room with my flashlight.

She was already talking softly to the machine as the monitor flickered to life. Kris's relationships with computers always turned into dialogues, with Kris giving voice to the binary being with which she was engaged.

I picked a file and leafed through it. Seeing nothing, I picked up another and another. Nothing jumped out at me in the several files I searched, although I wasn't really sure what I was looking for. I hoped I would know it when I found it. Kris chattered softly behind me.

Perhaps anything important—at least to Kayson—was buried

somewhere so as to keep it out of prying eyes. I set about lifting and pawing until I got to clusters of bulging files bundled together with heavy rubber bands and set along the bottom of the back wall. From the looks of the dust layer, they'd been there for several years.

I started through them and at first glance, it looked as if they contained old case material. Some of it dated back thirty years or more. Probably this had all been before the department switched to storing information on hard drives or on disks. Perhaps these had been slated for transition onto a computer, as soon as there were personnel available to do it, which may happen on the day the sun finally burned down to a glowing cinder. So they sat, probably in a damp room in the basement, taking up space.

So, how and why had they found their way to Kayson's office?

I sat down amid the dust and stacks to look more closely. I quickly realized that each bundle, comprised of perhaps two to six file folders, contained the records of one case. Some of them documented the entire life cycle of a case through several generations of people in a family. Here were the details of people who had struggled at the margins of society or who had been overwhelmed by circumstances that had left them without resources. I was vaguely aware of Kris tapping and muttering. I opened a tattered dark-brown folder and had to stifle a sneeze.

The first file introduced me to Christina and her three children, who had been discovered living in an abandoned building. She was twenty-five years old, unmarried, and trying to keep her family from freezing by starting a fire from some of the debris in the building. The building had gone up in smoke and one of her children was killed in the blaze. Christina should be forty-five years old now. If she'd made it.

Martha and Edward and their four children were evicted from their apartment when Edward lost his job of twenty years because the CEO had bankrupted the company. The CEO had done eighteen months at a minimum-security prison for illegal trading and Edward had lost his entire pension. After this blow to the family, Edward had started to drink. Later, two of their children, with children of their own, had also come to the attention of the department. Both cases had involved unemployment, alcohol, and abuse of children.

Alexandra, age five, was sexually and physically abused by her father and older brothers. She spent most of her early life going from one foster family to another but had trouble "bonding" with the various foster parents, who each gave up on her after a year or so. Here were the details of what we called an attachment disorder. She spent the last five years in a group home for the unadoptable. Alexandra would be forty years old. Again, if she'd made it. The file didn't say. Just like the others, she had left the system when she was eighteen years old.

Odetta's boyfriend beat her up repeatedly and she had her children taken away from her because she left them for days on end while she got high on heroin. Her own mother had sold her for sex beginning when she was five years old. Three of Odetta's four children also had their own files, as they got older and had children. One died in a drug raid, one became a prostitute, and one disappeared when he was fifteen years old.

Each file was thick with notes and forms providing a dense history of a family's sometimes endless relationship with the SSD. If they were around long enough they might have had several caseworkers. For some, the relationship with the organization was established before their birth through their parents and, in some cases, their grandparents.

I looked up from my grim journey to see what Kris was doing, and I suppose because I wanted a break from this stuff. "Damn busman's holiday," I mumbled.

"What?"

"Tragedy aplenty here."

Kris motioned for me to come to her. I stood behind her and she pointed at the screen.

"Most of what was on here was routine crap," she whispered. "Stuff like memos and correspondence to other departments, evaluations of people who work here, and stuff to and from the federal and state government about some grants. Then I found this. Look here." She clicked on something and a bunch of numbers appeared. "This guy has written a grant that gives him control of about five million smackers over four years and he got an 8 percent operating cost allowance. That's about $400,000."

"That's a chunk of change, but I don't know if it's unusual. What's the grant for?"

"Well, it looks like it's a huge project for helping women and children get on their feet."

"Something like that would cost a lot. Maybe five million isn't out of line."

She shrugged. "I'll keep looking."

As I turned to go back to my search, we both jumped at the sound of a noise in the hall. We snapped off our flashlights. I watched Kris in the glow of the monitor reach up to turn it off as I crouched down behind the desk. I heard rather than saw Kris leave her chair and squat down.

"I saw a light through a window down this way," a male voice said from the hallway.

My breath caught in my throat. They must have seen either my flashlight or the light of the computer through the window. Kayson had to have an office with a window to the outside. It probably meant that the guards made their rounds outside the building as well as inside. I cursed myself for not thinking about this before.

I heard footsteps approaching and sensed Kris reacting to the noise as well. What kind of trouble could we be in? I wasn't sure. I belonged here and Kris wasn't forbidden. Could I talk my way out of this? Were we better off just flipping on the light and acting as if nothing was wrong? I froze to my spot with indecision.

The door to the office slid open and a flash of light danced over its clutter. I was suddenly very grateful for Kayson's lack of house cleaning here.

"See anything?" The male voice asked from the hall.

My heart pounded. "Look at this shit. How can people work in this slop?" another voice said, standing in the doorway to our scene of deceit.

"I don't see anyone in here, man." As he pulled the door closed, I heard him continue, "Maybe it's the next office. I could have sworn it was in this area."

"Ah, yer seeing things again, Charlie," the other voice said more faintly, and their footsteps receded.

We stayed still for some time. Kris moved first and leaned over the desk to whisper in my direction, "We gotta book. If I'm caught here it could be serious."

"What about the stuff in the computer?" This felt like the only chance to search Kayson's computer we had.

She held up something, which I couldn't quite make out. I moved closer and she whispered, "I brought a bunch of disks to download the stuff that looks promising. I'm gonna finish it up in a few minutes and then we're outa here." She turned back to the computer and the monitor lit up.

I looked again toward the sagging stacks of files and wondered if there was any point in taking some of it with me. I remembered Georgia's story of Kayson's getting off on her early history. This may all just be his idea of porn.

But many of the files had nothing to do with sexual abuse. And why older stuff? I ran my hand along the spines, raising dust as I went. A large brown envelope was wedged between files and I caught my finger on something sharp. I pulled my finger back quickly and watched a point of blood form.

Was this a sign? I tugged on the envelope and it resisted as if to say I had no business there. I gave it a bigger yank and it released, pulling a couple of files with it. The envelope had been clipped to another one of those bundled files. I turned the envelope over in my hands. There was nothing written on the outside. The file was old and grimy, as dingy paper can be. It was labeled MILLER.

Just then, Kris whispered that she was finished, so I scooped up several of the files, including the one with the envelope and we moved quietly to the door. We stood face-to-face listening for sounds from the other side, and when there seemed only the quiet of the darkened building, I pulled open the door.

I was convinced that the police were following us, just waiting for their opportunity to grab us and throw us into some musty, urine-tinged jail. But then I stepped out of Kris's car, tiptoed by Mrs. Kaldione's and slipped into my apartment without incident.

I debated about looking through my booty, but I felt heavy with exhaustion and my foot was burning. So I set them down reluctantly and limped to bed. I needed to function the next day. They would have to wait.

CHAPTER 38

Two marked police cars were parked near the door of the SSD when I arrived the next morning. This wasn't unusual—the police were often an unpleasant but necessary part of Social Services cases. But that day, it made me very nervous.

I heard the distinctive crackle of a police radio as I got closer to Georgia's office and my heart started to hammer. A uniformed officer stood in the hallway and two people in street clothes were going through Kayson's old desk and piling files into boxes. Georgia was standing nearby overlooking the scene with her arms folded. All over Cubicle City people stood in clusters around their desks watching the action.

"What's going on?" I asked as smoothly as I could muster. Had our break-in been discovered?

"Isn't it obvious?" Georgia said. "These idiots have decided that the contents of Kayson's office are evidence in his murder case. I was making good progress sorting the stuff out and now they'll tear it all apart. They're even taking the computer."

I felt twinges of both relief and guilt—I wasn't going to jail as a burglar—but would the police have come here if I hadn't put a bug in Redstone's ear? "How long will they keep it?"

"Who the hell knows? I can't get rid of this creep no matter what I do. I'm doomed to be mixed up in his crap ..."

"Come on. Let's go to my office and rethink this," I said. I gently propelled her toward some much needed privacy.

"I'm so sick of that guy," she said, as I pulled the door closed. "Even after he's dead, he's still a part of my life." She swung around to face me, tears welling up. "Addy, I'm sorry. I … he was such a miserable son of a bitch and for some reason here I am cleaning up his shit. Again. And I don't understand why. I mean …"

"Georgia. Sit."

She slumped into the chair I pushed toward her. As she tried to talk, she began to sob. I had no idea where the anguish was coming from. I thought Kayson had just been a poorly chosen lover. But he'd evidently pushed some buttons that ran deeper than I knew.

When it looked like she was winding down, I said, "I didn't realize that it's still so painful for you."

"How could I tell you, Addy? It was so stupid. I was so stupid."

"So you thought that you could just joke about it and … what? It would just not be an issue? Come on, you're a social worker. You know it doesn't work that way."

"Yes, right, I know that was stupid. But I couldn't talk about it. It was bad enough that you and everybody else knew."

"I know because you told me. I'm not sure I would've found out any other way."

"Are you kidding? Almost before we went to bed, everybody was already talking about it." She practically spat out the words, using anger as a way of keeping her shame at bay. "I even heard a couple of students talking about it the very next day. You should have seen their smug faces."

"How did they know?"

"Hell if I know, unless he told somebody. I didn't say anything to anyone until we had been going out for a couple of weeks." She paused. "I just don't know why I didn't see him for what he was. I mean, I actually thought I loved him. Can you believe that? There was something inside me telling me to stop, but I just couldn't help myself. He was so goddamned charismatic."

I moved to stand next to her and touched her shoulder as she stared at the floor. She cried quietly for a moment and then shook me off and went to the desk to pull a couple of tissues to her face. "I've got work to do here." She sat back down and sighed as if to shake herself free of something unpleasant. "I guess there's a lot of other things we can do until I can get that stuff back."

"Like what?" Since this wasn't a therapy session, and she was clearly signaling that she had done talking, I let it drop. Besides, I'm sometimes wary of encouraging people to spill. There are so many people who will douse you with the most intimate details of their lives at any sign of plain old civility even if they've never laid eyes on you before. Perhaps especially because they don't know you. It can stir up all my professional instincts, but it's never the right place or time to do anything about it. Besides, it can really backfire, in that people may also avoid you if they're worried that they spilled too much. Who needs the aggravation and potential awkwardness?

"Okay." She cleared her throat. Her reddened eyes were the only evidence of her recent emotional struggle.

"Well, now, we can go through the supervisor's program files, since we have no choice but to put off organizing the main files."

We headed in the direction of Janice's cubicle, Georgia in the lead. As we passed Kayson's old office, Detective Arnold Redstone and I exchanged looks and he gave me a small smile. I smiled back trying to convey thanks without compromising his position, and then I hurried to keep up with Georgia. I assumed that Detective Kelley was somewhere close by, and there was no sense in going another round with her. Although I might have enjoyed it. At least a little.

When I joined Georgia, she was standing facing the locked cabinet that I had met earlier in Janice's cubbyhole. She actually kicked it and grimaced. "Goddamned thing."

We searched for the keys, but to no avail. I told her that I had already asked the secretaries if they had them. Despite that, Georgia marched over to the secretary's desk, with me trailing behind her.

"Where the hell is Janice?"

The poor woman jumped up from her chair, shaking her head, "I don't know for sure, but I think she's over at the complexes."

"Which ones are Janice's?"

The secretary warily held out a piece of paper and actually took a step back as Georgia snatched it from her.

"I'm sick of this," she said. "Let's go."

I felt the need to hold on tightly because of the mad woman at the wheel as we wove through the streets.

CHAPTER 39

Janice's unit of complexes—one of five spread across the city—was made up of three two-storied light brick buildings, each with eight apartments laid out in a parklike setting. The apartments on the second story had stamp-sized balconies, while small wooden decks extended from the back of each first-floor unit. A one-story community center formed the focal point for the units. Jungle Gyms and the outlines of sandboxes, two basketball courts, swings, slides, and benches formed clusters of activity areas, now mostly obscured by the deep snow. Blue shutters framed the windows, some of which had plant boxes hanging from them. Bits of dead plants dangled from a window box nearby. Neatly trimmed bushes and small trees broke up the expanse of what was probably lawn, now whitened and crisscrossed with tracks. I imagined the green lawn and the sound of children playing in the warmer months. It looked like anything but public housing.

Georgia and I stopped first at the community building in the center of the complex. Following the sounds of children, we found a large airy room strewn with toys and lined with short bookcases and shelving. Somebody had painted a brightly colored mural depicting a fire-breathing dragon chasing a group of laughing children across one wall. In fantasy, children can easily escape danger. Often, not so in real life.

A bank of full-length windows flooded the space with natural light. Cutout animals and shapes in primary colors frolicked across the windows. It was a children's sanctuary from the bleakness of their previous lives.

There were about eight children, ranging from infancy to five years old and being tended by two adults. The huge space dwarfed the small group. At the far end of the room, there were several cribs and cots as well as a kitchenette and a reading area set apart with an orange carpet and bookcases.

I didn't recognize the young man and woman who looked up in surprise as we entered. The man moved toward us and Georgia gave him a smile and held out her hand. He looked to be in his early twenties.

"I'm Georgia Enfield, the interim director." As she spoke, I could see the two relax. The woman, who was as young as the man, also walked in our direction. Most of the kids had stopped to watch what the adults were doing.

"We're here to see how the program is working," Georgia said, still smiling. "Is there anything you can tell us about how things are going?"

Neither Kate nor Daniel had any complaints. Both had been working for the project as child day-care workers for about three months. They didn't know what had happened to the previous workers. This wasn't all that unusual, since these kinds of jobs usually have high turnover rates.

"So, how many kids do you usually have here?" I asked.

"What do you mean?" Kate said. "This is it. The most we have is these eight kids."

"How many families live in this complex?"

"I think it's eight," Daniel said. "There are a lot of empty units now."

"How long have they been empty?" Georgia asked.

They both shrugged and Daniel said, "Since I've been here." Kate nodded. Just then, a child of about five ran up to Kate and began to pull on her arm. She looked at us as if to apologize and turned to go back to her charges. Another child began to cry. Daniel said he had to go, too, and we thanked them both for their time.

When we explored the rest of the building we came upon a large, multi-purpose group room with another kitchenette and shower rooms for men and women, which led to an outdoor pool, now closed for the winter. There was a small business office, which was also closed up and a TV room with the furniture arranged into small conversation spaces.

I think I was gaping. "This place looks, looks …" I started to say.

"Not like any public housing you've ever seen," Georgia said.

"Can you believe it?"

"That's the point of the program." Georgia talked as we walked. "It's to give people a sense of what's possible, and to do it in a dignified way. Not the usual hellhole that only makes people more discouraged."

"Well, I wonder how long this will last when we know everything."

She didn't answer, but after a moment pulled out a ring of keys. "Let's look in the business office."

"You have keys?"

"A perk of being the director." She searched through each key, looking at the label until she found the one marked Bldg. C. "There should be duplicate keys of each of the apartments in here. I'd like to see one of the empty ones."

"What are you thinking?" I asked as I followed her into the office.

"I'm not saying yet. But I have my suspicions."

I nodded at her back, wondering if we were thinking the same thing.

We soon found the locked cabinet containing the keys to all of the apartments, and with it a list of the residents of the complex and where each of the families lived. The records were legibly and neatly written.

"Look at this," Georgia said. "Nothing like the disorganization at the main office. I wonder who took the time to do this."

"I assume it was Janice's handiwork. In fact, this looks like her handwriting."

"How can you be so sure?" Georgia asked.

"I should recognize it," I said. "I've seen some of her records."

The lists indicated that there were eight families, each headed by a woman, with a total of eighteen children. That meant ten more kids who were probably in school or somewhere else. This was far short of what each complex could hold or what the program was designed for.

"Isn't this interesting?" Georgia said as she and I looked at each other. "Let's check this out."

We hurried through the beginning snowfall to the first apartment building.

The first unassigned apartments we checked seemed to be used for storage but the others were fully furnished. And totally, completely benign. I don't know what Georgia imagined, but I was thinking of little love nests, with satin sheets, candles, and porn. Or maybe racks, whips, and chains. But these were … ordinary.

"Georgia," I said, pointing at a print on the wall of the third apartment, "do you recognize that?"

She shook her head.

"This is the third copy of the same print. One in each apartment so far."

"Probably got a good deal at Walmart."

But there was something haunting the edges of my mind, something familiar. I opened the cabinets in the kitchen and found a few mismatched sets of dishes and just a smattering of canned food. Where were the half-full boxes of cereal or the opened jars of peanut butter? But the places weren't empty. A comb lay carelessly on the kitchen counter, an empty dog-food bowl sat on the floor. One had a teddy bear placed carefully on a bed in a child's room. In another, there were a couple of articles of clothing casually strewn and books laid on tables.

"They're like movie sets," I said.

"What?"

"The apartments. A quick glance, and they seem occupied, but look a little closer, and it's clear that nobody is living in any of them."

"Were they set up to fool an inspector?"

"Seems like you'd have to assume a lot of incompetence on the inspector's part."

Georgia opened the humming refrigerator. Three bottles of sports drink, and an empty orange juice carton in the door.

"You're right. This is weird."

"Maybe the incompetence is Janice's. Maybe she was supposed to make the apartments look lived in and just did a half-assed job."

"Well, whatever's going on, Janice is in the thick of it, and I'd try to avoid us too, if I were her. However, that's going to stop. I think that Kayson had a very cozy setup here, with the help of his staff. And we are going to get information out of her if I have to …"

I didn't say anything, but I heard the menace in her voice.

During the drive back to the office, Georgia ranted about the incompetence and chaos of the project. "Did you know that we are paying for day care for thirty kids in that complex? And there are only eight." She pounded the steering wheel.

"Well, I know that's a discrepancy, but that doesn't seem to be all that much money."

She turned to glare at me. "According to the project proposal, we are getting money for, let me see, five times twenty-four families. In the first year of the program, it was supposed to start with eight families per unit and then build from there to a full load. I think—although I can't actually say for sure, since the records are so goddamned confusing—that they never moved beyond the first year's goal. And this is only one complex. There's no telling what's going on in the others."

I relaxed as she tended to the task of driving and we drove for a short while in silence. I had let go of my tight grip on the seat when she erupted again.

"Do you know how much money that could be? I mean, for each family, each parent gets training and support services for a full four years, to get the family on their feet, if they need it, not to mention the supplemental income. And there are services for the kids, too. Of course, close to the end of each family's stay with the program, they are supposed to take over most of their expenses, as a way to transition into the regular world. Even then, they would get extra income to bring them up to a living wage. If we have been billing for a full group and there are only eight families, where the hell does all the extra money go?"

"Georgia," I said as calmly as I could, "I think it's time to call in the auditors, isn't it?"

She shook her head, "My boss won't be happy. I gave her a heads-up that there might be something hinky, and she wanted me to try to clean it up without going outside. But, how am I gonna do that?"

"And what if the police put two and two together?" Of course, Redstone was following my lead on Kayson's sexual predation, but who knew what he would find, or what the police might think was important.

"I guess they might be looking for a motive for somebody to kill him in all that mess," Georgia said. "But wasting government funds? I can't imagine …"

"There's something else."

"What?"

I took a breath, trying to figure out how to say it. "There's a possibility that Kayson forced some of the women to have sex in exchange for staying in the program."

"What?" She almost screamed it, and then slammed on her brakes for a changing traffic light.

"Georgia, please," I said. "I want to make it back without a detour to the hospital."

After a moment, she said in a tight voice, "I'm sorry. But you better tell me."

The light changed and the car took off with a lurch. I grimaced at a stab of pain in my foot. "I can't tell you where I know this from. It's confidential. So we have to find another source to confirm it."

"God, Addy. If this is true, you need to tell me how you know."

There was another silence. I have an obligation to protect everything that a client tells me. I'm freer to say something if the client tells me that he or she is going to hurt somebody, but Kayson was beyond hurting people. Until Cheryl gave me permission, there was no way to justify betraying this confidence.

But it couldn't be hard to confirm. Adding what Cheryl had told me to Virginia's tale about Kayson, it was a good bet that he didn't limit his tactics to students. He probably took advantage of all kinds of people whom he had some power over. Exploiting powerless people to try to solve a psychological dilemma means that you can't ever stop, because it never solves the problem.

"I'm sorry, Addy," Georgia said. "I know this puts you into a bind. But I need to know what you know."

"Georgia, I would if I could. Trust me when I tell you that I'm pretty sure Kayson used his authority to rape SSD clients."

She pounded the wheel again. "Shit. I wish that son of a bitch wasn't dead so I could kill him myself. After, of course, he'd been publicly humiliated."

"I should say that this is not confirmed. But it's hard to feel generous toward that guy."

"You don't have to convince me of that." Georgia hit the steering wheel again, but not as hard. She was calming down, and starting to think again. "Well, now we have to interview all of the clients and see what's what. And we are going to track down Janice and Kenneth. Those two have some explaining to do."

"Right."

"I hope the cops are finished by the time we get back."

They weren't.

CHAPTER 40

K ris's home was a showcase for her renovation skills. The Eastlake had been heading toward certain demise when she bought it and began restoring it. She attacked it—as she did all projects—with all her energy. It took her five years in between running her business and pursuing the ladies. And even now she could still find things to redo.

That evening, we had agreed to get together and Kris had insisted on using her own computer to look at the stuff we had "borrowed" from Kayson's computer.

"At least my computer is from this century," she said by way of argument. Why buy new when something still worked was my motto. So we were in her dark-paneled den, in the tower, where I settled down on an overstuffed chair while she booted up. I leafed through the material that I had, well, stolen. Hmm. A murder suspect and a thief. Both fine qualities in a social worker.

The first file introduced me to the Garcia family. They had been Mexican migrants following the harvest during the early sixties. The department of Public Health had been called to investigate an outbreak of tuberculosis at the migrant camp and discovered Mrs. Garcia and her three children sharing a shack with three other families. Her youngest was very sick and spending her days alone in bed, while the older children worked in the fields alongside Mrs. Garcia. Mr. Garcia's arrest two weeks prior to the report had left the family without its best earner. The authorities arrived to find the family slowly crumbling under the weight of too much adversity.

The story grew drearier. The youngest child died despite emergency treatment. During the investigation it was discovered the oldest child, a girl of thirteen, was made pregnant. Milana had been reluctant to talk, but the social worker's patience had finally convinced her to tell who had been forcing himself on her. It turned out that the man who had gotten her pregnant had also sold her services to men in the camp as well as to some of the bosses.

The middle child, Roberto, a boy of ten, had run away several times and finally ended up in juvenile detention. It was noted that it was also suspected that he had been abused. They had surmised this because he had refused to talk at all, but his medical examination had been positive for sexual assault. I could only imagine his humiliation and fear at being examined so intimately by Anglo strangers after being assaulted by the men that he did know. It would make it really hard for him to know other ways of being male.

Reading this story also brought Natalie to mind. She had never been eager to share her early history with me. What I knew was sketchy. Her beginnings were in Mexico and somehow she got to this country as a child. All I knew was that she came with an uncle. I never knew what happened to the rest of her family. She would change the subject abruptly if I ever tried to ask her about it. But I did notice how quickly the pain would show whenever I did dare to bring it up.

There was much more to the Garcia story, but I set aside the papers and began on another file. It held very different specifics, but once again it was the story of children and adults caught in the grip of deadening poverty and want. I skimmed it, looking for something, although I had no idea what.

"Why do you suppose Kayson had this stuff in his office?" I asked aloud, not really directed at anyone.

"Wasn't he somebody who needed to be in control?" Kris answered as she peered into the monitor.

"Yeah, that's pretty clear. But how does keeping thirty-five-year-old files around give you control over anything?"

"Do you recognize any of the names?"

"Not yet. But I'll keep looking. How are you doing?"

"I don't really know. What do you make of this?"

The screen was filled with a list of names, some of which seemed familiar to me. "This looks like people who work for the department, maybe on the project. Yeah," I pointed, "that's Janice and Ken and several others who are supervisors." But there was something odd about the names. "How old is this list?" I asked.

"I don't know. It's weird but nothing is clearly labeled. It's as if whoever put this stuff together was deliberately trying to make it so that other people couldn't understand it."

Kris continued to scroll down the list. "What was this guy hiding?"

Aha. There it was. "These are the names of supervisors and other people, but this is a list of students, not employees. See that? I pointed to a column with the entry ST99. That's probably Spring Term 1999."

"Okay. So why make it hard to see that these are students?"

"It doesn't make sense to me. SSD is a regular placement site for students. And sometimes placements will hire students once they graduate."

Kris swung around. "None of this seems all that incriminating or revealing."

"Well, let's—oh, damn."

Kris looked at me in surprise. "What is it?"

"I forgot to check with Marissa, Kayson's secretary. I asked her—or more accurately, pressured her—to get me some information. I gotta get over there tomorrow." Kris stretched, leaning away from the computer. "How will that help?"

"I don't know, but it looks like we could use anything we can find."

Kris went back to the hard drive, and I opened another battered file. Now the Miller family's sorrowful story unfolded through caseworker's notes and newspaper clippings yellowed by time. Robert Miller had left his wife, Katherine (Kay), and three children when the oldest, John, was five. He and his younger brothers, Luke and Mark, had come to the attention of SSD when John, at fifteen, had killed their mother by smashing a heavy water glass down on her skull.

According to a newspaper story, the mailman had thought things seemed too quiet and had peered into the windows of the small house. He described what he saw as "a terrible thing" and he wasn't exaggerating. John had been found sitting on the side of the tub, his mother sprawled at his feet with her head caved in. Shards of thick glass were scattered over the floor and clung to her bloodied scalp. Blood from a slash on John's hand dripped onto his mother's body.

Luke and Mark were sent into the foster care system and John was sentenced to juvenile detention until his eighteenth birthday. He remained silent about all of these events the entire time he was held. However, Mark, the second oldest, had been very forthcoming about life in their mother's house.

She kept them in the unheated basement when they weren't in school. He described to his caseworker how the three boys had huddled together, often burrowed into a pile of towels that John had run through the dryer for warmth. Katherine Miller also enjoyed playing games with her boys. One of them involved bringing them upstairs into the kitchen for a meal, only to feed two of them while the third one was forced to watch. More often than not, she chose John, and if she picked one of the others, John would plead with her to let him be the one to sit out. This would infuriate her, but she often gave him what he wanted.

Getting a satisfying meal was a rarity for the boys. Most of the time, she threw something down the basement stairs that only kept them going but did not kill the gnawing in their stomachs. The hunger was always with them. John was picked up one time for shoplifting on his way home from school. He was caught with two boxes of macaroni. According to Mark, they soaked it in water from the utility sink and ate it with catsup packets lifted from the local fast food places.

The caseworker's notes were full of Mark's stories of his mother's craziness. John had frequent broken bones, burns, and other injuries, but he always had a reasonable explanation for them when he and his mother arrived at the emergency room. There was a thick pile of medical reports laying bare Katherine's record of outbursts. According to the notes, Katherine kept a blanket chest where the two youngest boys had each spent many hours waiting for his mother to return. When a boy was too young to go to school, and Katherine wanted to go out, she would put the child into the chest, with a pillow and a blanket and lock it. "To keep you safe," she would say to the child as the lid came down.

Sessions with Mark also revealed that "the mother" would sometimes bring either John or Mark up from the basement into the bathroom. Luke had been spared this for some reason. Perhaps he was not yet old enough. From Mark's telling, Katherine would almost tenderly help the child urinate and then undress him, and often she would also take off her own clothes. She would run her hands over the child's body and sometimes lie down with him on top of her. The boys had come to dread the sexual rituals. On many occasions, Katherine would also take one of the older boys into her bed, while the other two spent the night hunkered together in the basement.

Mark also told his worker that his mother kept two bedrooms outfitted for children, with toys, books, and walls decorated with ships and baseball scenes. However, they were only allowed to peek into them when they were being herded by on the way to school. He had confessed that sometimes when "the mother," which is how they all referred to her, was out, they discovered that she had forgotten to lock the basement door and they would creep up the stairs and into those bedrooms. They would just stand there and take in the space, trying to etch the images into their memories.

It was then that my heart literally skipped a beat. I felt it.

"Addy," Kris said, "I think I've—what?"

I handed her the report. I was surprised to see my hand trembling. "Read this."

While she read, my mind spun, trying to take this in. It was John, it had to be John. Mark had talked, and Luke was spared, but John had taken the brunt of it. And he'd never said a word.

Kris put the report down, disgust apparent on her face. "Addy, this is … God, I mean … but what does it …?"

"Don't you see? He was trying to get away from it, but you never can. You always wind up reliving it—Katherine! Kay! His mother's name was Kay. Dear God, she followed him wherever he …"

"Addy, what are you babbling about?"

I tapped the report. "Don't you see? This is the early life of Professor David Kay- son."

CHAPTER 41

I sat at my table and cradled a cup of tea in my hands the following afternoon. I'd been too excited to think—or sleep much—the night before. I'd risen late, and then stumbled through the day. This was my first real chance to ponder the problem.

Knowing the truth about Kayson's past explained so much. The empty, too-perfect apartments in the units, and his pathologically neat office. These were the public face of his life, the perfect boys' rooms, neat and convincing and ultimately hollow. Then there was the time hanging out in the basement with the janitor, the slovenly office at SSD, the dark, messy, underground reality of David Kayson's life. And the exercise of power, sexualizing all relationships, especially those where he'd been in control.

But there was another side as well—John, caring for his brothers. Odious as Kayson was personally, he was, by all reports, an effective social worker. His clients tended to improve, and from what I could see, his SSD program was genuinely helping the few people who were in it.

And his psyche? I had joked with Natalie about not getting any on me, but now what I felt most was pity. He had been beaten and sexually abused by his mother. He had murdered her. His unconscious must have been a swampful of stuff that felt like it had no bottom. If I'd been he, would I have had the courage to face up to it, to let it all out? I like to think that no one is so badly broken that they can never heal, but he would have had to go through hell before getting to the other side.

But what did he do instead? He kept reliving the horror of his childhood, and inflicting new horrors on everyone around him. Virginia Early. The women in the SSD program. Who knew who else? And one of them had finally killed him for it.

Unfortunately, I was now no closer to knowing who.

I stared at the surface of the tea and watched the steam rise from the dark amber liquid, feeling the heat transfer through the cup to my hands. The envelope from Marissa lay in front of me on the coffee table. She had come through for me. When I dropped by the school, earlier, she handed me a manila envelope taped as if it contained top-secret information. I almost expected red block printing stamped on its side and a wad of wax to seal it. Her hand shook as I took it from her and I could feel myself begin to redden with guilt. I had pushed this woman to do something it was apparent she felt reluctant to do. I thanked her, vowing to try to make it up to her. Flowers, maybe?

I set down the cup and pulled out several sheets of paper. Each contained a class list. Kayson had taught two or three classes a term and Marissa had included lists from the last eight years. I taught one of the basic courses everyone was required to take, so I recognized many of the names. I wasn't surprised to see Virginia Early's name. I found Julie Pigeon and Donna Blare on another list. I saw Roz and Jerry on older lists, as well as several others I recognized. No surprises there. I noted that the supervisors from the SSD were also ex-students of Professor Kayson. And so was Amy Arnold. I wondered what kind of grades those students had gotten from him. And how many of them had been forced to share their favors in exchange for a grade? I wasn't sure if this was one more piece of the puzzle or just more information to clog up the mess that was this situation.

Leaving the pages on the table, I headed out to the Social Services Department offices. Georgia and I had divided up the SSD clients to interview. At least this made me feel as if I was doing something.

I tried to include as many of the women whom I had already met in the group meeting as I could. Hopefully, somebody who wasn't a complete stranger would make it easier for them to talk more freely.

It took me a while to decipher the schedules so that I could locate the women. Several of them were scheduled to be at their jobs. I didn't want to conduct such a delicate interview where they worked, so I set them aside until later in the day when they might be at the ends of their shifts. When I approached Lucinda, our having met earlier didn't seem to help her loosen up at all.

"I don't have anything to say to you. I need to get to work." We were walking along the sidewalk leading up to her apartment. By her pace, Lucinda was in a hurry, despite the icy footing, so I was forced to keep my eyes on the ground as I worked to keep up with her.

"I understand … you have a full schedule," I said as I fought for oxygen. "I remember that you said it felt like it … was too much. I'm interested in hearing more about … your experience with the project. It would just take a few minutes."

"What good would that do? Nothing ever changes. I'm just keeping my mouth shut, because nothing good comes from opening it. My mother used to tell me that."

"Your mother was pretty wise, huh?"

"You bet. And I ain't about to start changing the rules now."

We drew up to her door and, as she fumbled for keys in her purse, I gave her my final pitch between gasps, "I'm really interested … in your take on this program. You've been in it for about … two and half years now, right? And you've probably got some really good insights … that might help us improve things around here."

As she unlocked her door she laughed, "I doubt it. Things is always gonna be the same. Nothing changes, and nothing will change even if I say my piece. I gotta go. I'll be late for my job, and I've already been late once this week. You know how bosses can get, especially the ones paying you your $5.50 an hour."

She tried to duck into her apartment but I held the door. I was a little worried about what would happen if she got pushy with me. Although I'm tall and solid, Lucinda had both height and poundage on me.

"Lucinda, if you change your mind, let me know." I offered her my business card. "I'll be back around to check with you later."

"Don't bother."

She disappeared into her apartment, leaving me with my hand

outstretched, the card crumpled against the slammed door. Some people really like social workers.

When I approached another program client, Francine Childers, she seemed wary but cooperative. I stood in her kitchen, watching her prepare a pot of chili, while I looked for an opportunity to ask about Kayson.

We'd been talking about how well her kids were doing in school now that they all felt more settled—they'd moved eight times in as many months before she was offered a chance to enter the program.

"So this program has been really helpful."

"Oh, sure. I don't know where we'd be if we didn't get in here. I was pretty bad, with the drugs and no job, you know. I'm never going to be on the street again."

"Is there anything in the program that you would want to be different?"

"Oh, no," she said quickly. "There's nothing. It's all working out for us."

"So, you don't have any complaints at all?"

"No, why?" She turned to look at me, the knife with which she'd been chopping a green pepper poised over the cutting board. "Have any of the others said anything?"

Her glance was meant to be casual, but it had an undercurrent of something else. Francine walked over to a cupboard and took out two cans of kidney beans. She wasn't going to volunteer anything. She was probably too scared of losing her place.

And I couldn't promise her anything, since I didn't know what was going to happen with the program once everything was out in the open. All I could do was appeal to the side of her that wanted to deal with having been harassed into having sex so that she and her children could stay off the streets.

"Francine, I'm interested in anything you might want to tell me about your experience here. I've heard some things that are pretty troubling. That involved Mr. Kayson. If there's anything …"

Francine kept chopping while slowly shaking her head. "No, no, there's nothing I can say. Mr. Kayson didn't have much to do with the program and Janice, the supervisor, has always been good to me and the kids. I like them people who watch the kids, and you should see how my daughter is so happy with her art." Francine turned to indicate the child's drawings hung on the refrigerator.

"See, those over there. She's so proud, and happy. I think she's got special talent. Everything is fine for us."

Francine resumed her work, looking away as if to avoid eye contact. "But I'll let you know if I think of anything."

I left my card with her, all the while seeing her as someone who, given a little more time and encouragement, would probably loosen up.

I found Mona Sonoria in her second floor apartment. She cracked open the door and peered out at me across the security chain. I stood back so that she could get a good look at me and reminded her that we'd met before. Her dark eyes betrayed her fatigue.

Mona seemed to debate about letting me in. I didn't blame her. She may not have known what I wanted, but my being there didn't signal anything good.

Finally she pulled back the door and nodded for me to follow her in.

"I wasn't feeling too well, so I didn't go in today," she said. "My kids are over in the day care, and I thought that it would give me a chance to get some rest. I've been so tired."

She walked slowly over to the blue corduroy couch. I sat in a green flowered chair across from her. She wore a gray sweatshirt and sweatpants with a pair of fluffy yellow slippers that looked like Easter peeps.

She reached for a pack of cigarettes, shook one out, and then offered me the pack, which I reluctantly declined.

"I know I shouldn't do this, but they're hard to give up," she said.

"Yeah, I know. It was really hard for me to quit."

She looked at me through reddened eyes, her short brown hair in a tangle, as if she'd just awakened. "I couldn't go to work. I just couldn't go to that place today." She lit the cigarette and the smoke curled lazily up around her head.

"Mona," I said gently. "I'm not here about your job, or anything like that. Sometimes people call in sick from work because they don't feel well. And that's that."

She nodded. "So why are you here? You're another social worker from the project, aren't you?"

"Yes, I am. Remember, I attended the group meeting? But there's something else I want to ask you about that has nothing to do with you going to work."

It was as if she didn't hear me at all. "I get so tired, and after a while I can't stand that place, it's so greasy, and I come home smelling bad and covered with crud. My hair dripping with oil, my legs aching. So I just needed to be off just for this day. I mean, so I won't have as big a check, but it's just one day. I'm still going to finish this program. I know a couple of girls who made it out of here. One of them, she's a friend of mine, is going to be a social worker like you. And I'm going to get through this too. She made it and so will I."

"Really? A social worker? Is that what you want, too?"

"I don't know. I've still got my GED to get before I can go to college. I think she had only two more years to go for her BA before she came into the program. So all she had to do was get back on her feet, and then she just applied and they took her. We had such a party when she got her letter. You shoulda seen it. We got so drunk, and everybody was partying so hard." Mona looked to the right as she was remembering, a small smile playing across her tired face. "That was a good time."

"So her success has inspired you to keep going."

She flicked an ash. "You bet. I'm gonna make it."

I wanted to ask for her friend's name, but it was important to avoid getting her back up. Besides, there were other ways of discovering that piece of information. It could wait. "I don't see why you couldn't do it too."

She exhaled slowly. "So why are you here?"

There was no time like the present to forge ahead. "Actually, I wanted to ask you about your experience in the program, especially with David Kayson."

I was watching and I thought I saw her expression shift like a curtain dropping. "What about him?"

"Well, is there anything that I should know about him? Anything that might have happened that you want to tell me about?"

She shrugged, flicked her ash again, put the burning cigarette to her mouth, and inhaled deeply. "There's nothing to say. Why, has somebody else said anything?"

This was the second time I'd heard this response. Suggestive, but not revealing. I needed to take another tack. I shifted my position, trying to appear non-threatening. "Look, Mona, I need your help. I have heard some rumors about Dr. Kayson that weren't very pleasant."

She snorted at that.

"We need to know if anything happened so that we can make sure the program isn't in danger." What was I saying? It was probably true that the program would be in jeopardy if what we suspected was true and if it came out, but was I playing loose with the facts? Or worse, maybe I wasn't. Was my goal, that had nothing to do with this woman's life, going to threaten the program and the lives of all these women? I watched her face as she weighed what I'd just said. She stared out the window that overlooked the expanse of snowy courtyard between the buildings and then slowly stubbed out her cigarette. Following her gaze, I saw the pictures of her children arranged on the windowsill.

"I don't know if I should say anything. What I don't understand is that everybody knew and nobody did anything." She looked down and I saw a tear drop onto her lap.

I leaned forward. "This is really hard."

She nodded and stood up. I worried that she was just walking out on me, and as if to read my thoughts, she said, "It's okay, I'm just going to get a Kleenex."

I watched her walk into the kitchen and return to her place on the couch with a box of tissues in hand. She seemed to have resolved to talk. Even so, the words came slowly as if she had to physically force them out.

"When I started in the program, I guess around two years ago, Kayson told me that I had to follow all the rules if I wanted to stay here. My little girl was twenty months old, and I was pregnant with the twins." She stopped to light another cigarette and inhaled deeply. "I hadn't seen the kids' father for about six months and I was broke and drinking so much. I couldn't pay the rent where we were and my landlord was on my case. So when the caseworker told me about this program, I thought, 'What the hell?' When Kayson said that to me, I thought I would give it a try. But I didn't know what he meant by all of the rules."

"So you found out?"

"Yes, I did." Tears started to stream down her cheeks. "I found out that the biggest rule was that I had to sleep with that bastard if I didn't want to be kicked out."

"How long did that go on?"

She grunted, "It stopped when I got too big, and then it started again after I had my kids. And then it finally stopped for good when the jerk was killed. Finally, it stopped. I wish I could thank whoever did it."

"Did you know of any others that this happened to?"

"You've got to be kidding. He did anyone he could. I don't think he was picky."

"Did anyone else ever say anything to you about it? I mean, did any of the other women ever tell you that they were having to sleep with him too?"

"Nobody talked about it, but everybody knew. He used one of them empty apartments, and whenever he wanted to 'see' one of us we knew to go down there and meet him. Once when I was leaving the apartment, Birdy was going in. I looked at her and I knew."

"Birdy is another one of the women in the program?"

"She's the one I was telling you about. She's one of the ones who got out."

"Did he wear a condom, at least?"

"That was the first thing he brought up and it was a good thing. I didn't need another kid and he wanted to make sure, so we used condoms every time, even when I was pregnant. And after the kids were born too. I can't use the pill. It makes me sick, even the low dose ones, so I had a choice between the diaphragm and the condom. With my boyfriend, I had to use the diaphragm because he wouldn't use a condom, but I hated it. It's so messy, you know." She raised her eyebrows and nodded at me to indicate that we were sisters in the know. "So, Kayson was okay with it, condoms, you know."

I breathed an internal sigh of relief. I hoped this meant Mona didn't have to worry about AIDS or any other complications. Who knew what kind of bugs he carried?

"So at least you didn't have to worry about getting pregnant."

She shook her head then, as if to rid herself of some ugly image.

"What is it, Mona?

"God. He was kinda … kinky, you know." She looked at me and turned away, drawing on her cigarette.

I waited.

"He used to force me to, you know, do it in the ass. I have always hated that, but that's what he wanted most. Weird guy. I thought at first it was because he wanted to make sure I didn't get pregnant."

"You thought something different later on?"

"I don't know. The first thing he asked me was what I used, and when I told him that I couldn't use the pill, he says that he doesn't want no kid around, so that we better use the condoms." She shrugged, "But—"

"But?"

"He was a strange guy. I mean, he thought he was God's gift, you know, but he looked to be afraid of kids. He wouldn't ever look at 'em, or talk to 'em. I mean, some guys don't like kids, and you can tell because they yell at them, or they ignore them, or something. But Kayson always seemed sorta nervous around them, like he kinda wanted to get close to them, but he was scared of them or something. I don't know. It was weird."

Weird unless you knew his history. It was his little brothers, all over again. Or maybe he was shying away from his own impulses to hurt children, since he could have assumed that part of his mother's personality as well. In an odd way, it made him a better person than she. Kayson had never had children. In fact, he seemed to have had only serial short-lived relationships.

It hit me then that his history of relationships felt familiar. Too familiar.

"Mona," I began, and she looked up, her face drawn, the lines around her eyes carved deeply with her pain. "This has been an awful thing to have to go through. I'm here to get information about what's happened to you, but I think you should have somebody to talk to about this, to help you find a way to deal with it."

"How do I do that?" Her despondency bleached life out of her. "There are people who never get anywhere and people who get everything. I'm always gonna be a person that doesn't get much more than shit in my life. This is one more of those things. Kayson is the kind of person who gets what he wants and gets away with it. And I'm the kind of person who gets done to."

Except this time, somebody did it to Kayson. Again.

CHAPTER 42

The throbbing in my foot was a painful backdrop to thoughts of my recent journey through some of Kayson's history. Any of those women had a motive to kill David Kayson. I looked around my cramped little office at the SSD, waiting for Georgia to return, and tried to picture one of them actually ramming a knife into a man. I thought about the loneliness of that little huddle of children, waiting for one more terror to descend from overhead.

God, I had heard so many similar stories that sometimes I wondered if there were any normal people left in the world. At least normal in the sense that it never actually occurred to them to be overtly sexual with their children, or act out their anger violently. I felt worn out by it. Too much pain. Too much violence and too many people without internal braking systems. Images of my own childhood surged front and center. Remembrances of anger swallowed to avoid one more beating. The crimping of shame and sadness in my chest and stomach, forcing me take a deep breath.

Enough. I stretched my arms and shoulders and focused on the task at hand.

I decided to make some notes on the interviews I had just finished, but my mind drifted to the idea that there was somebody out there that had it in for me. Someone had it in for Kayson, and someone had it in for me. Kayson had done something bad enough to push someone to murder him. The brick thrower was obviously very angry with me. Anger was often an outward expression of unacknowledged fear or hurt. Was there anyone I had wounded so deeply or to whom I was such a threat that they would think getting back at me would solve the problem? Or was I just a stand-in for someone else? Those women that Kayson had forced into submission were stand-ins for the child he'd been. He'd become his mother and kept his charges controlled and in fear of him. It was hard to believe that I, too, could be perceived that way, although it happened all the time in my role as a therapist.

Had Natalie also been a target because of who she was, or had the killer viewed her through a distorting lens? I felt a tightening in my chest and I swallowed hard to rid myself of the sensation of tears just below the surface. I forced myself back to my notes, thankful for the gentle art of suppression.

But more so, I was grateful that Georgia arrived at that moment.

"Hey," she said. "So how'd it go for you?"

Was it my imagination or was there something on her mind? She seemed jumpy. I paused and looked a question at her.

She didn't pick it up. "So, what did you find?"

I told her about my conversations with the women, including how many didn't want to talk with me.

"That's okay. I had the same thing with most of them, but all it takes is one or two. And two of the women I talked with were pretty candid about that son of a bitch. Can you believe I ever went out with him?"

"Don't forget having sex with him." I instantly regretted having said it. Hostility is often not too far under the skin.

There was a distinct pause and then she shuddered, "Don't remind me. You remember that I told you that he was a clean freak?"

I nodded, thinking about the small boy trying to keep his little brothers clean in a dingy basement. Not to mention scrubbing away the dirty feeling of having sex with your mother.

"Besides having to practically clean my whole place before he could relax, he also used to insist that we, you know, do it a certain way."

I hoped silently that she wouldn't go on. I just didn't want to hear another confession at that moment. Or was it that I didn't want to hear anything more about Kayson? Being both sympathetic and repulsed was getting to be a strain.

"Yeah, he was always pushing me for anal sex." She glanced at me as if expecting that I might recoil in disgust.

I might have if I hadn't known what was coming. "And ...?"

"Well. I didn't ... don't particularly like to, you know. But he just insisted and insisted and you just have to give in or ..."

"Or you worried that you'd hurt his feelings."

"Yeah. Stupid, isn't it?"

"No. Not at all. I hear that all the time, especially from women, even smart ones. We seem to be more willing to give in to others to avoid hurting their feelings at our own expense. It sometimes explains the 'no means yes' phenomenon."

"It was as if he liked to see me feel sad and ... I don't know—"

"Humiliated?"

"Yes. It was humiliating."

She looked as if she was about to cry and I didn't want this to turn into a session. I had too much else on my mind. So I had to cut it off.

"I'm sorry, Georgia. I know it must have been rough. Did he really never say anything about his own childhood?"

She seemed startled by the question. "I don't think he ever did. He was too interested in my story." I watched her stand as she made an internal shift. "You know, enough about that bastard." She walked over to the desk as if to take care of something and then turned. "Anyway, my next step is to corner Janice and Ken and the two other supervisors. I think I have enough to put pressure on them to come clean. Either way, they're in deep shit."

I nodded. Social workers have a legal obligation to take action if they know that somebody, especially a client, is being hurt in some way. "Ethical charges?"

"And the financial fraud will likely land some of them in jail," Georgia said. "I can't see how they all didn't know about this crap. It makes me sick." She slid a couple of small boxes aside and sat on the edge of the metal desk, tapping it absently with her index finger. Again, I was aware that there was something else that Georgia wasn't saying. I thought about what I had learned over time about her. Georgia was a dedicated social worker and a very good administrator. She took a shelter for battered women, which had been limping along, and turned it into a model for such programs. I had not known much about her personal life, at least until that day. And I wasn't sure I wanted the information I now had.

"Addy, let's call it a day." She sagged against the wall. "I have to be more rested to think about what to do about all of this."

"Look, I'm sorry, but I'm not in a good place to hear any more, so it may have seemed that I cut you off. But if there's something else you want to say …?"

She chuckled then. "Nope. Thanks anyway, but I'm too far gone." She looked straight at me. "Addy, go home. You've got enough to worry about without taking on mine as well."

"Well, I'm around if you need to talk."

"I'll be okay. I'm gonna take in a meeting. And that will help."

I left the building feeling unsettled.

CHAPTER 43

The traffic sounds emanating from the receiver told me that Captain Redstone was calling me from a phone somewhere on a busy street. He was being careful. His call had caught me at home, just as I had limped through the door.

"I wanted to let you know that one of the witnesses recanted." He was semi-shouting to be heard.

"What?" I felt like I'd been dropped into a conversation that had been going on for a while before I arrived. "Who? And recanted what?"

"One of the students. I re-interviewed her and pressed her a bit. As I expected, she couldn't hold on to her story. The one about seeing you with Kayson."

"Oh." It was all I could muster, my sluggish thoughts beginning to slowly form a question like a photographic image emerging from a chemical bath.

"Yeah. It was a lie. She didn't see you with him at all. In fact, although she didn't actually come out and admit it, she was put up to it. Just wanted to let you know."

Donna. That's who he meant. I didn't know how I knew or rather felt it, but I did.

"Was it Donna?"

"Yes. The other one is sticking to her story, but that doesn't sound right to me, either. It could be that she was the one who got

Donna to go along with her. But Donna's the weaker of the two, so she broke."

The question finally emerged, "Why're you doing this, Arnie? The charges were dropped, so the case is over, isn't it?"

"Your case is over, but somebody still killed the bastard. And lying in a police investigation is pretty serious. I just thought you would want to know about this latest situation."

"Thank you, Arnie. And how is your lovely partner doing with all this?"

I sensed him retreat from me. "Addy. Just take this for what it's worth. Tell your lawyer. Do what you need to do. But don't ask me about my partner. Got it?"

I got it. "Sorry, Arnie." It felt awkward using his first name. "It's good to have you as a friend." Was this lame or what?

"Addy. Somebody wants to hurt you. That brick through your window and the note were not random events. Keep your eyes open."

Somehow, the same warning coming from Arnie sounded more ominous than when Kris had said it. Still, "What do you expect me to do, just sink into a hole somewhere? I've got a life and I'll be damned if some sicko is going to scare me into hiding."

"Sicko? Is that a technical term?"

"Yeah. It comes right before weirdo and wacko on the technical terms list."

I heard him laugh.

"Arnie, what did you get from your search of the SSD offices?"

He didn't answer right away and I squelched my impulse to ask if he was still there at the other end of the line.

"I can't really say anything about that, Addy. We've got a mountain of files to go through and we're just starting. So there's not much to tell yet."

"Anything that would help me, Arnie?" I knew I was pressing, getting dangerously close to the edge of what he was going to tolerate.

"Is there anything that you want to tell me about all of this? I mean, you were over there as well, and this should be a two way street."

I thought about Kris's warning and about Georgia, as well as my clients and the SSD women I'd talked with, and where my allegiances lay. "I ... suggest that you speak to some of the women who are in the program, specifically about their relationships with Kayson."

"Why?"

"Well, let's just say that you might find plenty of motives there to kill him."

"Can you give me more than that? Any particular woman? And what should I be asking about?"

"Actually, I'd recommend that a woman detective interview them. Carefully."

"I see. But Addy, I'm obviously trying to help you out here, because frankly I'm with you. I also think there's a link between Kayson's and Natalie's deaths. It's too weird a coincidence otherwise. But you've got to stop getting yourself involved in the investigation. It's okay that you want to feed me info, but it's not okay that you keep getting mixed up in this. Stay away from the investigation. Do you hear me?"

"Arnie, your warning is out of concern for me. I see that and appreciate it ... but the very fact that I was accused of this in the first place tells me that somebody in your office can't tell the difference between people who kill and those who don't. Besides, I'm not getting in your way. I'm just doing a little consulting."

"Addy. Don't get stubborn on me. You could be charged with obstructing an investigation. This whole thing could backfire on you. Leave it to the professionals."

"Thanks for the help and the advice," I said, having no intention of following it.

CHAPTER 44

Kris and I pulled into the driveway of a small blue-and-white California Craft-style house in a modest neighborhood of mainly rental properties. Its façade boasted faded, peeling light-blue paint. The houses were built as close together as possible, leaving yards the size of handkerchiefs for each. So far, winter had not been kind, with large dirty lumps of snow and ice lining the street and covering the sidewalks. It was a small side street that hadn't seen the plows very often, so people had to carefully pick their way over the mounds. A couple of larger hillocks suggested cars buried beneath them.

Even though Kris had called ahead and Julie Pigeon was expecting us, she scowled as she opened the front door. The tinny hollow sounds of laughter, applause, and voices emanated from a television in the back of the house. Julie led us into a cramped front room, jammed with worn, oversized furniture and bric-a-brac. There was barely room for the three of us to stand, so Kris and I settled into a deep maroon overstuffed couch while Julie perched on the edge of a stained pink-flowered wingback chair across from us, our three sets of knees hovering close to the small, scratched coffee table in the middle.

Up to that point, no one had spoken. When I looked across at the woman sitting so close, I was struck by her frail appearance. She was thin and pale. Her short auburn hair clung to her head in small, wispy curls. The pink oversized sweatshirt with images of butterflies exploding across her small breasts made her appear even more diminutive.

"Julie," Kris said, "we wanted to ask you a few questions about what you told the police."

"I told them everything. There's nothing else to say. If they don't believe me, then it's not my problem."

I couldn't be sure, but I thought her glance at me was filled with hostility. I searched my memory, trying to remember how our paths had crossed. Several semesters ago, she'd been in one of my classes. I had to work hard to even get that far, because Julie was one of those students who hadn't stood out in any way. Why would this sad-looking woman be angry with me? I also remembered our last phone conversation, when she expressed her dismay at the idea that she might have made a mistake. Was this woman such a good actor?

"Donna Blare has now told the police that she didn't see Addy— Professor van den Bos—with Professor Kayson at all."

"So she's wrong. Or maybe somebody scared her off. I told them what I saw. And I'm not changing my story."

"I'm not asking you to tell a story. I'm inviting you to tell the truth, since it's not in your best interest to make things up. Especially if you don't want to get sued for slander."

Sure. Like this woman had anything to sue for.

A frantic knocking at the front door interrupted us. Julie flinched at the first rap and rose quickly to answer it, brushing the coffee table. Two children raced toward the front of the house and Julie sternly told them to go back to where they'd come from. The small boy and girl protested loudly but complied, while the knocking became more insistent. A female voice called out from the other side of the door.

Julie yelled, "Keep your shirt on," as she opened the door and stepped outside, holding the door so as to shield the other person from our view. There was a brief muffled conversation on the front porch and then Julie came back into the house. A sheet was draped over the curtain rod so all I could see was a shadow of a figure hurrying away from the house. Julie offered no explanation and quietly sat back down while eyeing us both.

Kris began again, "Julie, what you told the police is not only slander, but it is also obstructing an investigation. And ..."

"That would be so convenient for you, wouldn't it, but I am not lying. I saw her leaving the school with Professor David Kayson." Defiance prevailed.

She pointed at me as if we were in the courtroom. I had to squelch an urge to duck.

"Julie," I finally said, "how could you have seen me, since I never got into a car with that man?"

"I don't know anything about your relationship with Professor Kayson." She seemed to smirk as she spoke. "But I know what I saw. And you can't talk me out of that. Besides I've heard things, and lots of people know about it."

"Know about what?" I shot back.

"You can't tell me you didn't sleep with him. Everyone knows that he got all the adjuncts."

I could have joined her in the seesaw "no I didn't—yes you did," but it looked like she was completely committed to her own version of the truth. There's usually not much chance of talking someone out of such a strongly held belief, so I just shook my head. "Okay. Looks like you want to believe that, whether it's true or not."

Her glower could have carbonized me.

Kris spoke quietly to her, "Julie. I encourage you to think carefully about this, because if I find evidence that proves you are lying, I will take you to court. You will be prosecuted."

"You can't do anything to me that somebody else hasn't already done. So your threats don't scare me. And," Julie turned to me, "you social workers are all alike. You promise to help people, but you're really just looking for ways to take advantage of people, to push us around. Maybe it's your own egos that you need to build, or maybe you get off on exploiting people, but either way, I won't ever trust a social worker. You people just like to fuck with other people's minds."

"So you've been betrayed by somebody who was supposed to help you," I said. "I'm surprised that you would want to now be one of those people."

"Don't pull that psychoanalytical shit on me. I am going to be a social worker who actually does help people. And people who need it." She wound down into silence.

"I hope that whatever happened to you doesn't lead you to create more pain for yourself," I said, thinking of Kayson.

She scowled in response. Did I detect a softening or was it wishful thinking on my part? I leaned toward her to and tried one more time.

"Listen, Julie, I understand how disappointed you are by the very person who was supposed to help you. And how hard it is then, to not expect that kind of treatment from everybody. Seems like a lot to carry around."

I could see that my words had touched her but she quickly hid her first reaction behind a look of disgust. "Good try. But I know what I saw."

"Well, I get the impression that you want to punish me for a crime somebody else committed against you. Perhaps there was somebody at the school?"

Did I sense a stiffening in her?

"I don't know what you're talking about." She stood up. "If that's all you wanted, then we're finished here."

I struggled to get up out of the soft cushion. "If you decide to tell the truth, let me know." I set a business card on the arm of the Julie's chair.

"Oh, and by the way," Kris said, "Donna's testimony that she didn't see what you say you did would tend to cancel out your statement. A lawyer can make you look pretty bad up there. It's not a fun time."

Julie didn't respond.

She stood by the chair, where she remained as we left. It was only when we were in the car and pulling away from the curb that Kris broke the silence.

"Wow. That woman's got problems, doesn't she?"

"Kayson used grades to blackmail her into having sex."

"She didn't say so."

"She didn't have to."

"Well what did we get?" Kris said after a moment.

"I'm not sure. But I didn't really know what to expect. It was a long shot. What we did get is that she wants to use me to punish Kayson. And perhaps others."

"So how does that tie in to Natalie?"

"I don't know," I said. "I wonder how much she knew about Kayson's death."

"It's a common enough strategy, throw suspicion off yourself by incriminating somebody else," Kris said.

"What was it that the person outside of the door yelled at her?"

"What? What, oh that. I don't know," Kris said. "But I am tired of this winter weather." She removed her gloves and dropped them between the seats. "I can hardly wait to do a round on the links in the warm sunshine."

"What made you think of that?"

"I don't know. All this snow and wet and cold, perhaps?"

"Yeah."

I couldn't shake the sense that I was missing something, right in front of me.

CHAPTER 45

Sometimes lying in bed staring into the darkness was just what I needed to understand a problem I had been worrying about. I wandered around several speculations, trying to put the puzzle together, feeling very much awake. A small, yet distinct, unfamiliar sound drew my focus back to my bedroom. I listened in the dark for the noise to repeat and when I was about ready to attribute it to a stray misfiring neuron, it came again. Tick and scrape. There had definitely been a sound that didn't belong to the small melody of creeks and groans that the old building tended to emit.

It was one thirty in the morning and I realized suddenly that it wasn't too late to make a phone call, especially to the Mounties. I reached for the phone and tried to dial 911. The phone was dead. No amount of shaking brought it back to life. Damn my aversion to cell phones. I set the receiver down quietly.

Tick. Unsure if I could make it to the front door, I grabbed my clothes and sprinted into the bathroom. At least it had a lock. It was the best I could do.

The grainy sounds of a window being cut with a glasscutter, the dull thud of the little circle of glass falling to the carpet, and then the sash being raised emanated from the front room of my apartment. I couldn't help but smile nervously at the thought of Mrs. Kaldione's reaction when she found out that yet another window would have to be replaced. I shook the thought away, but I could feel the giddiness of fear begin to seep in around the edges. I couldn't think about what to do next so I crouched in the tub, holding my clothes close to me. I decided not to try to dress, to minimize the noise, but opted to wait quietly.

My teeth began to chatter, perhaps from a combination of cold and fear, as I searched the quiet beyond my bathroom door for signals about what was happening. I sensed more than heard someone enter the bedroom. For a moment there was no sound and then I heard some unidentifiable activity coming from the direction of the bed. I was surprised to hear what sounded like sobbing, and then a muffled noise of something hard repeatedly hitting something soft, like an odd wrestling match. I tried to pace my breathing despite the urge to take in a deep breath and let it out in a scream.

A stab of pain shot through my bad foot because I was putting pressure on my stitches. Inching the foot into another position relieved it temporarily, but the pain soon started up again. I knew had to get off it, but I wasn't in any place to do that. The noises began to subside and then the person began moving around the room, pulling open drawers and doors. More things fell to the carpeted floor. Then there was silence, as if the intruder was considering the next move.

I jerked as someone yanked the bathroom doorknob. Please, let him think it was a door to the attic or to outside.

The few moments of silence might have indicated that the intruder was again contemplating the next step. Suddenly something seemed to explode on the other side of the door as the prowler banged on it and wildly rattling the doorknob. I grabbed the edge of the bathtub as if to lock myself into position for what was to come, but the racket stopped just as abruptly. My thudding heart filled my ears and I strained to pick up any sign that the invader was still around. Something slick and warm oozed under my foot. It felt as if someone had ripped the stitches out with pliers. I waited and listened. My left leg began to cramp and ache from the coldness of the tub and from being folded up under me, but the silence stretched out.

And when I couldn't stand it anymore, I hoped it was safe to venture out. Getting out of a tub without making noise is more difficult than one might imagine. Feet squeaked and slipped along the enamel, knees knocked against the side as I struggled out of my crouch. Each sound was like a shot cutting through the quiet fabric of night. Thankfully there was no response from the other side of the door. When I finally got out, I moved slowly toward it on my wobbly legs.

Mrs. Kaldione's voice called out to me from a distance, "Addy. Addy, what's going on?" Again someone rattled the doorknob and my landlady's voice called out worriedly from the other side.

I swung the door open and I let out my breath. "Mrs. Kaldione. What a pleasant surprise."

"I heard a crash. I thought you had fallen." She was breathing heavily. "What happened?"

I looked beyond the disheveled woman in her bathrobe for any sign of another person. We seemed to be alone. "Somebody paid me a friendly visit," I said, and then led her to my bedroom and I flipped on the light.

The aftermath of a frenzied attack on my bed was spread around the room. My shredded sheets, blanket, and pillows had been sliced into ribbons and flung everywhere. The nightstand that normally stood bedside my bed lay face down, the lamp shattered, the alarm clock in pieces. The whole thing had "rage" written all over it.

"My god, Addy," Mrs. Kaldione said, surveying the mess. "Somebody is trying to hurt you. We gotta call the police."

So, once again I found myself awake, wrapped in a blanket, being interviewed by the same third-shift police officer while his partner searched my apartment. Mrs. Kaldione hovered in the background after giving her statement. When the police had left and while Mrs. K. rewrapped my foot, I called Kris and left a message at her work. I wasn't sure why, but I had to take some action to fend off my feelings of helplessness. And rage.

Sometime during the night, when I was once again tucked into Mrs. Kaldione's guest bed, a moment from my childhood came flooding back.

I had crouched, shivering in my underwear, on the stairs, with my legs pulled up to my chest, watching and listening as they spewed back and forth and finally my father laid a roundhouse punch that sent my mother flying. He then lunged at me, drunkenly bellowing that I was a weight around his neck. I dodged his outreached arm and fled up the stairs into the bathroom, snapping the lock just as he got there. I cowered in the bathtub, calling for my mother, while he railed on the other side of the door. I thought I could hear my mother's voice from below, weakly calling to my father to stop. Perhaps I only hoped that she was there, at least trying. Whether she was or not made no difference to him. I shook the image of the scene away before he broke through and got to me. But not before I saw his arm punching through the panel and grabbing for the knob.

I was nine years old.

"Hey, Addy. How are you doing?"

"I'm fine."

"Like hell," Kris said.

"What?"

"You called me about your midnight visitor."

I was back in my apartment, getting dressed for work and trying to ignore the chaos around me. "Actually it was about one thirty."

There was a short pause. "You're a piece of work, Addy. Why can't you be straight with me, without putting me through this dance first?"

Another smart retort was poised on my lips, but I hauled it back in. "Sorry. I'm not much on talking about my own stuff. You know that." I thought about the memory that had flooded back last night. "It's not as well-charted a territory as it might be. But I'm okay."

"So why did you call me in the wee hours?"

"Look, Kris. You know I appreciate your support. I'm not sure why I called you; I felt like I needed somebody to know. But it was probably a freak thing."

"Addy, this is the second—or maybe third—time somebody has tried to hurt you and this is one time they actually got into your place. This happens after two other people associated with the school have been murdered. You have to take this seriously."

"What makes you think I'm not?"

"Okay. Okay. What can I do?"

I was thankful that she backed down.

"Actually you could help with something else. I told you about Mr. Garza, Natalie's attorney, didn't I?"

"No."

"Well he wants to meet with me and it would help me out if you came along."

We talked about what he might have to say and we worked out the details so I could get back to Enrico Garza.

CHAPTER 46

Virginia Early sat quietly, waiting. We had been talking about her struggle around going home to visit her family.

"So," I said, "you sound terrified about facing your parents."

"Christmas is the most important holiday in my family," she said. "My mom goes all out to make it one of those Bing Crosby Christmases every year. On Christmas Eve we watch *It's a Wonderful Life*, and on Christmas day is a big dinner with all the relatives. Can you believe that? People come from all over. We must have about forty people or more. My family lives in an old farmhouse and we pile everybody in. Only a few people ever miss it. This is the first time I wasn't there. That was a big deal. But she still wants me to come home for a few days. I'm going to have to just try to get through it. I will have to find something to keep me busy." She sat sighing, avoiding looking at me. "It'll be okay."

"It doesn't seem that it will be, but I get the impression that you don't want to consider the other possibility."

"You mean tell her? No, I can't. It would kill her." Suddenly she folded over and buried her face in her hands. "I can't and I don't, I mean, can we talk about something else?"

I waited, but nothing more was forthcoming. Just as I was about to say something, she spoke in a small tremulous voice from behind her hands.

"I think that I don't need to come here anymore."

"Oh?" This wasn't surprising. She wanted to see if I would take her up on her offer of getting out of my hair. "What brings that up now?"

"I don't know. I don't feel much better and I don't know what good any of this does. I shouldn't waste your time, anyway."

"You're concerned about taking up my time." It was a statement.

She began to cry again. "I just want to disappear."

"I get the impression that there's something else really troubling you."

She spoke haltingly through her hands, "I can't talk about it. Not here."

"Okay. What do you mean, not here? Is there something about this space?" I leaned forward. "Or are you afraid of hurting me as well?"

She lifted her head and sat back in the chair. "No. I mean yes. I don't know." Pause. "I can't tell you. It's too hard to say. You'll hate me. I hate myself."

I watched her struggle and knew that she wasn't going to be able to get it out. Not yet, at any rate. How much worse could it be than being raped by Kayson? Virginia sat paralyzed, staring away from me. It suddenly struck me that perhaps she was rendered speechless because whatever it was had some direct connection to me.

People in therapy will commonly see the therapist in light of their own experiences, and expect the therapist to behave like someone from their histories. This is routine, and in fact paying attention to how a client views me often gives me clues as to what their history has been. It's central to the work.

But … Virginia seemed to brace herself against some unseen threat. Just as she couldn't tell her mother about what had happened to her in the school, she was unable to reveal something important to me: Maybe I was being confused with her mother, but she had a genuine secret that she was afraid to reveal because it would kill her mother and destroy their relationship. Was she scared that telling her secret would hurt me in some way? Or herself?

"Perhaps you expect that I will want to push you away if you tell me," I said.

"You wouldn't understand. And, no, no I can't."

"What wouldn't I understand?" I was pressing in a way that I didn't usually do, especially when I knew this kind of fear. What she knew must be about Kayson's death or perhaps Natalie's.

She shook her head and turned to look out the window. "It's no good. I just can't."

I suppressed a sigh. It wouldn't help for me to show her my frustration. I had truly stepped out of my role as her therapist and made an effort to get back there. We soon ended and I watched through the window as she walked toward her car.

I was aware of a developing kernel of worry nudging me from somewhere distant as the rest of the day unfolded. What was she hiding? And would I press her out of my own need to know?

When I arrived at my small office at the Social Services Department, I found that Georgia had already caught Janice and ushered her in. Although I'd stacked some of the cartons to allow me some working room, it was still a tight fit. I got my share of the scowl that Georgia had been enjoying as I squeezed in.

"Let's talk, Janice," I said, after greeting them both.

Her eyes seemed to flutter with nervousness. "About what?"

"You know, it's time to step up to the plate, Janice. There's no running from this anymore because after you explain your part of this little party to us, you'll be invited to do the same with the police."

"I don't know what you're talking about."

Georgia seemed on the verge of standing, but held herself to her seat. "Janice. We know a lot of what's been going on here and we know that you've been involved. Soon the police will know it too because they've got the records."

"And," I added, "They're interviewing all of the clients. Maybe some of them won't talk, but I know some of them will."

"I don't have to talk to you." I could see that she was on the edge of tears. "I haven't done anything wrong."

I took a different tack. "Janice, I need to know what you can tell me about Kayson. I expect that you probably didn't have much choice but to do what he told you. If you can help us understand how he worked, then perhaps we—Georgia and I—" I glanced at Georgia to encourage her to go along with me. "—can put in a good word for you in the police investigation."

She looked tearfully from one to the other of us. "Professor Kayson was a good man. He would never do anything to hurt me."

"I'm sure he was good to you, but he was not so nice to others, especially the clients. And you must know that."

"I don't know what you're talking about. He was always doing things for us."

"Like taking you guys out to lunch or sticking up for you with the administration?" Taking his workers under his wing just as he had his brothers.

Janice glared at me. "Yeah. So he was a good guy. Is that a crime?"

"No. But you suspected something else didn't you? You knew he wasn't so nice to others. And you didn't do anything about it."

"I don't know what you are talking about."

I worked to keep my irritation in check. "So what did you have to do in exchange for his being so nice to you?"

Janice seemed to consider her options and then said, "You don't know how it was. He would ask me to do things and how was I supposed to say no? He was the boss."

Georgia asked, "So what did he make you do?"

"I didn't want to do it …"

"Yes, I imagine that it was a tough place for you." I almost choked on the words.

"It was. I didn't know what to do. But I had to."

"So you …?"

"It was Kayson's idea to make up the names."

"Tell us about that." I wasn't sure what she was referring to, but think I managed to hide the fact.

"He thought that if we made up a bunch of names … you know, created cases … we could collect the money for them and not have to spend it on the cases. Kayson made up the names and we were supposed to keep records about them as if we were working with them."

"How many cases are we talking about here?" Georgia asked.

"Each of us was supposed to have about twenty-four families and about three-quarters of them were fake cases. And we would submit reports for all of them and he would include them in his stats."

Georgia practically snarled her next question, "So how many of the supervisors were in on this little scam?"

It was Janice's turn to shake her head. "I'm not giving you any names." Her voice was shaky but she seemed determined.

"Oh now you're going to do the honorable thing," Georgia said. "Where was your integrity when you were ripping off the system?"

"I finally had enough time to do some good work with the clients I did have," she said. "I couldn't have with a full caseload. The paperwork alone is enough to make it impossible to do your work right. We weren't hurting anybody."

"Not hurting anybody? What about the people who weren't allowed into the program because of your greed?" Georgia's anger had finally erupted. "Or what about what happens to all of the clients once this gets out? Do you think we'll be able to get any funding for this kind of program again? Ever? And what about the money you stole? What the hell were you thinking?"

Janice cringed away from Georgia and began looking around as if searching for an escape route. "I don't care what you say. I didn't hurt anybody. I did good work with my clients. Just ask them."

"Yeah, well, how much did you make from your little fraud?" Georgia asked.

"I don't know and I'm not saying anything else. It wasn't my fault. Kayson was the boss. It was his idea and I didn't have any choice." Just following orders.

"If that's the case, Janice," I asked, "why didn't you come forward and report it after he was dead?"

She slumped in her chair, averting her eyes.

Georgia finally stood up, her anger fueling her need to move around the small space, which seemed to shrink as her rage grew. She ended up leaning over the seated woman.

"Another thing. What were you thinking when you kept quiet about his little sex scheme? I mean, where were your ethics when you stood by and let him use the clients in that way?"

Janice tried to appear shocked. "I don't know what you're talking about. What sex scheme? I ... I didn't have anything to do with anything like that."

"Look, you can keep up the lying as long as you want, but in the end, the truth will come out. And there isn't any way you couldn't have known." Georgia was leaning into her by now, working to control herself. I grew worried that she would actually hit Janice.

"Georgia, it's time to call the authorities in on this, don't you think?" I said, before things could spiral further out of control.

Janice whirled around to look at me. "With what?" she barked. "You don't have shit on me. And I'm not telling them anything."

I wasn't sure exactly what we could offer the police as evidence, other than what she'd just told us and our suspicions of her collusion with the sick system that Kayson had orchestrated. I wondered if Arnie had followed my suggestion to interview the clients and if any of them had talked.

Georgia looked as if she was searching for something to throw at the seated woman. Janice sat defiantly, all outward signs of fear or remorse swept away by her anger.

"Janice, you can pack up your stuff and go," Georgia spoke deliberately. "Leave your badge and keys with the secretary."

"But I've got a lot of stuff to do. I have some appointments today."

"Not any more. I will accompany you to your office. You will hand over all of your keys and you will pack up your personal stuff only. I want you out of here as soon as possible. We'll take it from here."

She opened the door and waited for Janice to lead the way. Janice glanced at me as if seeking some support but I wasn't in any mood to come to her aid. She stood and, making as wide a berth as possible around Georgia, walked out with Georgia trailing behind her. Despite her defiance, I assumed she knew that it wouldn't do her any good to fight this. She must have known that it was over.

About twenty minutes after our confrontation, I saw Janice leave the unit carrying a full cardboard box, accompanied by a couple of security guards. Georgia nodded to me as she stood, arms crossed, silently watching the small procession file toward the exit.

Georgia stopped by my office a few minutes later and invited me to sit in on her meeting with Ken. I declined, although it would have been interesting. I had to run back to my private practice office and see two clients.

My cheap plastic answering machine vibrated as Georgia's voice bellowed over the speaker. "So that son-of-a-bitch Ken denies that he had anything to do with the scheme. He sits there and coolly lies to me while I hand the stats over to him. I ask him to tell me where half his clients are since they haven't been seen by any of the clients actually using the program or anyone else for that matter. I mean, I tracked down fifteen clients that are on his roster and don't exist, and that bastard sits there and denies everything. Then he gets up and waltzes out as if I'd just given him a lump of sugar and a raise. I can't believe it. I've never seen anything like it." I heard her take a breath and I worried that my machine would cut her off, but she started up again, a little calmer, "So anyway, I talked to the rest of the supervisors. Now that the shit has hit the fan, I was able to get to most of them. It looks like there were only four of 'em who were actually involved, although everybody knew something about it. God, Addy, how can people be like that? Ripping off poor people."

"Not to mention taxpayers," I muttered. Where were the ethics of all those who knew about this?

Georgia's message continued, "Crap. Today is the closest I ever came to drinking in my eleven years of sobriety, so after this, I definitely need a meeting." Another pause and then she went on. "Anyway, I have talked it over with my boss and she consulted with hers. We've got the Attorney General's office involved and they're sending somebody over. You don't have to be here if you don't want to, Addy. I'll understand if you stay away. But give me a call anyway. There'll be a lot of cleaning up to do and I'll need your ..."

My machine beeped, indicating that she'd run out of space on the tape. I sat listening to the silence for long time.

CHAPTER 47

M r. Enrico Garza's offices overlooked the heart of the Hispanic community. For over a hundred years, countless numbers of people from Central and South America had made their way north to the orchards and fields surrounding Whitefield to labor seasonally to bring food to the tables of America. Gradually, enough were able to settle permanently to give the area an international flavor. The little shops and cafes in the Latin district exuding exotic smells helped make Whitefield less blandly monochromatic.

Kris and I sat facing Garza behind a cluttered desk. We waited while he removed a folder from the desk drawer, opened it, and arranged its contents in front of him. He had one of those mellifluous voices that reminded me of a rich full-bodied red wine.

"I'm so glad we could finally meet, Ms. van den Bos. As you know, Natalie Cruz named you in her will, and she requested that you and I meet in order to conclude our business."

"Mr. Garza, I don't know what to say. Natalie was very important to me, but I'm no relation to her and she never mentioned a will to me."

"Well, she was very clear about what she wanted. You see, Natalie had no living relatives. She had one uncle in this country and he died many years ago. As far as I know, she also had no relatives in Mexico, where she originated."

Originated? Such a formal word for something so much more.

"It's hard to believe." I watched his face, looking for something more. "How do you know Dr. Cruz?"

"Let's just say that we have a very long acquaintanceship." He spoke with the formality of an old-worlder.

I decided to let it drop for the moment. Instead, I nodded and waited, wondering what Kris was thinking.

He looked down at the folder and seemed to be reading. "This is a fairly straightforward will. She left a few specific amounts of money to some charities and groups. But the section that is pertinent here reads, and I quote, 'I leave my beloved house, all its contents and land,' and there's a description of the property, 'to Adrienne van den Bos,' as well as a trust with a fixed amount to be used for its upkeep." He looked up expectantly.

At first I wasn't sure I had heard him right. I knew I had when I turned to see Kris's expression of astonishment.

"There are no restrictions on your use of the property," Garza said, "but she did say she hoped you would keep it intact. She hoped also that you would want to live there and that you at least would consider using it for purposes consistent with her wishes."

"Did she add specifics?" Kris asked.

Garza directed himself to me, "Actually not in the will. But Natalie and I often talked about such things and I believe I understood what she meant. I assumed you would as well."

"You seem to know a lot about her," Kris continued, and I was happy that she did. I was still trying to assimilate what I had just heard. "Natalie, that is. You and she go back a long way?"

"Actually, yes. I owe most of what I have to her."

I finally found my voice, "How is that, may I ask?"

He didn't answer.

Oh, but of course. He didn't have to. I should have seen it.

I decided to take the leap. "Look, Mr. Garza, I—I mean we, Kris and I—are trying to find out who killed Natalie and it would help us if there's anything you can tell us."

"I thought it was a burglary."

"So do the police," Kris said. "We believe that this case is related to the murder of Professor David Kayson. I assume you heard about that one?"

He nodded.

"So, Mr. Garza," I said, "you know that Natalie was very important to me, as she was to you. Is there something you can tell us, to help us find her killer?"

He seemed to decide something. "I don't know how I might help you. How is it that you think the two deaths are linked?"

That stopped me. "I don't have anything in particular, but it is not a coincidence that two professors in the same school got murdered within days of each other. It is conceivable that she was going to tell me something about Kayson's murder. And somebody didn't want her to. I think that Natalie was killed by a student from the school."

"How could you know that?"

I told him about the quote Natalie had up in her home and office and about finding her with the plant in her hand.

"That must have been awful to come upon."

I felt tears threaten at his sympathetic words, so I was glad for a chance to brush his comments away. "I know this is a long shot, but are you related to a family named Garcia that worked in the migrant camps, north of the city, in the sixties?"

It was Garza's turn to be taken aback. He sat for what felt like a long time and then finally spoke softly, "How could you have known that?"

Kris turned to gape at me.

"It was a hunch. We have an old file on your family. It would have been easy to change your name."

Garza looked back and forth at the two of us. "I don't need to know how you got that file." He paused as if considering his next move. I got the impression that he, too, was in need of confession as part of his grief. "I met Natalie when she was a new social worker and I was ten years old. She was working in the migrant camp where my family would come to pick. I suppose she must have kept records. I can't believe you found them after all these years."

How had I missed this connection to Natalie? I had read the material quickly and never once glanced at the signature. Were those really her records?

"So she took a special interest in you," I said. "Why do you think she did that?"

"As she did with you."

Touché. "Yes. I suppose."

"Natalie grew up in the camps. Her family was killed in Mexico, except an uncle who brought her here when she was young, to live the life. So she knew it first hand, and she must have seen something in me. I don't know what it was, because I was a tough kid by the time she found me. But if she hadn't hung in there with me, I'm sure I would be dead. And I made her earn her money."

"Mr. Garza, why would your family's file end up with Professor David Kayson?"

"So that's it." He shook his head.

"That's what?"

"I knew she had trouble with one of those guys on the faculty at the school. She never told me his name, but I think that he … tried something with her. It was a long time ago. You know Natalie. She didn't beat around the bush when she told him she wasn't interested, and ever since, he was out to get her. She didn't talk about it very much, but I think it was on her mind."

"You think he was making her pay for saying no?"

"I got the impression that he wouldn't let it go."

"He had something on her?"

He shrugged. "Perhaps. I always wondered."

Kris asked, "Any ideas about what it might be?"

"I don't think we need to go there," I said before Garza could speak. I avoided Kris's gaze and hurried on, "So, how do we proceed with the will?"

I could see Garza make a psychological shift as he pushed a sheaf of papers toward me. "All we need is your signature on these forms, and perhaps Ms. Conner would be the witness."

Garza explained how the trust fund worked and then handed me an official-looking packet of documents and, finally, a ring of keys. Natalie's keys. But they were mine now.

Once out in the hallway, Kris said, "What the hell was that?"

"I'll tell you when we get out of here."

When we were safely away from the building, I turned to look at her. "I think Kayson found the Garcia records when he went looking for his own family's files."

"Yeah. So?"

"I think that he discovered that Natalie had worked with the Garcia family and that she had taken an interest in Enrico."

"So what's the big deal? That's not much."

"Yeah. But what if he discovered something about him or her that she wanted kept quiet? I didn't read the files that carefully. What if she wanted to protect Garcia from something Kayson was threatening to leak?"

"Are you saying that Natalie killed Kayson, or that he was blackmailing her?"

"I don't know what it means. Why did Kayson have that particular file? There has to be something more to it."

"Didn't you see it in the files when you read them?"

"Sometimes one has to know what to look for," I answered as we got into her car.

CHAPTER 48

Once again we were in Kris's den. We sat quietly reading case files for some time, occasionally reaching for the glasses of red wine she had poured. When I finished the Miller file, I looked up to find her staring out the window holding the Garcia files in her lap. "So?" I said to bring her back.

Kris turned. "Yeah, well. There are several different signatures, including Natalie's. But you were right; she was the main worker for the Garcia case. And you were also right about the other thing. Roberto (a.k.a. Enrico's father) sexually abused him. There may have been others as well. Although, his father wasn't in prison for that— his dad was put away for assaulting a prominent local landowner. I guess back then, it didn't matter much when a Mexican farm worker raped his own kid. How the hell did you know?"

"I had a hunch. But, look, according to this report, Kayson, or John as he was known back then, had been his little brothers' protector. But in the end, killing his mother had resulted in the family being torn apart. So he would of course think that it was his fault he hadn't been able to protect his brothers. John was sent to Cedar Hills. That's a state-run residential placement for tough kids. And his brothers were put into the foster-care system. The oldest, Mark, was what they call a successful placement, in that the family that took him in eventually adopted him. The youngest, Luke, had some kind of accident and died. It looks like he fell down some stairs.

So do you see? John would have decided that his brothers, his family, was torn apart because of what he had done. That one died could have sent him over the edge. He would have blamed himself for not protecting them."

"Okay. I get that. But how did this tie in with Natalie and Enrico Garcia or Garza or whatever his name is?"

"Well, I think that somehow, Kayson found out that Natalie and Enrico knew each other. What does your file say about what happened to Garcia?"

Kris looked back at the Garcia file and picked up a couple of pages. "Enrico got his own file when he was eight. Seems so young. He got into some trouble and ended up at"—she pawed through the file—"yes, here it is, at Cedar Hills." She looked up with a smile on her face. "Of course. They met there. But Kayson had to be much older than Enrico."

"So how old was Enrico when he went in?"

More searching through the papers. "It looks like they tried to work with him, but then he was sent to Cedar Hills in 1968, when he was almost ten."

"That's pretty young. But again, he was a poor Mexican kid and they probably didn't have many options for him, and racism allows you to overlook so much."

"So when did Kayson leave Cedar Hills?"

It was my turn to look at the file on my lap. There were actually several case files for Kayson, and one was from Cedar Hills. "It looks like he was discharged on his twentieth birthday, in 1970. At least, that was when his sentence was up."

"So John Miller met Roberto Garcia in Cedar Hills," Kris said. "Two abused boys, one quite a bit older than the other. One can only speculate on what went on between them."

"And when Kayson discovered the file, maybe when he was in search of his own files, he somehow put two and two together. He saw Natalie's signature and, out of his need to recreate his own failure to protect his brothers, he put her into a position of having to protect her surrogate son. I would guess that he threatened to expose Enrico's slash Roberto's past. Maybe that he had been abused."

"No," Kris said evenly. "That's not it."

"No?"

"He threatened to out Garcia. Enrico Garcia is gay. Or maybe he's afraid he is, because of what Kayson and he did together."

"And what his father did to him. But would that be enough? I mean, you're out of the closet and you don't have any ..."

"Whitefield isn't San Francisco, Addy. I do mostly corporate and estate law, working with better-off, and usually more liberal, clients. Judges are elected, and there aren't that many of them in the county. It only takes one or two with a bit of bias, and you start losing clients. Besides, it can be harder on gay men, and even more so with Latino men."

"So she worried about him even if it wasn't the worst thing in the world."

"No. But then, Kayson wasn't forcing her to do anything really egregious, was he?"

It made sense. "So that's why Natalie sometimes sided with Kayson on important votes at the school even though it didn't make any sense to me." I remembered the argument we had over the proposal to include an antiracism project in the internship. "It was like withholding food from one kid while the other two ate. He dangled that file over her head."

"Why didn't Garza or Garcia recognize Kayson?" Kris asked. "He must have seen Kayson's picture in the paper."

"People change after so many years. And remember, Garza only knew Kayson as John Miller. Even if Natalie told him who it was at the school, Garcia wouldn't have recognized the name."

"Ironic. Both of them changed their names to escape their pasts. They had so many things in common and yet their paths were so different."

I nodded, thinking about what Kayson had been turned into by his parents. And then I thought about my own need to take on the sorrows of others and how that was a reflection of what I witnessed in my family. I could feel myself cringing from the thought and what it implied.

"Kris," I said, "can you bring up the list of students Kayson had at SSD?"

"Sure, but why?"

"I've got a hunch about how we find out who killed Kayson. And maybe Natalie too." I was relieved to have something else to do besides go ever deeper into what David Kayson and I shared.

While Kris worked on the computer, I pulled out the lists I had gotten from Kayson's secretary, Marissa.

"Okay. Now what?"

When we compared the lists, we could see that everyone who worked for or was placed at SSD as students had also been in at least one of Kayson's classes.

"Look at this," I pointed at Janice's name. "She's been in four classes with him and so has Ken."

"Is that a big deal?"

"No, but it would interesting to see what kinds of grades they got from him."

"Ask, and ye shall receive." Her fingers raced over the keyboard.

"What the hell are you doing? No, don't tell me. I don't want to know about this."

"Don't worry, we'll be in and out. It's Saturday night. Nobody's home." I watched as she drew closer to her target site and with a few strokes, we were looking at the Rankin School of Social Work registrars' files. I shook my head, but kept looking. I couldn't turn away.

"They have an ancient protection system," Kris said as she slid around the electrons. "So who should we look up first?"

"Start with Janice Wolf."

Janice Wolf had a spectacularly bleak academic record. Her grade point average was barely a B, which is the minimum for graduation.

"Look at the incompletes she's had," Kris said. "I don't see where they were made up."

"Usually an incomplete is changed when the professor submits a change of grade after the student has finished the work. And you have to do that during the semester following the class." I peered at the screen. "And what's worse is that Janice also did both her placements at the SSD. That's a big no-no. Students are required to have two different placement experiences, for obvious reasons. It looks like Kayson took care of Janice in other ways as well."

"And did you notice that she also had one class with Natalie? She got a C."

"Oops. That's not good. Only the worst of the worst students get below a B."

"Who else?"

We discovered that Kenneth Braden, the other SSD supervisor, had a similarly lackluster record, as well as only having one placement site. What was also startling was how well both Kenneth and Janice did in Kayson's classes.

"How is it that you can get As in three classes with the same professor, and Bs and B minuses—and look, one C—in all the other classes?" Kris asked as she scrolled. "Here's a class that Ken had to repeat because he got a D in it the first time around."

Then I saw Amy Arnold's name. "Look her up."

Amy had taken only one class with Kayson and had done very badly. The rest of her grades were not stellar, but at least she was passing.

"How did Virginia Early do?"

"Virginia got an A in Kayson's class. She seems to be an average student, according to her record."

"That fits."

"It does?"

I suddenly remembered that I had no business talking about Virginia to Kris. "Yeah, look up Jerry Lake." It was the first name that came to mind, to distract Kris from my huge faux pas. I was really not firing on all cylinders.

"Here he is. Jerry also got an A from Kayson, while doing only so-so in his other classes."

"What? Jerry?" I sat back to digest this new piece of information. I vaguely remembered Jerry telling me about his educational experience being completed in an alcoholic blur. My sigh made Kris turn to look at me with consternation.

"What is it?"

"It's too bad you can't unring a bell. Me and my big mouth."

I watched the information take hold and the implications dawn on her. "Oh. Jesus, Addy." She stood up from the desk. "That guy was outrageous. Why didn't anybody stop him?"

"Somebody did."

She swung around. "Dammit, Addy. I didn't mean that. Why didn't the school do something? There are ways to get rid of corrupt professors. What a bunch of cowards."

"I imagine those who could had their own skeletons. Besides, he was a big name. He published. He got grants."

"When the hell did he have the time? Wasn't all that screwing around a full-time job?"

"Yeah, well, some people really liked him." I thought about Marissa, and Roz. I also thought about how Natalie would often ally with him on faculty votes and not always, I suspect, because of the Garcia file. And I was reminded of those little boys, left unprotected and used by the one person who was supposed to love them. "So it's all a cesspool. Did we think it was any different? I still have to find out who murdered Natalie."

Kris stood, breathing deeply. "Okay. What's next?"

I picked up the lists I'd gotten from Marissa and scanned them for a name. It wasn't there. "Look up Julie Pigeon."

Julie had never taken a class with Kayson.

"So what was her beef with him?" Kris asked the screen.

"What was it that Julie's visitor called her?" I shook my head slowly as if to loosen the answer from where it was hidden in my memory.

The thought of my dissertation popped into my head. That stopped me. Why was I remembering Burdy at that moment? And then it hit me.

"Julie Pigeon. Pigeon—bird. It's Julie's nickname, of course. And that's why you started thinking about golf the other day. What does every golfer want at every hole? A birdy."

"Julie Pigeon's nickname is Birdy." Kris said.

"Leave it to the unconscious. The old punster."

"So what does that tell us?"

"One of the clients I interviewed at SSD told me about Birdy a.k.a. Julie. She was a client at the program before she went to school. And while she was there, she got the opportunity of sampling Kayson's favors too. That was her reason for hating him."

"But kill him?"

"He's the social worker who betrayed her."

"Big time."

"You know the saying, that every time you go to bed with somebody, you're sleeping with all the other people that person has been with?"

"Uh-huh."

"Well, how about—when parents abuse their children they are violating all the people their children are going to mistreat in the future."

"What about holding people responsible for their own actions? Kayson wasn't a child when he was blackmailing students and clients for sex."

"To grow into a person who will act responsibly according to our social norms is a complicated process. We need our parents or somebody to socialize us."

"Yes, but come on. Not everybody who gets abused becomes an abuser."

"Some kids have a higher innate threshold. Some are able to find other adults who can help them. And there are kids who grow into people who take it out only on themselves—you know, cutters and the like. But just because kids succumb to the mistreatment, should they be discarded? I think the criminal justice system only heaps more abuse on those who couldn't protect themselves the first time around."

"Maybe. But what do we do then? Do we not punish somebody like Kayson who raped and humiliated people?"

I thought about those little boys in a psychological trap far worse than any locked basement. A wave of sadness caught me off guard and I got a glimpse of an internal image. A menacing figure looming. I shoved it aside.

"Maybe Kayson was too damaged," I said. "But for others, maybe the injuries could be treated instead of exacerbating them by locking them together so they only have each other."

"It's an imperfect world. Maybe we should let it go, Addy. We could go around with it forever. Where to now?"

I gathered all the papers and files together. "I know what I have to do."

"Can I help?"

"No."

She looked at me with surprise. "I hope it's not illegal."

"Yes, I know how much you worry about that. Will you be signing off the school's computer now?"

"Touché. Just be careful."

"Always."

CHAPTER 49

During my drive over, I made the mental transition from the sordid pasts locked in those dusty old files to a surprising present. Before getting out of my car, I took a deep breath and closed my eyes to ground myself. Then, clutching the unfamiliar key ring in my hand, I stepped out onto the virgin snow that lay blanketing Natalie's home. It was hard to believe that I was the new owner of an old rambling farmhouse, its outbuildings, and the land on which they sat.

As I approached the front door, I felt a fleeting impulse to search for the key in its hiding place in the rotting windowsill. I felt silly when I realized that it wasn't necessary, and even glanced around to see if anyone had caught my lapse. I swept the landscape with my eyes, taking it all in as a starving man might with a food-laden table.

Having only ever been a renter, I now had to find a way to make this landowner business my own instead of feeling like I was walking around in somebody else's clothing. So stepping over that threshold seemed like stepping into another life. Could I make it mine or would I just be pretending to be Natalie?

My footsteps tapped hollowly on the stone entryway. I moved hesitantly, so as not to disturb anything in case none of this turned out to be true, in case there had been some colossal mistake and I would wake up from the dream. I thought idly, as I wandered around, of what I knew about Natalie's background. She had pointedly avoided any in depth discussion of her past. What had been obvious was that she carried a deep sadness I had only been allowed to glimpse occasionally.

Instead, it was my sorrow that I encountered in room after room of her silent house; how could I ever think of this place as belonging to anyone but Natalie? I walked through the first floor, purposely avoiding the kitchen. I climbed the stairs and peeked into several rooms, all of which seemed at the same time familiar—throughout the years, I had stayed in all of her guestrooms—and strange. I entered her bedroom cautiously and surveyed it, feeling a bit as if I was breaking a rule. The bed was neatly made, covered in a multicolored tapestry and several corduroy throw pillows. I paused when I realized that the small uneven square of fabric lying on the bed was her nightgown, folded carefully and waiting for the next time it would be needed.

Natalie's home office was on the second floor next to her bedroom. It was lined with floor-to-ceiling built-in bookcases, all full to overflowing with texts and files. Her small, plain, blonde wooden desk faced a large window overlooking the area where she planted her garden every spring. I sat down at it and gazed out the window, seeing the places where I imagined Natalie bent over the small green things she coaxed from the ground. The wooded area in the back rose darkly against the foreground of the land now softened with snow. Small lumps of white indicated where the rows of vegetables and flowers had grown. Here and there, long dead plant stems poked above the pale blanket.

The desktop was a jumble of papers, journals, and books. Her computer sat on a table next to it, hidden by a plastic cover. The layer of dust on it gave testament to Natalie's devotion to pen and paper. Picking up papers laid haphazardly, I saw that they were full of notes for the books that she'd been working on. I knew that one was to focus on working clinically with Spanish-speaking people and the other had been about the immigrant experience. I couldn't remember her ever talking about her plans for the third. Now, we would never have the benefit of her wisdom. I wondered if there was some way that I might pull some of her material together for publication.

As I sifted through more papers, I came across a sheet with what looked like jottings, but at all different angles, as if it had been the paper that was handy when listening to phone messages or as reminders to herself. One notation listed three items that would normally be on a shopping list—olive oil, corn flour, and avocados. Another, perpendicular to this list, said simply, "call Marty, re: article." I picked up the paper and held it so that I could twist and turn it to read some of the other musings. There were several phone numbers with names, a set of directions to somewhere, and then I came across my name.

She had scrawled a note starting with "c Addy abt stud.con." I looked further on the paper for more information, but there was nothing. I couldn't quite decipher her code, but it was about something involving a student that would be of interest to me. Was this related to her mysterious phone call just before her death? There was no date.

I searched further into the piles, but found only more notes related to the two books, as well as what appeared to be outlines for presentations. But that scribble about the stud.con. had piqued my interest. I started in on the top drawer, rifling through the contents, looking for something that might give me a clue. More stacks of papers and files filled the first one. Nothing jumped out at me. The second drawer held office supplies, paper clips, pens, Wite-Out®, and such. When I tried to push it back into its place, it got hung up on something. No matter how I shoved and jiggled, it wouldn't go.

It was just as cantankerous when I tried to withdraw it completely from the desk. In my frustration, I pulled up sharply and jammed my knuckles against the desk. I let out a yelp, swore, and jerked at the drawer. With that, it came free and I had to step back to catch myself from falling on my seat.

The drawer's contents flew out all over the floor, and the drawer itself landed on my toe, corner down. Pain shot up my leg and I had to sit on the floor, hugging my foot, waiting for it to pass. With both feet throbbing, I knelt to dig around in the space left by the drawer. Something seemed to have fallen out of the top drawer, and had become wedged in the side. It took some doing, but finally, I was able to free the object and pull a small leather-bound book from its hiding place.

The notebook's front was covered with a finely tooled scene of a hillside farm. Tiny people toiled, bent over, in the field. It was the kind of cover that fit over a blank insert of empty pages waiting to receive the musings of its owner. The first several pages were filled with Natalie's bold sliding scrawl and the rest of the book was blank. I could see right away these were random observations on the academic world, in fictional form. Was this the beginning of another book on the life of a professor? A quirky way of keeping a journal? A way of understanding people by getting into their heads?

Professor June Wilson stood dazedly among the throngs of students as they wove toward their classes or the building exits and their lives beyond. She felt lost, unable to remember where she'd been headed before she found herself stopped dead. The professor had just come from a covert committee meeting where a self-appointed group of faculty had discussed a vote of no confidence in the Dean. She felt secretly delighted at being included in on the meeting, since most of those there had not shown the slightest interest in her for the past several years. Earl Boilerplate had seemed especially friendly. Suddenly she felt important again, as it had been years before, before things had begun to grow indistinct. She brushed aside the fact that it wasn't clear to her what the problem with the Dean was, but she felt reassured by the arguments the others made. They would know. It was best not to concentrate too much on it, but to think instead about how good it felt to be in the know.

Still, standing there amid the moving crowd, she felt slightly panicked at not being able to remember where she had to go next.

Fortunately, her secretary, Angela, happened by and gently helped the Professor toward her office only a few steps away from where she'd been rooted. The crowd parted as if responding to a silent signal. A few faces reflected amusement at what had become a common scene at the school.

It was Professor Anderson. Natalie had captured her perfectly. I'd witnessed such moments often enough to recognize it. I read on.

Flecks of unrecognizable food speckled his graying beard, which rested on his generous chest and stomach. Professor Earl Boilerplate drew in a breath to begin a new topic, and clicked onto autopilot, since he had given this same lecture for many years. He shifted uncomfortably in his seat at the head of the classroom, the chair creaking from the weight. A small cadre of students sat listlessly facing the professor, pretending to be focused on the lecture he pretended to give. The professor could conduct the class while at the same time contemplating his next move in the ongoing drama of academic life. He felt convinced that the Dean was a major impediment to his hard fought-for academic arrangement. Every time he thought about what would happen if she persisted, a tight knot formed in his middle. It had taken him close to twenty years to create this niche for himself. Nobody had the right to take away his supplementary income or to expect that he come in to the school any more than two days a week. And nobody had the right to interfere with his class content. It had been working for almost forty years and there was no reason to change it.

And worse, she had the gall to overlook his formidable skills and not award him the newly created position of Director of The International Social Work Institute. It was his! He'd earned it by virtue of his seniority. Besides, hadn't he traveled all over the world on his vacations, and didn't that qualify him for such a position? And to even suggest that he retire! His indignation rose the more he thought about it. He'd show her.

Suddenly there was a shift in the room. It took him a moment to realize that he had begun to weave his secret thoughts about the Dean into his lecture. Now he stopped, blinking and staring at the group, not knowing where he was in the lecture and worse, not knowing how much he'd actually revealed aloud. He searched his mental files frantically for the place to resume, but was unsuccessful. Glancing finally at the clock, he saw that there were only ten minutes to the end of class. Gratefully, he dismissed early.

Ralph Brewer. Natalie had surely been playing with fire. I remembered that look on Brewer's face when I accidentally swiped him with cake. If such a small thing could evoke that much fury, what would this unflattering description drive him to do? I knew that Natalie and Brewer hardly ever agreed, and that she had sided with the Dean about the new directorship appointment. And she had sometimes let slip her lack of respect for the man.

I stared at her notes. Was this the beginning of a book that was to be Natalie's revenge? To reveal the petty academic shenanigans that she'd witnessed in the school?

I turned the page. A new narrative began.

Sounds of a whispered conversation bled through the cracks around the ill-fitting office door. In the small foyer of the corner office, two people huddled together talking in low tones. Behind the office door, a professor stopped her work, straining to hear. In the silence of the mostly empty building, the words that were intended to remain a secret were spoken almost into the gap between the door and the frame.

How could they not see how wide that opening was? The professor held her breath and listened. Maybe they thought the office was empty.

"Don't be crazy," one voice hissed. "We're in the clear. Nobody even suspects us. They've got Alison van Dorne for it."

I gasped, loudly enough that the noise surprised me further. I found my place again as quickly as I could.

There was a pause. Another woman spoke, "That doesn't seem right, Robin. She didn't do it."

"It's our best chance of not getting caught. Besides, she's got money. She'll get a lawyer and make a deal. And she's like all the rest. She doesn't give a damn about us."

"But for what? She'll make a deal for something she didn't do. I don't know. It's not right." The woman sounded unconvinced, but it was the kind of sound someone who has no real backbone makes. To argue weakly for the right thing, all the while knowing that you won't do anything about it in order to remain safe yourself, was the ultimate in cowardice.

"You better not say a word ..."

The first voice left it hanging. There was another silence and then the sound of footsteps signaling their retreat from the doorway. The professor rose soundlessly from her chair and moved to the door. She pulled it open cautiously and stepped into the foyer that hid her from the main hall. Carefully she peered around the corner and watched the two women walking down the hallway toward the exit. The floor creaked beneath her weight as she shifted to turn away and one of them, Robin, swung around to look behind her. The professor ducked back but wasn't sure if she'd been observed. However, she had seen enough to recognize one woman as a student she'd had in her class.

I reread the passage several times, trying to wrap my mind around what it said. The first two vignettes were clearly actual descriptions of real people despite the changed names. Could the third piece also reflect something Natalie had actually overheard? Was she the professor craning to hear the confession? Or had she heard this from someone else? If it were she, could a dead woman's thoughts be admissible legally?

And, most important, what did this tell me? Robin was Julie Pigeon, of course, and I'd guess the other student was Donna. But had they acted alone? Was Julie the ringleader? Who else might be involved?

In any case, I was pretty sure how both Natalie Cruz and David Kayson had met their ends. The whys weren't too far behind. And who was to be held accountable would follow. Holding that notebook, I stared out the window and turned too late to find Amy Arnold standing in the doorway.

CHAPTER 50

I stood up to face her. "What are you doing here?"

"I lent Professor Cruz a book she never returned, so I thought I could just get it back without causing anybody any trouble."

It was thin. And reminded me of the story I had conjured up when Kris and I had broken into the SSD building. That seemed so long ago.

"And this you would do by breaking and entering?" I said.

"What about you?" she shot back. "You're doing the same."

"Actually, I'm not. You see, this is now my property and you're trespassing." I actually enjoyed saying it.

"I don't believe it."

"You're welcome to believe me or not. Would you like to check it out with the police?

"I wouldn't ..."

"You aren't looking for some book or anything you lent Natalie. I think you're looking for something incriminating and you're scared that your little scheme is falling apart."

"I don't know what you're talking about." Ah, the answer of last resort.

"I think you do. The police are getting close. And, very clever how you set me up to be a suspect for Kayson's murder. Your idea, I suppose?"

This time, a distinct smile flitted across her face. A perverse pleasure at my anguish? Or relief at my ignorance. I was guessing here, after all.

"You don't have anything on me," she said.

"You mean, except this breaking-and-entering thing and, might I add, perhaps a little larceny?"

"I was only going to take what was mine."

"If you're looking for something that Natalie wrote about a certain conversation she overheard, you're out of luck. The police already have it." The lies came so easily. "And how did you know she had it?"

"She told me."

It took a second for her to realize what her answer revealed. I saw her begin to panic, her eyes moving quickly around the room as if to search for escape. Perhaps I was pushing her too hard.

I worked to slow myself. "Amy. As long as we've come this far, why don't you just tell me about it? I'm sure that you did what you did for good reasons."

She glowered at me but remained silent. I was perfectly aware that I was attempting a manipulation, and at that moment I felt no remorse about it. Perhaps I would later, but standing there facing the woman who I was fairly certain had killed Natalie I felt nothing but abhorrence. But I didn't worry about it showing because Amy was not one who could accurately assess other people's motives. Besides, people also want to state their own cases, to justify their decisions. I would try to use this to my advantage.

Speaking slowly and calmly, I said, "It must have been scary to think that Natalie had something incriminating. And, of course, when you went the first time to see her in her office, you just wanted to talk. And then you came here. And she wouldn't cooperate, would she?" As I spoke, I moved slowly toward her. "I mean, you've got your hands full already, what with working, going to school and caring for your mother. And she was threatening to take it all away."

Amy stood for another moment and then said almost inaudibly. "She wouldn't understand. I mean, she told me she had to tell somebody about what she heard. She was going to wreck everything."

"You must have been desperate."

"I didn't know what to do. She was so unreasonable. I just sort of lost it. She said she had written it down and put it in a safe place.

And when I told her that I had to have it, she got angry at me. Can you believe it? She's gonna ruin my life and she gets mad at me. I mean, who was she to wreck my whole life?"

I could see her begin to rev up, as she settled into her rage at the injustice. "And so you picked up the brick and ..."

"I just had the brick to, to, I don't know, to ..."

"To threaten her?"

"I don't know why I picked up that brick. I was just so mad and scared and I just had to stop her, to stop this from getting out of hand."

I could imagine the scene. Natalie could be piercing if she felt herself in the presence of ineptitude, and Amy wasn't wrapped too tightly. The two women squaring off, both believing that they were in the right. This made for a volatile situation. Only Natalie hadn't counted on the fact that Amy had no internal braking system and she got a caved-in skull for her miscalculation. I had to be sure not to make the same mistake.

"It wasn't my fault," Amy said. "She pushed me to it. What did she expect? That woman made me jump through hoops in her class, and still she only gave me a C. And then she tells me she's going to the police, thinking that she knows what she's talking about."

I thought I'd take the chance. "Do you remember what you did with the brick?"

Amy's expression suddenly changed. "Oh, no. You're trying to do the same thing. You and her are both the same. You're trying to get me into trouble. Why are you doing this to me? You don't care about your students. You don't know how hard it is to try to do all of this. Always ragging at us about all that work. Never thinking about how much else we have to do."

She straightened up and I could see in her face that the fury was controlled and focused. I tried to step away. Was she seeing me or had I taken on the role of someone else? Did she want to harm me, to punish me for the actions of someone else?

"Look, Amy," I said in my most soothing voice, "you don't want your situation to get any worse, do you? I mean, who would look after your mother if you got put away?" Actually, it already seemed guaranteed that Amy would be going to prison for a long time. But perhaps throwing her a bone would be enough to convince her to control herself.

"Forget it. I'm not going anywhere, and you aren't either." She pulled the door closed, standing between me and my only escape. Amy seemed to grow with her rage. Now it was I who was starting to feel the panic. I saw her glance around the room until her gaze settled on a small stone statue on a shelf next to her. She grabbed for it and lunged at me.

And then another figure was bearing down on me, fist cocked, an angry sneer on my father's face, his breath soured by alcohol. My heart started to thunder and I ducked to avoid his blow. It was Amy's that missed my head, but caught my shoulder. I stumbled as the pain tore through my arm and neck, but managed to scramble out of her reach. I struggled to focus, but waves of long-buried fear blurred the boundaries and I could only see him in his fury and recede into the ten-year-old that I had been.

Someone came at me again, grunting with the effort, and I was able to avoid the second swipe. But terror and helplessness washed through me as my father's voice screamed that he would teach me a lesson. I was in an old dark hallway, the scene of my father's most furious beatings, where he trapped me against the front door and all I could do was curl up in a ball and wait for it to stop.

I cried out, "No, Daddy," and felt the tears begin to flow. I could only focus on keeping away from the source of the pain. And wanting to call out for my mother. My foot ached and I was breathing raggedly.

I know that she got me a couple of times on the back and arm. But it was my father whose fists I felt landing and it was my father's face glaring at me with murderous intent.

And then the fury started to rise.

"You son of a bitch."

I grabbed a book and threw it hard at him and he stumbled as it found its mark on his head. I felt surge of joy at his grimace and was even more pleased to see the small trickle of blood start at his temple. I wasn't helpless. I wasn't a child. I would beat him into submission.

I started hurling anything within reach and felt some wisps of pleasure as I made contact. He came at me with fury in his eyes and I grabbed a lamp and swung from the hips.

I connected with him just above the belt, and he went down.

And I was on top of him, fists pounding, his eyes, his teeth, his nose. I think I was laughing.

"Addy!"

My mother trying to stop me. But why hadn't she stopped him all those years?

Hands grabbed me from behind. "Addy! Addy, snap out of it!"

Wait. My mother never called me "Addy." That was a name I began to use in college. My grown-up name.

I looked down. I was sitting astride a bruised and bleeding Amy Arnold. My hands hurt. I looked at them. The knuckles were bleeding.

"Did I do that?"

Someone reached past me to check Amy's pulse. I slowly turned around and found myself staring into the eyes of Georgia Enfield.

CHAPTER 51

"I think she's all right," she said. "Unconscious, but not permanently damaged."

I stared back at Amy, trying to take in Georgia's words, to get myself back into the present. As the reality of what I'd done sank in, I began to tremble.

Georgia took me by the arms and helped me up. We stared at each other and then she spoke, "Oh, god, Addy. This is all my fault. None of this should ever have happened."

I could feel the shaking in my legs. Standing amid the shambles of Natalie's den, I put up my hands. "I ... wait. Just wait. I ... I'm not ready to hear this." I had to regroup and find some way to keep from exploding into a million pieces. "Let's go downstairs and make some tea and we'll sit somewhere and then you'll tell me everything."

"What about her?" She indicated Amy.

"You're sure she's all right?"

"Yeah. I think so."

"Let's make sure she can't go anywhere."

The search to find something to keep Amy immobilized gave me a further chance to calm down. While I looked, I was trying to tell myself that it hadn't been what I knew it had. But it was a losing battle. The flashback had been real and I was stunned by its implications.

For the time being, I would rely on suppression. I knew that it wouldn't work in the long run, but I had to attend to things at hand.

String Natalie had used for tying up plants came in handy for our purpose. We left Amy unconscious, breathing, and, if she came to, unable to leave.

The flashback and Georgia being there swept away my unease about being in the kitchen. As I went through the ordinary motions of preparing our tea, questions whirled around in my head, but I held off asking until we could sit. It was as if I was watching myself make the tea. I remembered this was the ritual my mother would use to ground herself after yet another of my father's tirades. After he had beaten me, he would storm from the house to cleanse himself at the local tavern. No doubt to rid himself of the images of being a child abuser. Guilt is rarely far away. Amid the debris of the latest battle, she would calmly fill the teakettle and wait by the stove while it heated. Sometimes tears would spill down her cheeks, blending with the clear, hot water as it turned to a ruddy brown in her teacup. Tearcup.

Georgia sat wordlessly waiting at the small round table, just as I had sat with my mother so often years ago.

My mother was right. The guilt of my own recent violence danced around the edges of my consciousness. So I concentrated on the small simple ritual of tea making. It now made such visceral sense to do so.

Finally, we settled in the living room, the tea brewing hotly under the flowered tea cozy and two mugs resting on the tray. Georgia sat in a dark green wingback chair and I sank into a square green-and-black plaid chair facing her. The coffee table, on which the tea sat, was within easy reach between us.

I broke the silence, "How the hell did you know to come here?"

Georgia poured the tea as she spoke, "Amy was at my house and she just flipped out when we were talking about the school. When I couldn't calm her down and she started ranting about Kayson and you and what she might do, I followed her. I didn't know what else to do. And I know what Amy is capable of."

The teacup shook in my hand. I tried to keep calm, but it was a battle. "If you were right behind her why did it take you so long to get here?"

"I'm sorry. But I parked away from the house so I wouldn't be seen. Don't ask me why. I'm no outdoor person, so I got lost getting here."

"What? It's only half a mile in and there's a driveway for God's sake."

"Addy, I tried to take a short cut and I got disoriented in the woods and it took me a while to find the house. I'm sorry. Everything looked the same. I'm sorry."

Not only did I have a headache and an aching foot, but my shoulder, arm, and various other areas on my body had started to throb. "I think she got me in several places," I said massaging my shoulder and then my arm. But I got her as well. Oh, so unsocial-work-like.

"Addy. Like I said, I'm sorry and this is really all my fault. Do you think anything is broken?"

I waved her question aside. "So, Georgia, tell me how this is all your fault."

She held the cup to her lips and blew on the tea. "Amy was in a couple of my classes. She confided in me once that David had propositioned her in exchange for a good grade. She turned him down and she said he retaliated by giving her bad grades. She told me because she knew I had been involved with him; she thought I would understand and maybe help her out. I felt bad for her. So I made some … mistakes."

"What mistakes?"

"She began to think that we had some special bond because of Kayson," Georgia continued, "and she treated me with more familiarity than I was comfortable with, but once we had started down that path I didn't know how to come back. You see how unstable she is. I couldn't figure out how to get back to teacher-student relationship. I know it was stupid but I was afraid, I didn't want to set her off. I thought she might be dangerous. And now I see that I was right."

I think she expected sympathy. I just looked at her and waited for her to go on.

"And then she brought two other students to me who both had been hurt by Kayson. Addy, I felt some responsibility to them, because they were students and I thought I should have been able to protect them. I thought they would get some support from a group. So one day after class, they invited me to go to dinner. I didn't think it would do any harm. Just dinner out. I thought I could be of some help to them, you know, a mentor or something. In fact, one of them is placed at my agency and I referred her to you for therapy."

Virginia Early. But as Virginia's therapist I couldn't acknowledge that she was my client. So I didn't say anything and waited for Georgia to continue. I did, however, begin to sense the makings of an ethical dilemma.

She seemed a little put off at my silence, but went on, "Anyway, we went out that night to a local bar and this is mistake number two or three, depending on how you're counting. I drank. It was stupid. I know. But apparently the conversation turned to Kayson."

"That's not surprising, since it seems to be the thing you all had in common." I didn't try to keep the sarcasm out of my voice.

She looked as if I had slapped her. "Addy, it was the dumbest thing I've done in a long time." Her voice had taken on a trembling quality as if she was struggling to fight off tears."I know I should have at a minimum encouraged them to go to the authorities and I know that my apology doesn't mean anything right now, but what can I say, Addy?"

"You can go on with the story."

She breathed in, "Okay. So, we talked about Kayson. I don't remember this part clearly because I put away several glasses of wine. Once I get started, you know. Anyway, when one of them, I swear I don't know who, said that she thought Kayson should be punished for what he was doing to women. I guess we went on and developed an actual plan for it."

"What do you mean, you guess?"

"I was drinking. I don't remember it clearly. God, Addy. I am so sorry." She took a sip of her tea. "Blackouts are my specialty."

And now mine as well.

"So what was the plan?" I asked.

"I think it involved inviting him to party with all of us, promising a little group sex. The plan was to drug his drink and then I think somebody said we should take compromising pictures. Anyway that's what I figured out." She shook her head, "I swear, Addy, it was all fantasy as far as I was concerned. I can't believe that some of them thought it was real. And then he was killed. God. I was scared. I was pretty sure it was them, but I never thought they would take it that far."

Ah, damn, there was the ethical dilemma. Georgia had just told me that Virginia Early might have helped kill David Kayson. I stared at her, not wanting her to continue, but hoping she would. It was as if I was looking to her to give me some relief from holding what I had just heard. How was I going to deal with all of this?

"So then, Natalie overheard Birdy—a.k.a. Julie Pigeon—and one of the other women talking about it. And Amy took it upon herself to warn Natalie to keep quiet. And something went wrong there as well."

"I guess so. Amy didn't tell me, but I wouldn't be surprised. She's not wrapped too tight. Well, at least mentally." She attempted a weak smile at her pun.

I just nodded. "So tell me, Georgia," I used her name deliberately, "how did the knife with my fingerprints end up in Kayson?"

She shook her head. "Addy, I swear I don't know anything about that. We never talked about that as far as I can remember. I even tried to talk to Amy about it, but after Kayson's murder, she kept her distance from me. And frankly, although I wasn't sure that she'd done it, I didn't want much to do with her either."

"Do you see her as the ring leader?"

"Of the three of them, she strikes me as being the most forceful and unstable. The other two seem to defer to her a lot, especially Virginia. Birdy isn't as passive, but she's a little too scattered to have planned something like this and then pulled it off."

"And why for God's sake did you invite me to work at the Department? What was that about?"

"I felt bad that you'd gotten caught up in all of this. Remember that I didn't know how much I had contributed to everything. It was all very hazy, but I figured that I might have made life hard for you, so I thought if it would help you out, I wanted to do it. I know it was lame, but it was the best I could do." Her chagrin was obvious. "I was scared. I thought Amy would claim that I was in on it from the start; she as much as said so. I couldn't risk it. And I hoped that you'd be able to get out of it. After all, you didn't do it."

I couldn't decide whether to scowl or smile. "Okay. I'm going to call the police now. And you are going to tell them everything."

She nodded and sat quietly while I got up to call Arnie. He wasn't at the station and the dispatcher promised to give him my number. We sat and drank that entire pot of tea as we waited for his call. During our vigil I went upstairs once to check on Amy and found her groggy but awake and nonetoo happy to be bound like a roast loin of pork.

When Arnie did call, I explained where I was and gave him an overview of recent events. It took him only twenty minutes to arrive.

CHAPTER 52

We sat facing each other. Virginia Early appeared composed, for a change. I supposed that she had heard about Amy's arrest and was waiting for the confrontation. Arnie said that he would charge Amy with breaking and entering and then hold her until they were sure they could also charge her with the murders of David Kayson and Natalie Cruz. Amy refused to give any other names. He said that anyone else associated with these crimes would not be picked up until the police had enough evidence to do so and he expected that it wouldn't take long.

Virginia had agreed to bump up our appointment. Over the phone, I told her it would work out better for me if we didn't wait. She, too, had seemed almost eager to come in.

But, instead of beginning with the obvious, she started talking about a conversation she had with her mother.

"I'm still having nightmares. I didn't go home at all and my mother was really angry about that. Every time I talk to her on the phone, she's really cold and it's just hard to talk to her. I feel really bad."

Ah, she was introducing the theme of betrayal and guilt. "Virginia, I think it would make more sense for us to talk directly about what's happened."

I could see the alarm begin and expected that she would go into retreat mode. "Virginia," I said quickly, "I usually let people take their time to talk about the difficult material, but this isn't something that can wait. I assume that not talking about it is worse for you, and I know it is for me. This is about Kayson's murder and I think you know something about it."

She started to shake her head slowly back and forth. I expected a string of denials to follow but instead, she let out a low moan that transformed into a long sob. She wasn't fighting me off, she was fighting off terrifying images.

"Oh, Addy, I don't know what to do anymore. I'm so scared and I just can't keep doing this."

"If you mean keeping quiet and hoping it will all just go away, you're right. It will haunt you forever unless you face it."

"I know. I know. I'm just so afraid."

"I can't say I know what it's like for you, although I have some idea"—the memory of my own childhood terror came to mind—"but I can't collude with you by ignoring it as well and acting as if we could together do something meaningful in spite of it."

She appeared to be struggling with the question because she didn't respond despite the tears that were threatening to flow. I sat with her and waited for her decide which way she could go. She wept silently.

It felt like an interminable wait, but finally she spoke. The tears had dissipated. "You seem to know more about this than I thought you would, so I don't know where to begin."

"Assume I don't know anything," I said.

"Ok. Well." She paused. "You remember what I told you about what Kayson did? I mean that I let him have sex so that he'd give me a passing grade."

She searched for an answer from me so I nodded.

"So, anyway. I met a couple of other students who he also did things to and we got together. I felt so much better when I was with them. They really helped me a lot and I felt grateful to them. One girl had been in one of the SSD programs and Kayson had forced her to have sex so she could stay in the program. Can you believe that? I hate that guy."

"What are their names, Virginia?" This was outside the scope of the therapy, but I wanted to hear it.

She looked up at me, as if considering whether to answer or not. She sighed and spoke, "It was Julie Pigeon and Amy Arnold. And me, of course."

"So these women were supportive."

She nodded and blew her nose. "One night, we were out to dinner with Georgia Enfield, and somebody came up with the idea that we would pay him back. We talked about inviting him to have sex with all of us and then instead drugging him and maybe taking pictures of him in some embarrassing poses, or something like that."

"What did you think about that conversation?"

"I didn't think we would actually do it. At least not at first. It was so unreal. I mean, we were laughing about it, and I thought it was us joking and being crazy. And then it just sort of got more real.

"But it didn't turn out the way you thought it would."

She shook her head and bit her upper lip. "No it didn't. We did invite him to go with us one night up in the school and we got him drunk. It was so scary and he was so pathetic. I mean we were dancing around and he really thought he was going to do it with each of us. God, it was disgusting. One of the other girls put drugs in his drink and he fell asleep."

She began to cry. "Then somebody took out a knife and I freaked. I wasn't drinking because I was so scared and I just wanted to see him hurt like he hurt me. But I didn't want to kill him. I felt so sick."

"Hadn't you talked about that?"

"No, I really thought we were just gonna take some pictures. I just couldn't believe it."

"Then what?"

"I don't know because I told the other girls that I didn't want anything to do with this. I tried to talk them out of it. God it was so awful. By that time he was awake, but he was just sitting there looking so pathetic, I think he was drooling, and we were arguing, but they were so angry. They wouldn't listen. I really tried. And then I went to the bathroom. To be sick."

"What happened then?"

"I don't know what happened because I couldn't go back there. I tried but I couldn't go back in there."

"What else do you remember?" I asked.

"What do you mean?"

"Was there anything else that you remember about that night, after you left the classroom?"

She looked up as if recreating that night. "I'm not sure. I thought there was somebody else there, but I couldn't say who."

"How do you know that?"

"I ran up to the third floor, to one of the bathrooms up there. I didn't want to see anyone. One of the offices on the third floor was open. But I don't remember whose. There was a light on. The rest of the doors were closed."

"Which end of the hall?"

"One of those closest to the stairs. But I don't remember which one. I wasn't really paying attention, you know."

"And then what?"

"I went home."

"You're saying that you didn't actually see anybody kill him? That you left before that?"

"Yes. I couldn't do it. But they made me promise not to tell. They said I would be just as guilty of whatever happened even if I wasn't there. I didn't know what to think." She buried her head in her hands and cried quietly, with the occasional snuffle.

I sat back and drew in a deep breath, letting it out slowly. "Virginia, what have you decided to do about this?"

She looked up at me, her red-rimmed eyes shimmering wetly, fluids running down her cheeks and from her nose. I handed her a tissue that she used quietly.

"I don't know what I'm going to tell my parents. This will just kill them." She let out a disheartened chuckle at the unintended pun. "But I guess I'll have to tell the truth. Oh I just don't know anymore." She buried her face in her hands.

"Have you thought about hurting yourself, Virginia?"

She sat up slowly and shook her head. "I could never do that." She took in a deep breath and let it out forcefully. "I've ruined my life. What do I do?"

"There are ways to come back from the worst things we do. It is possible to get to the other side of this. But it will be tough going."

"How do I do that? I'm a murderer. How do I live with that?"

"It seems impossible now. You see yourself as the most horrible of people."

She nodded.

"There are ways to come to terms with it."

"I don't want to. I want it to all go away."

"What do you think will lead you to a different place with it?"

"I just want to get away."

"Do you imagine you can outrun the images?"

"What are you saying? I should turn myself in? And then what? How would that help anyone? He's dead. It won't bring him back. And who would want that, anyway?"

"Virginia, you should find a lawyer for the legal questions. And you and I will sort out the rest."

"You think I need a lawyer. Oh, god."

"And you need to talk to your parents."

She cringed as if I had hit her. It took the rest of the session to help Virginia find some footing. She had a very hard road to travel from there. To get to where she had to go, she would have to face the very worst in herself and then embrace the idea that she could live with it.

I know just how she felt.

EPILOGUE

A my Arnold kept quiet about who else had been with her, but Julie Pigeon finally caved and told the whole story to the police. However, neither woman admitted to switching the knives, no matter how they were pressed. It seemed an odd thing to deny given that they were already facing charges of premeditated murder. Both pleaded not guilty by reason of insanity. The trial strategy was going to include dragging out both of their abuse histories and the jury trying to balance a soul-twisting history against personal responsibility. And so it goes.

The knife used in the murder was found under the driver's seat of Amy's blue car, a souvenir of that wild night. Amy confessed to writing the warning, as well as being my brick tosser and midnight visitor. It would have been difficult for her to deny since her fingerprints were all over my apartment.

Virginia Early turned herself in to the police, accompanied by her lawyer and her parents, after we had another session. She had been offered a reduced sentence in exchange for her testimony about that night. She wrestled with this decision, feeling guilty for selling out Amy and Julie. We explored the dimensions of integrity and false loyalty as well as what telling the truth means, especially when it involves other people's lives.

Georgia and I were able to maintain a collegial relationship, however carefully. She came through and testified as to her role in all of what had transpired. But I wasn't too eager to work toward repairing our shredded relationship and so I kept my distance.

The Feds pulled the rest of the funding for the parenting program, so the women were put back into the regular client population. Pictures of Janice and Kenneth's bent-over figures, handcuffed and being led from the courthouse, were splashed all over the front page of the *Whitefield Chronicle*, as well as the local television news. And my name was back in the newspaper, but this time because of my role in solving the two murder cases. Better than a retraction. As expected, there was no call from my mother. She didn't know how to share the spotlight. We heard about the scandal for months and then it faded into the oblivion of all such sensationalized stories. Periodically, I reflected on how those women at the SSD were doing.

Too much suffering.

I decided that I wasn't really cut out to be in private practice, although the hours were great and the freedom to be my own boss was alluring. I missed Bertha's place, and the camaraderie of the staff in spite of the hardships. I got some help from Kris in convincing the board to take me back. It didn't feel at all like going backward, but more like coming home. I found that I had returned in the nick of time, since the supply of tissues was dangerously low. Jerry greeted me with a warm hug, while the rest of the agency threw me a welcome-back party. Even Edith came around. At the party, Jerry and I held an embrace for an extra long time, as if to communicate something. Thereafter, I never mentioned what I knew about his nasty brush with Kayson. He knew that I would be available to talk, but I would leave it up to him. If he chose not to, he would have to make his own way with it.

There are truths, as we see them, outside of us that are difficult to give voice to. There is also the inner truth, or something closer to it than what we might be living. David Kayson had showed me something about myself that I didn't like. Not one bit. So Dr. Fisher and I have been examining my internal truth for some time now, a fragment at a time. It felt awkward and sometimes frightening to be on the other side of the process. The forest was still difficult to see. But I made a commitment to stick it out, at least for a while.

Midway into the following term at Major University, I entered the elevator on the way to my class and found Professor Ralph Brewer already inside. He nodded wordlessly. The gold chain around his neck reminded me of the attacker in Virginia's dream. We rode up in silence until just before the doors opened onto the third floor. He turned to me and said, "It's too bad about Natalie."

And then he winked.

As he stepped out, over his shoulder, he added, "Especially since she so much enjoyed the chocolate cake at her retirement party."

I stepped out and felt the elevator doors hiss closed behind me. Standing there with a small knot forming in my middle, I watched him make his ponderous way down the hall.